This book is dedicated to my parents. Their work ethic and moral compass were instrumental in my writing of this story. My parents love and dedication to family are interwoven in all aspects of my life.

THE CURRENT
OF
SILENCE

Charleston, SC
www.PalmettoPublishing.com

The Current of Silence
Copyright © 2022 by Anne Elder

First Edition

Paperback ISBN: 978-0-578-24559-1

THE CURRENT
OF
SILENCE

ANNE ELDER

Acknowledgments

There are so many factors involved in writing a book, but the biggest one is the people that help you along the way. I want to thank all of those people who were inspirational to me in their own way.

I owe this whole experience of writing this book to my dear friend, Maria Erwin. The confidence she had in my writing, the many hours she spent pouring over the words understanding the story and helping me put the right words in place are so appreciated. This book would have not come to fruition without her.

My family cheered me on even when dinner was late or I spent weekends thinking and writing. They are my biggest supporters and understand the words in this book are very important to me.

And last but not least, I want to thank my husband for loving me and giving me the time and space to live out my dream.

Special thanks to Dana Klein of Photography by Dana for the awesome book cover of my first novel.

Driving beneath a crystal, clear blue sky I wonder now what changed in me that made me decide to come back here. I can see the farms beginning to dot the landscape and I know I am getting nearby. They remind me of the days when I rode my bike across these fields on my way into town, glancing at the ever-changing pictures in the clouds, and imagining what kind of life was in store for me. A shiver slithers down my back from the remembering.

Suddenly I become anxious wondering if this time I have chosen to return is the right time. How many of them will remember? It seems so long ago sometimes I wonder if the events those many years ago ever really happened. I wonder will they recognize me. It's doubtful with all the changes I've made to myself, I think with confidence or so I tell myself, no one will know who I am. I will be using my camera to document my journey and being a photographer will give me cover. My first thought as I pull into town is to find a place to stay where I can plan and decide what to do next. I want to know about the town's plans for the present, for the future and those who are the principals involved with an interest in decisions. I spot a parking place right in front of an internet café which has replaced the old Deli where you could buy absolutely the best pastrami sandwiches anywhere. With a deep breath, I begin my journey from the present to the past and back again.

Walking along Main Street is surreal. I can almost imagine myself walking here many years ago when the street was lined with a drug store, local bar and grill, post office, town hotel, small restaurant, deli, bank, hardware store, bus stop and other quaint locally owned shops. The street has hardly changed at all, although the trees are much larger than they were those many years ago. Spring is here and they are full of leaves shading the sidewalk from the sun. Some of the same storefronts are here although many of them are closed now. I am surprised to see the old bank has become a microbrewery which displays things have changed. An internet cafe has opened in the old deli and a tattoo parlor hangs its shingle next door. The Hotel is still here with the townies hanging out on the front step watching the town's fate swirl around them while they are wiling away the time with drink. I wonder if they still rent rooms upstairs because I need to find a place to stay while I begin my journey back in time. The Hotel does not look as if it has changed much since I left, so my stay there will have to be temporary. Right now, though, I must go to an ATM and get some money.

With my hat pulled down low, my hair a different color, and thank God for colored contacts, I think once again there is little chance anyone will recognize me. I changed my name from Misty Jenkins to Morgan Kiernan a few years after I left, trying to escape the memories buried in this seemingly sleepy little town.

It is very quiet along the walkway up to the bank's ATM machine which gives me a sense of relief. My relief is short-lived when no sooner do I withdraw money but find standing right in front of me is Mrs. Hardaway, my 5th grade teacher. I say excuse me and begin to walk past her. To my dismay she taps me and says, "What a beautiful afternoon it is, isn't it?" I mumble an answer and hurry along with my heart beating so hard I feel as if it may leap into the street. After a few minutes I calm down and realize she was just being friendly and did not recognize me.

Getting a room at the Hotel provides no excitement and I rent a room without a hitch. After unpacking my small suitcase, I lie down and close my eyes. Lying there, the noises from the bar downstairs remind me some things never change. People have been hanging out in the Hotel's bar for as long as I can remember. I drift off to sleep remembering the good times I had living on the farm, before things changed and before Jonathan ruined it all.

My dreams take me back to my childhood years on the farm to days filled with all kinds of chores typical of a successful working farm, cows needing to be milked and fed, younger calves bawling as loud as they could to let us know it is time for them to get fed as well, the scent of home cooking finding its way into the air and each season painting the landscape with the colors of a rainbow.

Warmth infuses into my body and I struggle into wakefulness not wanting to leave the warm feeling. My dream had transported me back into my world years ago and my visit there is still with me. Stretching, I rest my hands behind a pillow, and I lie awake there remembering more.

It was early one morning when I saw my Dad out in a field with a divining rod walking along very slowly. Running into the shed I grabbed the keys off the hook to the farm truck and took off to the field where he was walking. My brother Jonathan had taught me how to drive it when I could barely see over the steering wheel or reach the pedals. Now, at least according to me, I was accomplished in the driving of the truck, sometimes overconfident I confess. Dust tended to travel with me so when I pulled up next to him, he already had his handkerchief covering his nose and mouth. "Misty, are you trying again to hotrod that old farm truck? You know it might be yours someday when you get old enough to legally drive," laughed Dad. Jumping out of the truck, I look up at him and say, "Drive that! Are you kidding me! I won't be getting my license for another few years, and this truck will be ancient by then. Over my dead body will I be seen in this old thing," I complained. Laughing, he said he still wanted me to help him with what he was doing. I noticed he had two rods in his hands. Trying to understand, I asked what he was doing. He chuckled and looking at me as if I should have known said, "Why Misty I'm looking for water". Research showed me much later "dowsing" (as it was sometimes referred to) was a centuries old technique to find water. What I also found out was not everyone had the ability to do it. As I grew up there were many times when Dad was asked by well drillers to find the best place to drill for water.

MY PARENTS (Past)

My Dad was tall and broad of shoulder, with large and powerful hands. An accident on the farm had permanently curled his little finger on his left hand and another accident with a corn picker had taken the top from his middle finger on his right hand. As a little girl I can remember being frightened of him, like a moth is to a flame if you get too close you could get burned. His persona led one to believe no matter what, you needed to do better, transform yourself into a more important person, one who people would pay attention to, but his methods were instilled in him with insidious determination by those who came before him.

My early memories of him were like looking through a kaleidoscope, colors warm and inviting then stormy and frightening. As we became older, Jonathan and I became his workers. There was nothing on the farm he felt was too much for us to do. No matter what we had going on in our life, the farm came first. Day after day, I would complain to my Mom about not being able to stay after school and be part of one of the clubs or go out for a sport or cheerleading. The answer was always, "It won't sit well with your Dad, and there is work here to be done." Finally, when I went to high school, he agreed I could stay there for a function, if it was involved with a club or team of which I was a member. So, I went out for cheerleading and made the team. The condition to it however was my work would be waiting for me when

I got home. No one else was going to do it, so after the games, I came home. It was tough, but he was tough and as his children, we became resilient.

His demeanor, his size, the scowl more often resided on his face, are all memories which quickly come to the minds of most people who knew him. But then, you hear the quiet diatribe of what a decent man he was, his honesty and his appreciation for his fellow farmer, the way he could make someone feel at ease and open up to him about their farming and their families. As his children, we were always in awe and somewhat doubtful they were talking about our Dad. The people he helped and saved became his salvation and absolved for him and probably for us the anger and resentment which occupied most of our family life.

Looking back to that time and knowing what I know about my Dad in his later years, I realize he was paving his way in the world and caring for his family the only way he knew how, with hard work and decency to those around him. I remember the few times he freed the part of him he fiercely protected and shared delight and tenderness which brought us all together. Our memories of the hard times fled and were lost in the rows of waving cornstalks which could be seen as far as the eye could see. I find myself thinking about him more now that he's been gone so long. I realize the impact he had on Jonathan and me. It made me strong, but cautious in my relationships and life and shaped Jonathan's lack of confidence and ambition.

My Mother wasn't a very tall person, but her stature was majestic. Her hair was chocolate brown with waves scattered perfectly and her eyes were an Irish blue. I used to think she looked like she had been in the sun because her cheeks were always so rosy. But most impressive were her hands. Though they weren't long and slender, her nails just an average length and not manicured, with the same measure they could play beautiful music, hug her children tightly, or milk a cow. Somehow her hands are always what I think of when I remember her because it was her hands which held us all when we were hurt, made beautiful music, and worked the soil and the farm.

She had many roles, wife, mother, farm worker, pianist, choir director and music teacher. All these roles she performed as if each one was the only thing she had to do. She had unwavering dedication and commitment to everything she did. Nothing would keep my Mother from going to church every Sunday. The strong religious doctrine of her Catholic upbringing was always in the background when discipline or advice was being issued. Every morning I would come down for school and she would just be finishing up her rosary. This was her routine after she had come in from working in the barn since 5 AM. Somehow, she always managed to maintain a positive attitude and she had an inherent desire to help anyone in need.

Music always filled our house. Its sound embraced every waking hour on the weekend. I would come down in the morning and my Mother would be sitting at the piano, her hands making beautiful music. Music resided in her soul, and when life began to crumble around her, playing music was her salvation. Jonathan and I were both schooled in music, each playing an instrument. Jonathan played the clarinet, and I played the piano like Mother. We were just a regular entertainment group or at least that's what Mother liked to think. In reality, she had us play for our family and friends during the Holidays. Every October she would want us to spend Saturday mornings practicing with her getting ready for the holidays. When Jonathan was small, she taught Music at the local school but when I came along, she quit teaching and became a farm wife and full time Mom. Her music influence continued with piano lessons held in our living room every day after school.

Her relationship with my Dad was somewhat tenuous at best, though they loved each other very much. The pressures of raising children, and running a farm were sometimes a catalyst for an uneasy relationship, however, her dedication and love for her children was something close to amazing. They spent more than

40 years together working their farm and trying to make the lives of so many people better. My brother and I did most of the work on the farm with the help of neighborhood boys who needed jobs during the summer.

Edmond (Present)

As I turn over and stretch, I hear an awful racket coming from the hallway. I slide out of bed with the blanket wrapped around my naked body and quietly open the door just far enough to peek out. Coming down the hall is a Hispanic man in a wheelchair. He is attempting to get out of the chair to work his way down the stairs. Moving out into the hallway, inconveniently forgetting I am wrapped in a blanket to hide that I am naked, I offer to help the man. "Will you wait just a minute while I throw on some clothes, I ask?" He agrees and I hurry back to my room.

Leaning against the door in my room, I realize the man I am offering to help is actually a man named Edmond. Resigned, I quickly slide into my jeans throw on a T-Shirt and go back to the hallway. "Ok sir, now let's get you down the stairs! I will help you. Let me get you down there first and then I will come back up and get the chair for you." He looks at me so intently I am nervous thinking he might recognize me, but after a minute or so, he nods and lets me put my arm around him to start down the steps. His hair is curly but disheveled and his eyes are the color of dark chocolate. He smells of stale cigarettes and beer with those over-powered with the need of a bath. We slowly make our way down and I have the feeling he is sneaking looks at me from underneath his ball cap. At the bottom of the stairs is a bench, which has seen better days, however, looks strong enough to sit him on while I go back for the chair. On my trip up the steps, I decide to see if he will sense any recognition by introducing myself. I clamber back down and sit down on the bench, thrust my hand out and say, "Hi I'm Morgan. Who might you be?" He looks so stunned I might want to know his name he just sits and stares at me for an indeterminable amount of time. With his mouth curling up slightly, he finally says, "Hi, Morgan, I'm Edmond," while slowly extending his hand for me to shake.

We quietly sit there looking out the window at the busy street. Since neither one of us is very trusting this is a time to assess one another. After a little while, he begins to talk, almost as if I am not there, but talking, nevertheless. Memories of his youth are flooding into a verbal barrage of all the times this crazy town was full of his friends and how the passage of time has left him crippled and alone.

The rumbling of my stomach makes me realize how much time has passed sitting here listening to Edmond, so I put my hand on his arm and ask him if he is hungry. The look he gives me says a thousand words, but what I hear is he probably has not eaten a good meal in weeks. Without any warning he suddenly becomes very agitated and wants to get into his chair and go down the steps to the sidewalk. I move him into the chair and wheel him out and down to the sidewalk in front of the hotel.

Since it is Saturday, traffic is heavy and if my memory is serving me correctly this is when all the Monday through Friday workers does their grocery shopping and drop off their dry cleaning. Some are hustling to soccer games at the Recreational Park, while others are hurrying their kids to the Midget Football game. More memories come flooding back and I realize I have spent way too much time sitting with Edmond.

Frantic but trying to hide my distress, I stand up and say I will make sure someone brings him out lunch and it will be on me. Then without any more than a backward glance I run back up the stairs to my room. Once I open the door, I lean on it and take a deep breath. What the hell am I doing? Was coming back here the right thing to do? After several deep breaths, I can think clearly and realize I have been working toward this moment for many years and I am determined to see it through. One of the positive things which transpired this morning is Edmond who has been around this town forever and knows me, has expressed no sign of recognition.

Nick (Present)

It's Saturday morning and Nick is hurrying as usual. In a few hours he must put his game face on so 40 young football players will want to hang on to his every word. He runs into the bank to talk with the bank president, Tom Fraser about the upcoming board elections. Over the past few weeks, he has been working diligently with Fraser in pursuing candidates for the board which will be installed next week for loan approvals. So many of the local businesses have suffered over the last few years, but there is the plan for a new business complex being developed on the Jenkins property. With the development of the new complex, things are going to improve, and money is going to be needed.

Tom was just finishing a phone call when Nick poked his head into his office. "Got a minute, Tom?" asks Nick. "Sure Nick, you look intense, what's going on?" Nick realized at that moment how worried he had been since Fraser notified him about the progress of the business development project. "I just want to reassure you I will be behind you 100% at the election meeting on Tuesday," explained Nick.

"Also, I am curious, have you run into any interference from the Jenkins family regarding the sale of the property?" Fraser contemplates how much to say to Nick, knowing the relationship he had all those years ago with the Jenkins girl. "So far the discussions have been productive. Fraser says. Jonathan Jenkins is desperately holding out for as much money as he can, but I detect some weakening." Nick nods thoughtfully and says, "Well if you find yourself up against a roadblock let me know because I think I can lend some assistance. Jonathan and I haven't talked with each other in a long time, but we have a mutual respect." "Thanks Nick but I feel confident Jenkins will see his procrastination will be a detriment to a successful transaction".

Rushing out to the street, Nick's mind is racing. What the hell is he thinking offering to talk to Jonathan Jenkins? There is history between them and most of it is not good. If he was going to be honest with himself, he didn't want Jonathan to know he was even remotely associated with the deal. Suddenly his cell phone rings, and he looks at the screen and sees his wife is calling. Silencing the phone and putting it back into his pocket he walks back to his car realizing he needs to get home to pick up both his sons and get them to the field. More than likely this is why Whitney was calling him. The relationship he has with his wife is not a happy one. As he pulled up to the stop light, a woman steps out to cross the street. Nick pays little attention to her as his mind is preoccupied. While he is waiting at the light his gaze wanders back to the woman now standing across the street talking to of all people, Edmond, from the Hotel. Her hands are moving a mile a minute and suddenly he is reminded of Misty Jenkins whom he hadn't thought of in years.

Nick and Misty (Past)

Nick and Misty were high school sweethearts and most of the town assumed they would marry someday. Nick was the star quarterback, good-looking and from a prominent family. Everyone thought he would go on to the Pros after college. Misty was everyone's sweetheart, popular and easy to know. Her family was made up of hard-working farmers and strong community people. Misty and her brother, Jonathan, worked hard for the family farm and Nick helped at the farm when he wasn't practicing.

Misty's best friend was Whitney Miles. During their grammar school years, they were sidekicks, together in school and after almost every day. All through high school, Misty and Whitney remained friends. However, as the years went by their friendship became strained. High school politics often change the relationships between childhood friends and Misty and Whitney were no exception. Whitney's insecurities and jealousy of Misty were metamorphosing her into a wicked devious young woman. During their senior year, Whitney was always milling around the hallway near Nick's locker. Every time Misty would walk down that particular hallway, Whitney was there. Seeing Whitney lingering around Nick irritated Misty, but she knew Nick was true to her and would never be unfaithful. All through high school they were inseparable. She believed with all her being they would be together forever. However, life took a different road and the next thing she knew he was married to Whitney.

He is so distracted looking at her he doesn't see the light change. He hears a horn blow. "Why the hell I would be reminded of her, he mumbles to himself. It must be from talking about Jonathan with Fraser." Nick's cell phone rings again and this time he answers it, "What's up Whit? "Nick, do you know what time it is, the boys are chomping at the bit wondering when you are going to be back to take them down to the football field," snaps Whitney. Nick tries to keep his patience "I know I know I'm coming right now. I got held up at the bank talking with Tom Fraser." "Ok well try to get here soon because they are driving me nuts." whines Whitney. Nick hangs up and says to himself, "most people drive you nuts Whitney." His mind started to wander and suddenly Misty's eyes are staring right into his. He tries to put his thoughts away about Misty. Her memory had haunted him for many years until finally he was able to find a place for it. He had tucked it away behind the years in between and the present where he would no longer reach for her. The impact she had on him had been so powerful he had never really stopped loving her, even after all these years. Now, sitting in his car, in the middle of town and in a hurry, he had let himself drift back in time and found her there. He struggled to put these thoughts away, put his game face on and turn toward home to pick up his boys for the football game.

Morgan (Present)

My stomach is letting me know it is time to eat, so the question is, where I should take the chance to go? Walking along Main Street there are all kinds of familiar faces, but none of those faces seem to recognize me, which is a good thing but leaves me with a desolate feeling. The diner is the safest place to go I think, because there will not be as many local people eating there, or at least that's how it used to be. The familiarity of the town has left me with a sense of déjà vu. But eating is quickly becoming a necessity so surveying the diner quickly I spot a stool at the counter with no one sitting nearby.

Keeping my head down, I slowly scan the diner trying to see if anyone is looking a little too much in my direction. Susie Mitchell is standing right in front of me, "Hey would you like to sit down and what would you like to drink?" There are a few more wrinkles, a little bit of gray hair, but the eyes and the voice are the same. Susie had a voice which sounded like fingernails on a blackboard, but she had a heart of gold. All at once it strikes me 20 years have passed since I last saw Susie, and if my memory serves me correctly it was right at this diner. She looks directly at me and doesn't show any signs of recognizing me.

Susie was always a talker and that hasn't changed a bit. I watch her quietly as she goes along waiting on people. She is talking and laughing with most of the patrons and soon works her way back to me. "Are you new to the area? she asks. I haven't seen you around here before." "Yeah, I'm just passing through. I don't really have anywhere to be soon, so I might stick around for a few days and explore. It seems like a really nice town." I tell her. Susie beams with pride "Yeah good old Millersville, where everything stays the same. "If you would like to see the area, I will be glad to show you around on my day off." Trying to not sound ungrateful I say, "No, please don't trouble yourself with taking time to show me around on your day off. I'll wander around by myself and who knows what I might see or who I might meet." "Well, if you change your mind, just stop in and let me know. Where are you staying while you are here? There isn't any place nearby to stay except the Hotel and I don't know if they even have any rooms to rent." Susie said. Quietly I assure her, "They do," and abruptly stand up. Susie looks at me with a little uncertainty and says, "If you decide to spend more time here than you planned, you might want to try to find another place to stay."

After finishing lunch, I venture out onto the street taking in the smells and images of bustling Main Street. Walking back to the Hotel, I realize if I am going to continue and find the proof I will need, I will, as Susie said have to find a more permanent place to stay. If things are anything like they used to be then the Town Tavern, a local drinking establishment, is the place where there would be assistance to find a more permanent place to stay.

Trying to be as nonchalant as possible, I hurry back to my car so I can catch the afternoon football crowd at the Tavern. But first I double-check my appearance, because going out to the Tavern could possibly be a mistake. A glance in the car mirror rekindles my confidence. There is very little similarity of the woman looking back at me in the mirror to the girl who lived here so many years ago. The changes I made to myself are enough to fool almost anyone. I did hang out at the Tavern with Nick before, but it's a risk I need to take.

Slightly breathless, I hurry upstairs to my room, grab a ball cap and sunglasses which will help disguise me a little better. I am running down the steps to the landing in front of the Hotel, when I hear someone say, "What's the matter with you, someone chasing you?" It is Edmond, sitting out in front of the Hotel enjoying the sights. I hurriedly walk by and nervously laugh, "No, no just need to be somewhere and I'm late." He laughs and says, "Then you better get your ass moving, because you know you might miss something. You are here looking for something or someone aren't you?" Swallowing my annoyance, "why would you say that?" "I don't know you just seem to be very watchful, almost on a mission" "No, Edmund, I laughed. I'm a photographer and passing through. I definitely don't know anyone, and I certainly wouldn't be looking for something I haven't even lost. I'll see you later, Edmond."

Walking back to my car, I wonder what the hell that was all about. I think I may be too much in a hurry and intense in my behavior since I have arrived. I decide I will slow it down and be a little more nonchalant in my demeanor, more like someone passing through. Maybe Edmond needs to talk like he knows more than he does, but I am not taking any chances my behavior will somehow give me away. Enough worrying for now, I need to get to the Tavern and see if I can hear any gossip and find a place to stay.

The Town Tavern (Present)

The Town Tavern is Millersville's local drinking establishment and had been the place to go for as long as I can remember. When I was in my late teens, it was owned by Mr. Owens and was one of the local bars which would turn a blind eye on underage drinking. With gunstock wood floors, a glossy mahogany bar and the smell of stale cigarette smoke, it drew all the locals. It was a place where they kicked back and relaxed with their friends. As I walk in 20 years later, it still has a faint smell of cigarette smoke, which is odd because smoking has been banned for five years, and the wood floors and bar are still the same. There is a different atmosphere in here than in the past, TV's are hanging all around and the low tables which used to surround the perimeter of the bar are now high-top tables.

It's the middle of the afternoon on a Saturday and the clientele sitting around the bar is mostly male. Scattered throughout the stools are a few women with some of the old regulars sitting at the tables. College football games play on the TV's without the volume and the jukebox plays loudly in the background. Pulling my hat down and making sure my hair is securely through the back of it, I grab a stool at the corner of the bar. I want to be sure I sit facing the door so I can watch the different people come and go. Looking around, thankfully, I only see a few people who look familiar, so relaxing slightly I order a beer.

A few people glance in my direction, but no one is paying me much attention if I don't make eye contact with anyone. A conversation is going on near me that pique my curiosity. A man and woman are talking about their neighbor who has just up and left her husband and he is taking his children and moving in with his parents. As I continue to listen what I hear next is music to my ears, the house is going up for rent. Taking a deep breath, I lean over. "Excuse me but were you both just talking about a house for rent." I'm new to the area and I am looking for a place to stay". The couple turn and smile, and I realize the faces looking at me are none other than my Brother Jonathan's two friends from high school, Seth and Olivia. Seth and Olivia look the same just older and it sounds like they have their ears to the ground and know everything going on in Millersville. Trying to keep myself together, I hear them say, "You're new to the area? Where are you staying now, and where are you from? What brings you to Millersville?" All these questions were coming rapid fire from them, and I know this could be the informational pipeline I need to help me with my plan and to eventually accomplish my goal. They end their questioning by Olivia asking me "What's your name dear?" With a tentative smile I say, "Morgan Kiernan and you are?" We are the Palmers, Seth and Olivia, and it is very nice to meet you." Breathing a sigh of relief, I realize they don't have the slightest inclination of who they are talking to. "Do you want to know about a house to rent?" Nodding I answer. "I overheard you talking about your neighbors and the situation they are in and I was wondering if their house would be available to rent." "Well, Morgan the problem is we aren't sure what the plan is for the house. Our neighbors are splitting up and no one will be living in the house temporarily. As for long term, we have no way of knowing what the plan will be."

I don't want to appear too desperate, so I just nod and listen to the Palmers. As the conversation progresses, I find them to be very informative about events in Millersville. A couple of hours pass, and I realize I have relaxed a lot and am thoroughly enjoying my conversation with old friends of my family.

Suddenly the double doors which lead to the kitchen swing open and, a tall good-looking guy with dark, wavy hair walks through. Normally, I would not have noticed him, but surrounding him as he moved was this invisible but perceptible charismatic energy, the kind which startles you without warning. My eyes follow him while he strolls throughout the bar stopping and talking with several of the patrons. People yell out, Hey Brett how's it going? Brett, I shortly come to find out is the owner of the Town Tavern and now he is making his way over to where the Palmers and I are sitting. He smiles at them and says, "Hey Seth, Olivia, how's it going? "What's the deal you two, bad service or just nursing your beers?" "No Brett we have been getting great service and you know it. Stop fishing for a compliment. You know the Tavern has been going great since you took over ownership," quips Olivia. Brett laughs "You guys are great for my ego. So, who is this very pretty girl sitting next to you?" I look up and Brett is looking right at me or should I say right into me. I find myself looking away and unexpectedly blushing, which is suddenly accompanied by a startling, tender sensation. When I turn back around, he has the biggest smile on his face and bowing slightly says, "Hi, I'm Brett, your humble servant." Stuttering just a little, I somehow get out that my name is Morgan. "Well how do you do, Morgan. Are you new around here, I pretty much know everybody and haven't seen you around here before?" Still caught off guard by my reaction to him, I immediately say, "Yes, I'm just passing through. I may not be here very long." The Palmers look at me with something close to astonishment knowing full well I was just inquiring about a place to rent. Thankfully I am saved from any further discussion with Brett because his attention is pulled to another part of the tavern where some new customers have just walked in.

Seth turns, gives me a questioning look and says, "Morgan were you not asking us about our neighbor's house just a few minutes ago." "Yes, I was, but I'm not going to be here long, and I really don't want to become immersed in the community. "This place". I throw my hands up and around, "is definitely woven into the fabric of this town and which is great, but I don't want to become a part of it." Olivia looks hurt but pats my arm, and says "We'll see dear, Millersville has a way of growing on people." I just smile and say to myself, *"you have no idea"*.

The next hour or so passes by uneventful. We order some sandwiches and I listen while Seth and Olivia gossip about the town. What I find out just sitting there listening is very interesting but probably will not have any impact on my plan. Apparently, the high school is trying to raise money to expand through a referendum, while the old food store stands empty and a new development is being planned which would be around the corner from the Tavern. I enjoyed listening to them and after the small awkwardness we experienced while talking with Brett, they are as friendly as they can be. Suddenly in the distance, I hear someone call out "Hey Nick, did you guys win today?"

Quickly I look over at the door and see Nick walking in with a bunch of guys, laughing and hitting each other on the back. My stomach is doing flip-flops and I am staring as if I have a seen a ghost. Nick Darlington was my high school boyfriend and to most people in Millersville, was going to become my husband. But many events transpired and we never married. Here he is 20 years later, and I am going to have to deal with it. Nick is walking all around the tavern talking with everyone and I'm starting to wonder how I can quickly take my leave of the Palmers. Instead, I feel trapped on my stool and before I know it, Nick has made his way over to Seth and Olivia. "Seth, how have you been? I haven't seen you in forever. Olivia, you are looking as beautiful as ever." "Oh Nick, stop flirting with me," laughs Olivia. I take that moment to get up and excuse myself to the restroom.

Walking to the restroom I am now contemplating leaving the Tavern without saying anything more to the Palmers, but logic takes over and having confidence in how different I look, I decide to go back and sit down for a few more minutes. Nick apparently is too caught up in himself to pay much attention to me or at least that's what I am counting on.

In the restroom, I fix my makeup, redo my hair, and take a good look at myself in the mirror. Morgan Kiernan, the woman looking back at me, has red hair and blue eyes. Over the past 20 years, I transformed myself into Morgan Kiernan, cosmetic surgery helped and some due to the burden of the past haunting me. Probably the hardest thing to change was my voice but lowering it some and the effect of living in the Midwest have given my voice a slightly different accent.

Misty Jenkins was, what some would call, a Tomboy when she was younger. Growing up on the farm most days were spent out in the fields working which had her brown as a berry by the end of the summer. Freckles were speckled all over her arms and legs and her hair looked like the sun had dropped small star bursts of light through her dark hair. Some people would say she was cute when she was younger, but nothing to write home about.

Putting my game face on, I walk out of the restroom and head back over to where Seth and Olivia are still chatting with Nick. As I walk up, Nick turns and says, "So you must be Morgan. Seth and Olivia have been telling me how pleased they are that they have met such an interesting person, or at least Olivia thinks you are." Nick let me in on a little secret. "Olivia is quick to make friends even though she just met you about an hour ago." I feel myself getting hot and uncomfortable, but I cover it with a quick laugh, and say, "Well I like Olivia and Seth as well. I've enjoyed their conversation and all their stories about the people in the area." Everyone laughs and then the conversation gets very general. Nick decides to take a seat next to Seth, so I keep myself calm and continue to talk with Olivia while Nick and Seth are talking about the game earlier in the day.

Out of the corner of my eye I see Brett spending a little too much time looking my way. It seems like every time I look over toward him, I catch him looking at me. At that moment I decide I have had enough of sitting at the Tavern and it seems I now may have a possible place to stay so I get up to leave.

"Olivia, please let me know if you find out anything about your neighbor's place. You can leave word for me at the Hotel bar" I said. "I'm going to take off now but I'm sure I will see you around." "Ok, Morgan, it sure was nice to meet you. We are usually out here every Thursday and Saturday night, so stop in again." I make my way around the bar to the door and just as I get to the end of the bar, Brett is standing right in front of me. "Excuse me, I'm going to head out now." Brett smiles devilishly and says, "Before you go, I want to know how to find you again." "Oh, I will be around, I may be staying in Millersville for a little while. Catch you later." I go around him and out the door to my car. Once in my car I need a few minutes to catch my breath.

I learn later after I left the Tavern, Nick was grilling Seth and Olivia about me trying to find out who I was. Seth was being as close-mouthed as possible, but Olivia was full of opinions about me. "Oh Nick, she is so interesting. She's from the Midwest and has been traveling and has decided to stop in our little town. She thinks she might stay for a while. She's interested in finding a place to rent. Isn't that great?" Nick laughs, "Olivia, it sounds to me like you may have found a new friend. She seems very quiet, but she certainly is beautiful." Clearing his throat Seth cautions, "Nick, don't get ahead of yourself. She is just passing through. Plus, if Whitney ever saw your eyes straying elsewhere, I would worry about your survival. Sometimes I wonder what you were thinking all those years ago."

"You know, Seth, at the time it seemed like the right thing to do," he says remembering. "Misty's family's reputation was deteriorating plus her Dad was into crazy stuff with electromagnetic fields. I was young and selfish and made some bad decisions. I took the easy way out and I'm not proud of it. By the time I figured out how wrong I was Whitney and I were getting married and Misty was gone." Seth frowned, "Did you ever try to find her? Do you know why she left in such a hurry? Come on Nick, Whitney was her best friend so finding her should have been a priority since Whitney would probably want to know where she went as well." Nick laughed, bitterness creeping into his voice. "Whitney could have cared less and would not hear of me doing any digging as to where Misty went and why. It became not worth the fight, if you know what I mean. But I've been thinking a lot more about Misty lately what with the land development deal with the Jenkins property."

Seth looked over at Olivia and smiled. "Nick, is Jonathan really going to sell his property? It seems like such a shame the place has been in his family for generations." "I know, Nick said, but he has mismanaged it so badly this seems like his only choice. You know today I thought about the Jenkins' more than usual, and I swear I thought I saw someone today who reminded me of Misty. I was at the stop light in town and this woman was standing on the corner talking to of all people, Edmond, the town drunk and she walked just like Misty. She was tall and thin with red hair, so it couldn't have been Misty." Olivia laughed, "You just described Morgan, she's tall and thin and we have never seen her take off that ball cap she wears but I can swear there is red hair underneath it." Nick chuckled, "You know Olivia, you might be right, we may have found the mystery woman who was standing on the street corner earlier."

Nick, Misty and Whitney (Past)

Senior Prom was fast approaching, and everyone was getting their dates lined up and jockeying to get the prettiest girls to say yes. Misty was obviously going with Nick, and Whitney was hoping one of Nick's friends was going to ask her. The girls went shopping for their dresses and were constantly talking about how much fun it was going to be after the Prom when they all went to the Shore.

The Prom was going to be the second weekend in May and as of the end of April Whitney did not have a date. Whitney could talk of nothing else when they were on their way to school one day. "Misty, what the heck, what is it about me so far no one has asked me to the Prom?" Why isn't anyone asking me to the Prom? Nick keeps telling me Chad is going to ask me but so far he hasn't even looked at me," whined Whitney. "Just relax Whitney, one of those clueless jocks will ask you. They are so caught up in themselves they aren't even thinking about the Prom. I will talk to Nick about it tonight and see if he can put a fire under Chad to pop the question to you soon." "Ok thanks, Misty, I'm sure worrying about it isn't going to make it happen any sooner." The girls got to the student parking lot, found a parking spot then hurried up to the school before they were late. Meanwhile, Nick had gotten to school early because the football coach wanted to have a word with him before school started.

Nick's stomach was in knots as he walked to the coach's office wondering if this was going to be his break and Coach was going to tell him he'd been accepted to Michigan. Michigan Wolverine football is what Nick had dreamed about his whole life. Watching TV with Keith Jackson commentating and sitting with his Dad watching games every Saturday were some of Nick's best times. While other guys were hanging out with their girlfriends or just goofing off, Nick was on the couch every Saturday watching football with his Dad. Misty understood if she wanted to spend time with Nick, she needed to love football and Michigan as much as Nick did.

When Nick reached Coach's office, he was on the phone, so Nick waited outside in the hallway. Finally, Coach got off the phone and motioned for Nick to come in. "Hey Nick, what's happening?" he joked.

Coach Nelson was a great coach, good with the athletes and very in tune with their needs, from their academic successes and failures to their success and failures on the field. He had an open-door policy with all his athletes and even other students would drop in to talk with him now and then. Nick smirked "Nothing much Coach, just watching the mail for any acceptance letters which might be coming in. Keeping my eye out for the Michigan letter hopefully." Coach Nelson frowned a little but then smiled quickly and said, "Yes I hope it comes soon." Nick saw the frown but passed it off to Coach's quirky personality, thinking he's already missing the wins which had been stacking up since Nick had become quarterback.

Coach asked Nick to sit down but didn't start any kind of conversation just stared at the floor. Nick started to feel uneasy knowing Coach was never at a lack for words. Coach hesitated then said, "Nick you know I think the world of you and believe in your talent completely. You are the best quarterback to ever play at Millersville High and I mean that sincerely. I have great expectations for you and your future." Nick smiled, "But?" Coach Nelson shook his head and smiled but the smile looked sad, if that makes any sense. Then he began "I'm not sure what you are experiencing in life now will be something which will carry you into the future you deserve." Nick looked bewildered and said,

"Coach what is it you are trying to say. You have been beating around the bush about something since I walked in here. Now I think it's time you just say what you have on your mind because I don't think it's going to be any announcement about where I'm going to college to play ball." Coach suddenly laughed, "You know Nick, you're right. Make sure you let me know as soon as you hear anything. Is the coach from Michigan still in touch with your parents?" Nick nodded his head and said, "Yes he is, but my financial aid packet hasn't been approved yet so I'm still officially waiting to receive the acceptance letter." "I'm sure you will and Millersville will be so proud of you." Nick decided it was time to leave. He started to leave the office and Coach suddenly reached out grabbed him by the shoulder and said, "no matter what remember I've always believed in you."

After Nick left Coach Nelson's office, he decided he really needed to see Misty so he drove to the farm to see if she could go for a ride. On the way over to the farm Nick decided to stop at the local convenience store to get a soda. As he pulled into the store's parking lot, he saw Whitney's car parked by the store's entrance. "Damn I hope she doesn't ask me about the prom again. This is getting ridiculous I should have to find her a date to the prom," he mumbled. Nick quickly got out of his car and walked into the store trying his best to avoid Whitney. But just as he turned to go toward the cashier, Whitney wandered over and said, "Hey Nick, what are you doing today?" "Nothing much, Whitney, I am getting a soda and heading over to pick up Misty. What are you up to today?" Whitney groaned, "Helping my Mom with her cleaning service. One of the girls called out today so she asked me to lend a hand." "Well, its good you can help out once in a while," said Nick. Whitney lowered her head, Nick, can I talk to you for a minute, I think something is up with Misty." "Alright, let's go out and sit in my car and you can enlighten me as to what is going on with "my girlfriend". We have been closer than ever lately so I think I would know if something was up with her."

The Farm (Present)

I had decided to go for a drive and take some pictures, so after leaving the Tavern, I stopped at the Hotel to get my camera. Now back in my car, I decide to take a ride past the farm, my childhood home and see with my own eyes how things truly are. It's late in the day so there shouldn't be anyone out in the yard working, not that there is much work left to do with only Jonathan there to do it. Nervous jitters are running a marathon in my stomach, but I put my car in gear and head out of town.

Turning onto Jenkins's Lane where the farm is located and seeing how changed the houses are is an earth-shattering moment for me. Deep down inside I want the last twenty years to have left no indelible stamp on the neighborhood, but reality cannot escape our consciousness and I knew it was going to be different. The houses look so worn out, as if time had waged war on them and they have not been able to recover. I arrive at the beginning of our farmland. The fields of the farm are empty, no animals are in the pasture, the tractors are all rusted and sitting lopsided with flat tires. As I drive farther up the road other places are empty as well. I turn the car around to go back. The Smiths who lived next door are out in their front yard sitting enjoying the warm early evening. As I ride by, I wave to them in a friendly gesture knowing they have no idea who is waving to them. I stop down the road a bit and pull over. Getting out of the car with my camera and walking back toward the farm, I am snapping photos. With the long-range lens I purchased before coming back home, I see Jonathan walking out of the farmhouse toward the barn. He looks defeated, but he always did walk like he was in no hurry to get anywhere.

A feeling of homesickness washes over me. I see a couple of dogs running around in the yard of the farmhouse and two young guys sitting on the trunk of a car. It is as if the moment has stopped in time. They are my two great nephews Steven and Chase, who were just little boys when I last saw them.

I wander into memory where I see our moderately sized farm milking about 100 cows and farming approximately 400 acres. When I was a kid, my father and brother would do construction projects to offset the lack of work they had during the winter months. Jonathan was the oldest, and the only boy, so he spent a lot of time working with Dad and learning all aspects of construction and building maintenance. It was always assumed by my parents Jonathan would stay at the farm and eventually take it over so when Jonathan got married, he and his wife Sarah moved to the family farmhouse. But as the years went by Jonathan began to resent our parents never fully understanding what it meant to be self-employed.

During the next few years while I navigated my teens, the farm prospered, and things became easier for my Mom and Dad financially. They began to attend concerts at a theater located in a nearby state. These concerts ran every month and my Mom, having a musical background wanted to attend as many as they could. One night while waiting for the concert to begin an older couple sat down next to them. Dr. and Mrs. Sebastian were scientists and had been working with the theory electromagnetic fields were scattering the stray electrical current which was produced by the utility companies. The friendship which developed during these cultural moments was the root of the change transforming my father and mother and the lives they had made for themselves.

Over many conversations Dad explained to Dr. Sebastian how water acted as a conduit for the stray current, a centuries old technique of dowsing was the tool used to detect and expose the electromagnetic fields running through a person's body. He had discovered electromagnetic fields are enhanced by stray electric currents which penetrate the body leaving behind a negative footprint. He believed the stray currents coming from the electric towers were strong enough to affect the health of those living nearby; most vulnerable were the children, those with weakened immune systems, and the elderly.

Dad was doing quiet research on the electrical towers which were scattered all around our area causing the families living near them to have more health problems than normal. Many of the residents already had struggles with cancer and other serious illness. His internal need to help people was beginning to overcome him. As time went on, he focused his energies on finding evidence the electric company knew just how much stray electric they were producing and the effect it had on the families in proximity to the towers.

As time passed my Mom noticed they weren't being invited out as much by the group of friends they had for most of their married life. When we would go into the local stores, I noticed people looking at us with questioning expressions on their face. Nick who had been a part of my life since I was a little girl in knee socks, and who was considered by everyone, including me, to be the good-looking neighborhood boy was constantly teasing me about my Dad and what he was doing. To add insult to injury, my brother Jonathan wanted nothing to do with it. He felt about Dad the same way as all the other people, a simple farmer whose belief in his fight had overwhelmed rational thought. I wonder what would have happened if he had just believed the scientific studies of Dr. and Mrs. Sebastian and the findings of my father.

One day many months later I overheard my parents talking about the electromagnetic forces and what would happen if Dad could effectively authenticate the impact the electromagnetic forces had on people's health.

More and more people were calling and asking for help and what Dad was doing was starting to spread around the county.

After years of living in such close proximity to the towers, the health of many of the residents was in jeopardy. Most people didn't understand why they were getting ill or in some cases why they just didn't feel well. Electromagnetic fields can be very detrimental to the health of our population and the biggest offender in Millersville was the electric company.

Looking back on all of the controversy surrounding their methods, I believe this was the beginning of the problems which led to the worsening condition of the farm and Jonathan becoming more discouraged and ultimately to the death of my parents. In a way he was captured. My father could not manage the farm without him.

Since I don't want Jonathan getting curious and coming down to see who is pulled over on his property. I jump in my car and head back into town. I would have to bide my time and find a way to get back to the farm. By the time I pull into the parking lot of the Hotel it is getting late and finding a parking spot is a problem. There are cars parked everywhere causing me to wonder what is going on. Then it hits me. It's Friday night and the Hotel has a bar downstairs. I recall earlier I had seen a poster advertising Friday and Saturday night entertainment, which seems to be why there are so many cars in the parking lot. Not wanting to see anyone, I slip into the building through a back door uneventfully and get up to the second floor.

Jonathan (Present)

Jonathan tossed and turned most of the night so when the alarm went off at 5:00 am he felt as though he had hardly slept. Staggering out to the kitchen to get some coffee, he plopped down in the chair and lay his head down on his arms wondering why he was up so early when there was nothing to go out to on the farm. The cows were all gone and working in the fields was pointless but old habits persist. Probably his lack of sleep was due to the uneasiness he had about the meeting scheduled for 10:00 this morning.

He had been putting off the meeting with Tom Fraser at the bank for weeks now, but time was running out and so was the money. Negotiating a price for the farm and the land was something he never thought he would have to do, but with Misty gone and no one else to help salvage what was left of the farm, he felt he had no choice. What was really getting to him was he had finally realized he had failed his family, his parents, and most of all, Misty. She had tried to tell him their Dad's belief in the electromagnetic fields and the stray electrical currents were real. Jonathan had been skeptical about the whole process and had concluded his Dad was just short of being a little crazy. He had been angry for so long about how the farm was deteriorating and had spent years blaming everyone but himself. Now all he could think about was getting rid of all the bad memories and moving on. Not that any of this was going to assuage his guilt but at least he would be able to make a new life for himself and his family with the money the property would bring as a result of the sale.

The last twenty years had taken its toll on him both emotionally and physically. He had always been steady just working and never having much of a social life. Already being somewhat of an introvert, he internalized the times he fought his dad over the years. As the time went on and with the farm struggling, he became distant. Now this was eating away at him and enveloping him in tons of guilt. Working the farm again was not possible and the realization was very hard for him to swallow. His lackadaisical attitude along with his neglect of certain aspects of the farm over the years was instrumental in the farm going downhill and losing money. Now there was barely any money left and Jonathan needed the property deal to come through if there was any hope of a new life for himself and his family. Jonathan was determined Tom Fraser, the bank manager, would come to the realization the land was worth far more than he had been offering. With the meeting time becoming imminent Jonathan hurried downtown to the bank to meet Fraser.

Misty and Nick (Past)

It was the weekend, and the weather was great which meant Nick would be over in his jeep with the top down. Usually, they hung out together starting Saturday afternoon and couldn't be separated until late Sunday night.

Nick pulled into the yard around 4:00 and Misty was just a little irritated. Nick had said he would be there around 3:30. She clamped down on her anger knowing there would be a good explanation. Nick looked aggravated but Misty tried to be cheerful by giving him a smile. "What's up, did you get held up somewhere?" laughed Misty. Nick shrugged and said, "No I just got tied up." Misty frowned and said, "Ok, has something happened I need to know about?" "No Misty, you don't need to know everything, just let it be." Misty thought to herself, "*yeah ok I'm really getting angry now, so he can just come clean with whatever is bothering him.*" "Since when do we keep things from each other? If something is bothering you, talk to me." Nick gave her a little smile and said, "You know Misty you can be a real pain in the ass, but sometimes you just make me laugh. You are trying so hard not to be mad at me for being late. I'm sorry, I got stuck talking to Coach. He was talking in circles which got me amped up, so I rode around for a little while before coming over." Misty looked concerned and said, "I thought you talked to Coach the other day at school? He wanted to see you again?" "Yeah, I'm not sure what the deal is," Nick answered. "He keeps talking about my chances for next year at a big-league school and he sounds like if I don't get in it won't be entirely my fault, like something or someone would stop me from getting accepted to Michigan. It is making me nervous because I really don't know what the hell he is talking about. The more I talk to him the more I think he doesn't really know if I will be accepted to Michigan. Tomorrow I'm going to find out what exactly is going on in that guy's mind."

"All this talk about next year is confusing to me as well Misty, because I don't know what you are going to do. Have you decided anything yet, Misty?" "No, not yet. My Mom and Dad aren't being too cooperative about whether or not they are going to help me with tuition," she answered. "Knowing whether or not they are going to help me has a lot to do with where I can go. I've been accepted at some small schools, but I want to go to Michigan with you and I would never be able to finance it by myself. Since I don't play a sport, I have to get accepted purely on my academics." Nick laughed, "Well there shouldn't be any trouble as smart as you are. Any school should accept you with your grades as good as they are." Misty shrugged and said, "You would hope so, but I don't think that is how it works all the time."

"Let's change the subject, Nick, this conversation is beginning to unnerve me. It's the weekend so let's go out and have a good time tonight. Which reminds me, have you talked to any of your buddies about taking Whitney to the prom? She is driving me nuts about getting a date. You might think I was her social director as much as she is going on about it." Nick laughed, "Whitney needs to get a life and stop worrying about going to the prom and start thinking about next year." Misty frowned, "Whitney isn't going to try to get into college anywhere. Her ambitions have more to do with finding a husband and settling down and having children. Every time I talk about school, she changes the subject. Going to the prom with some popular guy is all she can think about right now and somehow it's become my job to get her a date." Nick laughed nervously and said, "You know, Misty, pretty soon Whitney is going to start looking my way for a date. We don't want her doing that, so I suggest you and me figure out how to get her a date and be done with this."

"I need to find out what is going on with Coach, all these little talks he is having with me are starting to drive me just a little crazy. So, I will call you later and we'll go out and get some dinner."

Jack Callahan (Past)

More people were contacting Dad to help them with the problems they were experiencing. Every one of the families had health problems which lived within two miles of the large imposing electrical towers. With the use of the dowsing rods Dad had determined their homes were being exposed to stray current which was contributing to the exposure of electromagnetic fields which can cause a myriad of diseases and health issues. Dad knew the electric company was not properly controlling the stray current emanating from the towers, but proving it was a whole other matter.

There was a sequence of events which catapulted my family's undoing, and it began with the first visit from a "so called" salesman named Jack Callahan. It was a rainy day and Dad was in the house longer than usual in the morning. It was very common for visitors to pull into the yard on days the weather was not conducive for farming. Don't be fooled, some of those visitors were not very welcome on a working farm because they were salesman trying to sell nonsense. Dad had a keen sense of those salesmen who were trying to swindle money out of hardworking farmers. This day, however, a gentleman showed up in a pickup truck and was dressed more like a farmer than a businessman. Jack Callahan, a name I will never forget and to this day gives me chills up and down my spine.

Even though it was raining that day, and Dad still had a multitude of chores to do on the farm, the visitor had a little more time than usual, but it still wasn't going to be enough by his standards. Jack Callahan, a representative from the electric company, portraying himself as a local supporter of the hardworking dairy farmer was planning to make an impression on my Dad.

Looking back his presentation was very smooth, he talked the farmer's talk. Crops, milk prices, weather and the government were all the key words he used that day. Those were what we call hot buttons which would get most farmers very animated and talkative. Jack was able to ingratiate himself and wrangle his way into our world by visiting every now and then. Never too much or too often, but just enough to have my Dad looking forward to his visit and the fabulous tasting container of his wife's peach sun tea he brought each time he came. It was probably how he got to have any time with Dad. Jack provided conversation for Dad which a lot of people couldn't do. He wasn't a farmer, but he had a keen understanding of what the farmer was up against. Little did we know, he was gathering his information by gaining the trust of my Dad. This was his first goal and his trust he was going to find out exactly what my Dad was up to.

On one of those many visits, my Dad began to loosen up and tell Jack all about the dowsing rods and how he used them to find water. I was on my way to the barn early one morning to give my

Dad a message from my Mother when I saw Jack's truck parked in the driveway. Just as I was getting ready to walk into the barn, I heard Jack's voice. Quickly but quietly, I turned and tucked myself behind some hay bales beside the barn door and listened. "Jack, I've been doing this for all kinds of well diggers for many years. Farmers need to know where water is on their land so they can install field tiles.""

"Over the last few months, I've found other uses for the rods I haven't quite perfected yet." Jack's eyebrows raised and he said, "Really is there some big breakthrough in using dowsing rods." "Well, no, they still are used to find water but I'm finding their ability to find water is also becoming effective in determining whether water is acting as a conduit for electrical current," said Dad. Jack laughed and said, "You're kidding right? Those rods you use find electrical current, how is that possible?" At that point, Dad felt he had said too much and changed the subject with Jack.

Over the next few weeks, Jack made several stops at the farm and really worked Dad for more information, but Dad became very closemouthed after that conversation. Jack Callahan continued hanging around asking all kinds of questions and Dad knew now there was more to his frequent visits than he was admitting. He was suggesting he accompany my Dad on some of his visits to the families which were suffering. Jack's persistence in this belied his normal casual attitude. During one of Jack's many visits to the farm, he spent more time than usual talking with my Mom or should I say interrogating her. To make it seem casual, he kept intercepting it with conversation about the peach sun tea Elizabeth, his wife, always made and how he would always bring Dad some. He mentioned it was a family recipe. Somehow, we needed to find out more about Jack Callahan and what was behind his constant visits.

Right now, though, my problem was how to convince my parents to help me pay for my college. With all these people relying on my Dad for his help the thought of asking him about college seemed insignificant. Somehow, I needed to figure out how I was going to get enough money to pay for college on my own. While I was contemplating my dilemma, I heard my parents arguing about how the farm was being neglected. What bothered me about the arguing was Dad being so insistent what he was doing would only help the farm in the end. I realized that day he thought he was going to change the world. If there was only some way to prove the electric company was responsible for all the sickness, then Dad would be able to move on and get back to farming. At that time, I was determined to find out something which would help my family.

Morgan and Brett (Present)

The colors of fall are breathtaking. I decide to wander downtown to walk amidst the autumn beauty which had transformed the foliage from one splendid array of colors to another. As I walk, I realize how calm and serene I am now feeling. People say time heals all wounds, and I may be beginning to transform my colors as well. Looking at all the comings and goings of the Millersville townspeople makes me feel content.

Walking along I suddenly feel like I don't have a care in the world until I find myself stumbling over a raised sidewalk because I wasn't paying attention. I feel myself falling down. Taking a minute to realize I am not hurt, I just sit there thinking about all the events which led me here. Suddenly my eyes filled up. I don't see Brett, the owner of the Tavern coming toward me walking determinedly. He leans down and pulls me up into his arms, and in a comforting voice he says, "I'm glad I came upon you when I did. Are you hurt Morgan?" "No, just my pride that's all. Thank you, Brett, for coming to my rescue." "Well Morgan, I was headed to get something to eat when I came upon you, and since you are not hurt, I would very much like to take you to lunch." I quickly come up with an excuse, "Brett, you don't have to, honestly it is not necessary besides don't you have a bar to run?" "Well Morgan, I want to get to know you and what better way to do to that than through your need to eat. You do eat, don't you?" Instead of getting annoyed with Brett, I surprise myself by smiling and agreeing to go with him to lunch. "Ok, you're on - so who has the best food in town?"

After riding for a while through the countryside, I wonder where we are going since it is definitely not to the Tavern. "So, Brett, where are you taking me? It's not to some quiet no name restaurant where I won't even be able to get a decent glass of wine is it?" I laugh. No sooner do I say this than we turn into a small parking lot in front of a brick building. ""What do we have here, Brett, some kind of hidden treasure you are going to tell me has the greatest Italian food ever?" Brett grins, "Exactly. Welcome to Botero's, the best kept secret in this area. It just so happens I have an inside connection with the owners, so we are going to have lunch before they even open." "How is that possible?" Brett smiles, "they only serve dinner, but as a favor to me they are making us lunch." Brett pushes open the door and the aromas which assault my senses are enough to make my mouth water, and for me to become suddenly tongue tied.

A small but robust woman heads our way, "Brett, Brett what are you doing? Get in here and stop letting all the cold air in here. Who is the beautiful young lady you managed to bring in to see me?" laughs Mrs. Botero. "Oh, so I don't warrant having a pretty girl on my arm, is that what you are insinuating," smiles Brett. "Morgan, it's my immense pleasure to introduce you to

Mrs. Botero, owner and matriarch to the Botero empire. Isn't that right, Mrs. B?" "Oh, stop trying to butter me up, Brett. Come over here, Morgan, and let me look at you. Don't pay the least bit of attention to Brett; he is just a big overgrown kid." Smiling warmly, I go sit down at the table with Mrs. Botero and as promised, she gives me the once over. Laughingly I say, "Will I do?" Interestingly enough she nods solemnly, and says, "Finally he has listened to me and has found himself a lovely girl." "Oh my, I don't know about all that. We just met a few days ago and we are far from being a couple. It was just a chance meeting which brought us here together." Mrs. Botero just smiles, turns and quickly barks out orders to get lunch brought out to us. Brett comes sauntering up to the table and somehow gets his long, lanky physique into the other chair at the table. "So, are you two getting acquainted and Mrs. B, I did good right?" "Oh, my boy, rest assured you have outdone yourself this time, so don't screw it up, Ok?" There is nothing more annoying than to have people talk about you as if you are not in the room, let alone sitting right with them. I clear my throat, "So whenever you two are finished discussing my qualities I would like to sample some of what is creating those delicious smells. That is if you two can break away from your conversation." Both of them laugh and Mrs. Botero says, "Morgan, don't be upset, I've known Brett all his life, he is like a son to me and I just always want the best for him. Now let's get down to business and eat."

After stuffing ourselves with some of the greatest tasting Italian food I have ever tasted and saying goodbye to Mrs. B, we leave and head back to Millersville. Both Brett and I are pretty quiet in the car, both absorbed in our own thoughts. I can't help wondering if this small interlude is the precept to something bigger between the two of us. Shaking my head, I tell myself you are *crazy woman, you aren't even being truthful as to who you are. How are you going to even begin a relationship!* Brett starts to say something but instead leans over and grabs my hand massaging my palm with his thumb. Then he looks at me with these beautiful expressive eyes the color of chestnuts with the biggest smile on his handsome face and starts laughing. In spite of myself, I laugh along with him. We spend the rest of the ride uneventfully and next thing I know we are back in town. "Where are you living Morgan, I'll drop you off," asked Brett. "Well, right now I'm staying at the hotel, but Olivia and Seth said their neighbor's house might be available to rent. I will have to catch up to them tomorrow and see if I can find out more about the availability and who to contact for the rental information." Brett frowns and says, "Ok, but please don't spend too much time staying at the Hotel." "Why what is the issue with staying there, so far I haven't had any problems," asked Morgan. "I know, but some of the clientele there leave something to be desired," said Brett. "If you are talking about Edmond, he has been nothing but nice to me especially when I didn't know anyone here," said Morgan. "It's not Edmond, Morgan. I want you to move into something else more comfortable and safer. Haven't you figured it out yet, you and I are going to become inseparable," laughs Brett.

Jonathan and the Bank (Present)

Jonathan finds himself wanting to delay his visit with Tom Fraser yet knowing it is inevitable, he goes ahead and gets ready to go to the bank. His trepidation concerning the sale of the Farm had been occupying every waking moment and each day went by he became more anxious. This whole process was eating away at the very fiber of him and now the day was upon him, there was no way to avoid Tom Fraser waiting to make a deal. He needed to walk into this meeting with confidence the offer on the table was one he could live with… *Wow it was almost funny! Live with selling the family farm because I couldn't make it a profitable business, because I let it deteriorate into a shell of a farm. Who was I kidding?* Jonathan took a deep breath and with feigned confidence said to himself, "*this is going to work out and when it does, I'm going to find Misty and tell her how sorry I am for what happened and hope she will be able to forgive me.*"

When arriving at the bank, Jonathan is required to wait for Tom Fraser which was not helping his mental state. The longer he had to wait the more nervous he was becoming, causing him to sweat and become increasingly irritated about sitting there while customers were coming in and out of the bank. His imagination kicks into high gear wondering if all of the customers know why he is waiting there.

Finally, a bank clerk motioned to him to follow her to the back offices where Tom Fraser was located. "Jonathan, come in and have a seat, can I get you something to drink." asks Tom. "No, Tom I'm fine, but thank you anyway. I'd rather just get down to business." "Oh of course, I'm sure this has been weighing on your mind. I want you to relax though Jonathan, the bank is here to help you with this sale. We are dedicated to get you the best price possible for the land." "I know, I know, Tom you have no idea how hard this has been for me. Deciding to do this has been something I never thought I would have to do." Tom tried to appear concerned but was ready to get this deal signed, sealed and delivered. This sale would help the economic outlook for the area and will also increase the bank's bottom line because of the construction loans which may develop. If the Jenkins deal falls through and Jonathan has second thoughts about selling the land, it will not bode well for Tom with the Board of Directors. The investors were getting impatient for the completion of the sale and were putting pressure on the Board to complete the sale. So, there is no way Jonathan is going to back out now," thought Tom.

"Tell me Tom, how much of this sale will help the Bank and what is in it for you?" asks Jonathan suddenly. "Well Jonathan, I'm sure you are aware the plan for the land is to develop it into a Town center, with homes, stores, and a golf course. The future of Millersville is connected to this project. Your farm constitutes 800 acres of prime real estate and there are investors lining up to get in on the project. Our plan is to get you the best offer possible which will help not only you but the Bank as well and of course, I will benefit from the sale in some way. I know how hard this must be for you, Jonathan, especially with Misty gone and the weight of the sale entirely on your shoulders. I know the farm was left to you but having her here surely would give you emotional support." "If Misty was here, Tom, we wouldn't be sitting here even having this conversation because there would be no sale pending," utters Jonathan. "Yes, you are probably right", states Tom, "but why are we even talking about Misty. You haven't heard from her in years and I don't see any reason why she would show up now." "Misty has been known to do some unexpected things in her lifetime, but right now showing up here doesn't seem likely," replies Jonathan. *"How I wish Misty would somehow let me know what she thinks about this sale and give me some kind of absolution for what I'm about to do," says Jonathan to himself.* Suddenly Jonathan realizes he might not be ready to do this after all.

Looking at Tom, he speaks very slowly, "I want you to get me the list of investors and their phone numbers. Also, I want to have the sale of the land postponed another couple of weeks." Tom replied with just a little rancor, "That might not be such a good idea, Jonathan. There is a lot of money at stake here and we wouldn't want the window of opportunity to close for you." Stunned at his own resolve, Jonathan responds "I don't think this will happen if what you say is true about the interest in the land.

A couple more weeks won't hurt anything, besides your commitment to the success of this sale will help convince the investors to cool their heels just a little while longer. What I think is I've taken a very apathetic attitude about this situation and it's about time I become a bit more invested in it. So, what I want you to do is get me the list I asked for and we will revisit this later."

Jonathan gets up, shakes Tom's hand and leaves the Bank finally feeling better than he had in months knowing he didn't just acquiesce to Fraser. Meanwhile no more than two blocks from the bank, Morgan is getting out of Brett's car and heading up the steps of the Hotel.

Morgan (Present)

Heading into the Hotel, I decide to wander into the bar and see if Edmond is anywhere around. I figured out quickly he didn't leave the hotel area very often, so I was sure he was sitting somewhere inside. Sure enough, he was sitting in his chair by the pool tables watching a couple of guys play. "Edmond, what have you been up to this glorious day?"

"Morgan, what in God's name are you so happy about? There is nothing more annoying than someone who is overflowing with good cheer." "Oh, come on, Edmond don't be such a bore, there is a lot to be happy about. We're living aren't we, and believe me things could be a lot worse, I don't know about you but I'm going to do whatever I can to stay happy." Edmond shakes his head and laughs, "You know Morgan, I've only known you for a week or so, yet somehow I feel like I've known you forever and you are right things could be a lot worse. So, humor a disabled pool shark and let me beat you in a game of pool unless you think you can beat me."

While playing pool with Edmond, I notice some commotion on the other side of the bar. Trying not to look too interested in the event transpiring, I try to concentrate on Edmond and the game. Suddenly I hear a familiar voice, or at least one I had known as well as my own. "Nick what are you doing here, I'm not ready to go home yet. If this is why you are here, you might as well go the hell home," Whitney shouts. Slurring her words, she continues berating Nick, "Can't a girl spend a little time just having some fun without worrying about her husband tracking her down. But oh, I forgot, you are great at that aren't you Nick? Always the perfect Nick, don't let Whitney cast a shadow on the great Nick's reputation" Quietly, Nick whispers, "Whitney, knock it off, you are making a spectacle of yourself again. Please get yourself together and I will take you home." As Whitney stumbles off to the restroom, Nick looks around the bar and ends up heading over to Edmond and me at the pool table.

"Hey Edmond, what's up. I haven't seen you for a while, how are things going?" "Same as usual Nick, but things could be worse isn't that right Morgan?" Eyeing Nick, I say, "That's right Edmond." With some astonishment and embarrassment, Nick says, "its Morgan, right? I saw you with the Seth and Olivia at the Town Tavern a few days ago. I'm surprised to see you here. Are you and Edmond friends? I thought you just got into town not long ago." "Hey man, she did, what's wrong with her befriending a stranger," states Edmond indignantly. "Settle down man, I'm just surprised to see her here. Besides, I really need a drink right now so I'm good with whatever you guys have going on," declares Nick. "Whitney doesn't look to me like she is ready to leave, Nick. So, you're right you might as well kick back and have a beer," offers Edmond. I sneak a look over toward the restroom and see Whitney coming out, and she looks like she is ready for a fight. Quietly, I say to Nick, "Don't look now but it looks like your wife is on her way over here and she doesn't appear to be very happy. Nick disgustingly laughs, "Who Whitney? She'll get over whatever has her ire up, besides come tomorrow she won't even remember being mad or possibly even being here." I look down at the floor quickly before Nick can see my eyes tear up. Finding my voice, "Edmond, it's time I get out of here, I've been out all day exploring and tomorrow is a new day so I'm going to head upstairs." "See you around Nick."

Quickly working my way over to the exit, I come face to face with Whitney. Before I can say anything or move out of her way, Whitney grabs my arm, "Who are you? I saw you talking with Nick and Edmond like you know them and I've never seen you around here, so again, who are you?" With as much kindness as I can muster, I say" My name is Morgan and I am staying upstairs for a few weeks which is how I know Edmond and as for Nick, I don't know him from Adam, so do you mind letting me by." Whitney lets go of me and rushes over to Nick, mouthing off about how she thought he was going to leave her at the bar.

I discreetly get out of the bar and head up the stairs to my room all the while thinking 'that was a close call. Facing these people from my past and seeing how their lives have evolved is starting to take its toll on me. I came back here for my family not to become entangled with Whitney and Nick. It is starting to get late and my eyelids are getting heavy. Hopefully I can get a good night sleep and not be plagued with dreams.

Nick and Misty (Past)

Nick Darlington wasn't always the popular guy in school. He grew up out in the country and was the only boy among four sisters. His youth was spent trying to avoid them and all of their boyfriend stories and makeup sessions which went on every weekend. His parents were hardworking people who dealt in real estate. It had them spending a lot of time away from home showing properties all over the county. He was a scrawny kid who until reaching puberty didn't care one cent about girls. Having his sisters breathing down his neck all the time was enough to put girls completely out of his mind. Then when he was just about to turn thirteen, his neighbor Jeff stopped over and asked him if he would be interested in going out for football. Nick definitely had some interest but was hesitant because he knew how small he was. But Jeff assured him there would be a place for him on the team as long as he worked hard and was committed. This was the beginning of the transformation of Nick.

Throughout the next couple of years Nick excelled both academically and athletically. By the time he was a sophomore in high school he had earned the starting position of quarterback and with the accomplishment came a lot of attention. Some would say all of the accolades and attention garnished on Nick changed him, but Misty knew different. They had been friends for a very long time and their friendship had evolved into a serious relationship by the time they were in high school. Nick went from being the scrawny boy in the neighborhood to being the most popular boy in school and the best looking. His physique was now far from being scrawny and his cinnamon colored hair and crystal blue eyes were just a couple of the traits made him irresistible to most of the girls at Millersville High.

A month before the Prom Nick and Misty were spending a lot of time together, studying, hanging out with friends and trying to dissuade the sexual tension they felt between one another. The nights they spent alone were getting intense with how much they loved each other and wanted to feel closer to each other, but both of them knew they wanted to do things differently. College and Nick's football career was keeping them honest, but they were struggling daily with their want for one another.

One Saturday, a few weeks before the Prom, they were hanging out at the bowling alley and Nick was acting very antsy after they got there. The whole time they were there he was surrounded by all of their friends laughing and goofing off, but the more Misty watched him the realization came to her he was putting on an act. Finally, she got him by himself and tried to find out what was going on. "Nick what's up with you today? I swear if I didn't know you so well, I would think you are trying to be annoying. It's not like you to be acting so crazy. Your friends normally get on your nerves only when you think they are acting immature, so what gives today?" "Misty, please don't start on me today, I'm not acting like anything, just having a good time with my buddies. Is this alright with you or are you too good to be hanging out with us now you've gotten accepted to college," snapped Nick. Misty had finally been accepted to Arizona University with a full scholarship. "What are you talking about, you know I don't feel that way and you're going to hear very soon as well. All the acceptance letters are starting to come in and yours won't be any different. Michigan has been talking with Coach for months and you've been out there twice, plus all your financial aid was accepted so I say again what you are talking about?"

Suddenly Nick pulls her close and says "Misty, I'm going to miss you so much, I thought we were going to be able to stay together while going to college. There isn't going to be time for us with me hopefully playing football and you maintaining your scholarship. We are going to be too far away from each other. If only your parents could have given you some money for college, instead you have to concede attending Michigan and go where you were offered a full scholarship." Misty gathered herself closer to him. "Let's get out of here and go somewhere so we can be alone and talk," she whispered. Nick smiles, relaxes a little bit and then yells over to his friends, "Hey, we are getting out of here."

As they are riding down the road, Nick starts to laugh, "Misty, so what is bothering you. "Nick, there is so much I want to tell you and haven't had the time, let alone the nerve to do it. Why don't we drive over to the lake so we can talk?" The rest of the ride was spent listening to the radio and Misty couldn't stop thinking about how it would feel having Nick make love to her. Nick pulls into the lake picnic area and shuts off the car. Turning toward Misty he kisses her so tenderly she wants it to go on forever, but she needs to tell him how she feels about their commitment to each other. "Nick we are in such a good place right now. We both have had so much pressure about college and money which has been so nerve-wracking. I feel like our time together now is on a timer and I don't want a second of it to go by without us being together." "Misty, don't worry," Nick begs. "We have the whole summer ahead of us before either of us has to leave for school. I want to spend every minute with you as well and I also want more with you. It seems like we have been dating forever and we have been so careful about taking our relationship any further. There is so much love between us Misty and I want to show you how much I love you. Every day I dream about making love to you." "Oh Nick, I want that too, more than you know. We don't need to wait any longer, I can't stand the ache I have every time we are together," Misty whispered. Nick pulled her close and kissed her deeply. "Misty, I love you and I want you so much." The moment reminded her of the conversations with her mother about staying a virgin until she was married. They moved in and out of her mind at a snail's pace as the desire she felt overcame them. Nick reached for her and Misty slid beneath him. He gently moved his hand to separate her thighs. For the first time she did not stop him.

Looking down at her face, almost losing himself with the expression of desire and love he sees there, he entered her with his fingers. She moaned with passion. He feels as if he will weep with the sweetness he finds there. He realizes he is unable to wait any longer and enters her, careful to be easy knowing it will be her first time. Feeling the tightness surround him and the pulsating wetness almost taking him to climax, he struggles for control. He hears a whimper which almost breaks his heart. "Oh Misty, I don't want to hurt you, sweetheart. I can stop," he says softly. Smiling through tears, Misty shakes her head, "No Nick, I don't ever want it to stop," she moans. Moving slowly, he strokes her until he feels her hips moving in concert with his own. Filled with the thirst of desire neither has known before, her eyes darken, and he feels her breath quicken. He waits for her. Her body shutters and he feel her tighten around him. Lost in one another and the passion, he murmurs how much he loves her and that he will never leave her.

The next few weeks were like heaven. Neither one of them could be without the other one for very long. Misty was pretty sure her Mother knew what happened because she was always saying how different and grown-up Misty looked. Something started to change as the end of the school year loomed. It was subtle but somehow their relationship was changing. Misty couldn't put her finger on it but somehow Nick wasn't as attentive as before. Little did Misty realize that summer would be one she would never forget nor would Nick, but it would take 20 years for him to admit it.

Stray Current

Many of the times Dad visited people who were suffering from different health issues he was by himself, but as more and more people were calling on him reinforcements was necessary. It was an extremely warm day in August when I saw what stray current could do to a person. We were visiting a young family who lived about a mile from huge electrical towers which were scattered throughout our county.

On this day, the family was having their air-conditioning replaced by a local HVAC business and the incident which happened that day was not only witnessed by my father and me, but the HVAC technician experienced it himself. While the new system was being installed, all the electric in the house had been turned off to keep the technician safe while he was hooking up the electric to the unit. Never had I seen someone sweat as bad as this guy did who was working outside on the units, his hat was wet, his shirt soaked, and I'll bet if asked he would have said all of his underclothes were wet as well. The heat and humidity of the day was extremely high. While standing outside the technician felt little tremors of shock going through his body, he immediately thought someone had turned on the circuit breakers to the air conditioners. After determining all the electric was off, he went back outside to finish the installation of the air-conditioning. Again, he felt the shocks going through his body but this time they were stronger, and the technician was becoming concerned. Dad went out to talk to the gentleman to see if the shocks would affect him as well, but of course they did not. What we realized was the technician was so sweaty and wet he was being shocked by the stray current that was in the air, due to the proximity of the electrical towers. Those towers were emitting stray current which was sizzling within the air and shocking the technician. We believed the only way the technician was not seriously hurt was because he was grounded, yet the impact of the electrical shocks he was feeling were scary enough.

This incident only confirmed for my Dad there was a lot of stray current in the air but was especially strong near the electrical towers. After more investigation he found a significant number of families experiencing health problems lived within a few miles of these same towers. Proving this was going to be more of a problem than he was going to be able to handle. He needed hard evidence if he was going to be able to legitimately do anything about the current. Talking with the people who were living near the towers, he found most of them were very apprehensive of living there. They were redesigning their homes, so their bedrooms were as far away from the towers as possible. The struggle they were all facing was financial. Their life savings were put into the land they built their homes on and the electric company denied any of the accusations stray current was floating in the environment.

After talking to one of the families even I realized they truly had a complaint. They would stand outside and hold a light bulb and it would light, literally light up with no power connected to it. If nothing else confirmed the problems which were facing our area this did.

As time went on, he became more agitated because he felt so helpless. Beyond helping the families cope with their illness there didn't seem like there was much else he could do unless he could convince the electric companies to admit they were producing stray currents. But how was he going to get the proof he needed? What was he going to have to sacrifice to find this information?

Jonathan (Present)

Jonathan left the Bank and instead of going home decided to head out to the Tavern and have lunch, something he had not done in a long time. Riding out to the bar, he reflected on the meeting with Tom Fraser. He smiled to himself realizing Tom helped him even though that was not his intention. Bringing up Misty and what she would do if she were here had renewed Jonathan and maybe just maybe things were going to start looking up. Telling Tom to provide him with all the investors' phone numbers might give him some leverage.

For now, however, he was going to the Tavern to get a beer and catch up on the news of the town. Maybe even get to see some of his old friends who usually hung out there on a Saturday afternoon watching football. So much of his life had been caught up in the farm so this afternoon's activities were different to say the least. Who does he see as he walks into the bar but the one person who has always had his back and somehow, he became so involved in his own misery he had forgotten the relationship they had shared?

"Hey Jonathan, long time no see. Where the hell have you been? We haven't seen you in ages," yells Seth. "How are things going? Olivia was just asking about you the other day and I was thinking then, how long it had been since I had talked to you." "Seth it is always great to see you. I have been busy but that is no excuse for not keeping in touch with friends. How is Olivia? Is she still as crazy as ever or is she just driving you crazy?" Laughing out loud, Seth said, "Man you've got her pegged don't you, but actually she is as great as ever. Sometimes I wonder how she puts up with me but I'm definitely not looking a gift horse in the mouth. She's supposed to be meeting me here in a little while, I hope you can hang around until she gets here because she would love to see you. You know back in the day we were inseparable the three of us."

Grinning, Jonathan leans over and gives Seth a man hug, "I will definitely stay until she gets here because she would never let you live it down if she knew I was here, and you let me leave. Man, I'm just looking out for you like always." Amused Seth looks around the bar and says, "You know this place hasn't changed much since we came in here twenty-five years ago. But I guess that is what makes it so popular. People just keep coming in, some of the same people, yet new younger people are coming all the time as well. How Brett juggles all of it is amazing. Who would have thought Brett would turn into the owner of a successful sports bar?"

Suddenly the door opens and like a whirlwind Olivia comes in. "Hey Seth, I thought you were going to save me a seat?" As she came closer, she got a smile on her face which would light up any room. "Jonathan Jenkins – I can't believe my eyes, is it really you? Where in the world have you been?" Playfully, Olivia tapped

Jonathan on the back, then grabbed him in a hug and whispered, "It's so good to see you out, we've missed you." Hugging Olivia back, Jonathan replies "Right back at you "Liv". You don't look a day over 30 but then you always did look good. Have a seat and tell me all about what is going on with you guys. Seth has been bursting with information but didn't want to update me until you got here. He has been practically holding me down so I wouldn't leave." "Well, we've been busy with the business but finally we are finding time to enjoy each other a little bit. The economy turned around in the last few years and we have grown the business enough to where we have had to hire some guys." Jonathan laughs, "Grow, I guess you did—I see your trucks everywhere. So, I know you have been doing well. "We finally get to have more free time to do some of the things we've always wanted to do but couldn't because the business required so much of our time." explains Olivia. "I guess having your son David working for you has been helpful since growing up in the business must be a plus. So, instead of going on vacation you're hanging out here?" laughed Jonathan. "But then again, what better way to spend an afternoon than hanging out with friends, especially ones you love right, Liv?"

After a while, the tavern began to slow down, and Jonathan wanted to head home. He was itching to start the process for getting the highest possible price for the land. "Well guys it's been great seeing you two but I'm going to head out," said Jonathan.

"Don't make yourself such a stranger from now on ok? Seth said. It's good to see you out and about because we were beginning to think you had become a recluse." "I know, I know, and you are both right I was becoming way too caught up in my own problems instead of trying to solve them. But something woke up in me today and I am going to do whatever I can to make good on the mistakes I have made. There has been so much bitterness it had taken over my life and has been controlling everything I do. It's about time I wake up and begin to live my life and be productive in society which I have definitely not been doing lately," said Jonathan. "Well, we are all in support of you Jonathan and we will be behind you all the way. The first thing you need to do is try to contact Misty. No one here believes she just up and left for no reason. We will help you if you want to find her and bring her back here to help you with this bank deal."

"If there is any chance you could save the farm by presenting a unified front to the bank, then you should do everything you can to bring Misty back." Frowning, Jonathan responded, "Olivia, that may be easier said than done. When Misty left, she made sure she left no trace of herself. So, finding her after twenty years may prove to be just a little difficult, don't you think?" Olivia smiled, "Well Jonathan, I guess we will just have to do some investigative work, but you can bet I will put everything I have in to helping you find her."

Callahan (Past)

Jack Callahan did not completely understand what was happening within the local community, but he knew many residents had a feeling of unease about the electric company. The project to erect higher towers was on the table and he was due to attend several township meetings where the community would be in high attendance. Having someone stir the pot and get the natives riled up was not consistent with his agenda. He needed to put his nose to the grindstone and find out who was causing all the disruptive noise he was hearing. He had befriended a farmer, Carl Jenkins, who seemed to be onto something using dowsing rods and finding stray current was emanating from the existing towers and hitting a little too close to home. Maybe he needed to go back to him and find a little more about what he was exactly doing with the rods he used to find water. Jack had a sinking feeling Jenkins was at the root of the problem and finding out what he was up to had now become his top priority. Somehow, he needed to get closer to Mr. Jenkins and have him share his thoughts and learn exactly what he was researching.

Elizabeth continued to badger him about the amount of time he was spending at the Jenkins farm, and lately seemed more determined than ever he would be moving on to another case. He did not know whatever gave her the knowledge he would be successful in this case because right now headquarters wanted to know what the residents were saying. It was becoming harder and harder to ingratiate himself to the community. His one accomplishment was getting close to the Jenkins family but now he felt the pressure of finding out more from Carl. In the beginning he had felt it was a dead end.

Most of the time there was not much to be derived from his visits there but lately he felt the tide changing. The last time he was there, Jenkins was excited about the effects of some stray current which caused an incident with a local contractor. He had the feeling his thought about dowsing rods would be able to produce proof of the currents. When pressed about what had happened, Jenkins had become very closemouthed and Jack was able to find out little about the incident. The more he thought about that day, it became clear to him he needed to pay the Jenkins family another visit. He would bring Jenkins his favorite drink since he was very fond of Elizabeth's sun tea. Maybe Jenkins will feel more communicative he thought, because he needed to understand the rods.

Morgan (Present)

I love the beach. I love the feeling of sand on my feet and the salt air blowing in my face. There is so much activity on the beach, with families playing paddle ball and Frisbee, children running, laughing and yelling happily along the edges of the water, and building castles in the sand. Suddenly a horn blows and sirens are in the background, and I realize I was dreaming, and the noise was coming from right outside my room. Moving deeper into the covers I try to go back to sleep so I can stay in my dream and continue to walk on the beach.

My dream will not return and finally, I give up trying to sleep. I roll over and spin myself out of bed so my feet hit the floor all in one motion. Standing up I look outside the window of my room, which looks down onto Main Street and there are all kinds of people milling around. The sidewalks are full of easy up tents and vendors are set up all along Main Street. Right away a sinking feeling comes over me. What in the hell is going on today and how am I going to get out of the Hotel without being noticed? Then I realize the crowds may work to my advantage. With so many people milling around, blending into the crowd should be easy. This might be the perfect chance to mingle with people and find out any information I can gather about the farm and what is left of my family. One person I do not want to run into is Brett. I hope he is busy at the bar and will not have time to hang out on Main Street.

Standing before the bathroom mirror, I take a hard look at myself and try to see if there is any of Misty Jenkins looking back at me. Remembering, I realize how much I have changed during the years. As a young girl before I was in my teens, I preferred jeans, sneakers and a white shirt, untucked of course. I was definitely not the girlie type. As a teenager I was still more comfortable in jeans and work boots or sneakers than in lacy dresses. When I became a young woman there were still no fancy dresses for me. I was most comfortable in casual dress, and hairstyle. Makeup was neither here nor there for me. Now I have become comfortable in sophisticated dress and style, but me, the real me is still a casual, sporty, jeans and shirt kind of woman.

There was not much I missed at the farm where I lived with my parents and my brother, Jonathan, whom I adored. There is six years between us, but we were as close as a brother and sister could be growing up in a farming environment. We had to work hard and working out in the fields was just one of the many chores we were required to do. Our family farm was the pride and joy of our parents and not until much later did we understand their dedication. Most Saturdays Dad came in and asked what I was doing and could I come out and work the fields with my brother. Most of the time, Mom would say she was going to have me cleaning or baking, but Dad always demanded I come out and work.

Some people would say my eyes were what would make me a beauty someday. They are a unique shade of green which could be called hazel, and when the light is right, they take on the color of an emerald. It could be called a fault by some but they tell everything. If I am mad or upset, one can just look at my eyes and know something is seriously wrong. They are the windows to the passion which may not have been as apparent when I was an adolescent though years later it would become obvious how passionate I was then and still am about life. Some would say I held myself with a subtle dignity which was rare in someone so young. My Dad and Mom were always supportive of my brother and me and instilled in us honesty and integrity along with strong family values.

I changed the color of my eyes with the colored contacts which were available now and all the different hair products had taken care of the color of my hair. Thanks to the fitness craze which has swept through the country, I have slimmed down considerably from the slightly plump senior who attended Millersville High.

Smiling at myself I turn back into the room and wander over to the window once again, this time with more confidence I can walk among the people and no one will be any the wiser that they are looking at Misty Jenkins. Hurrying to get on with my day I dress quickly and head downstairs to find something to eat.

Edmond is sitting in his usual place watching the people walk by. "Enjoying the sights are we I ask? It seems like every time I walk down here you are sitting on this bench watching the world. It is a beautiful day so where else should you be but outside enjoying all the sights and sounds. What's going on today anyway?" Edmond looks hard at Morgan, then softening his view says, "It's called a Fall Festival or something. It has been going on for a few years now where businesses and crafters set up tents, sell things and give out information. It's annoying to me because there are so many people walking up and down the sidewalks asking for information. Half of the things, they are asking me I don't know the answer to, nor do I care what the answer is." "My guess is you really would like to move about a little more, but you are too stubborn to ask for any assistance." I say quietly. "It must be nice to know everything, but you just met me a few days ago so I would appreciate it if you would keep your opinions to yourself," Edmond responds in a somewhat grumpy tone.

This is my exit. I can see Edmond is becoming agitated and I want him as a friend. It is time I take a walk. Trying to be friendly, I say, "Well I'm going to take a stroll around town. I will catch up to you later, ok?" "I will not be moving from this spot, so I will see you later," Edmond answers.

With that I take my leave and begin walking around town smiling and nodding to all the people I pass making sure I keep my eyes peeled for Brett or anyone else who might look familiar. As I cross the street, I hear someone yell, "Hey Morgan wait up!" I quickly turn around and see Olivia running across the street I just crossed, so I wait for her to catch up. "Hey Olivia, it's great to see you but slow down before you hurt yourself." I laugh. "Morgan it's great to see you, I was just talking to Seth about you last night. We have been wondering whether you are still interested in seeing our neighbor's house. It looks like the house is going to be available sooner than we thought. We wanted to get in touch with you to let you know but weren't sure if you were still in town." Nervously I laugh and say, "I've been a little preoccupied lately and it's been so busy I don't know where the days have gone. However, it is great running into you today. I've decided to stay in Millersville for a little while and it would sure be nice to have somewhere to stay besides the Hotel." "Well Morgan this is the best news I've heard. Seth has been telling me how much he thought you would fit in here and we know you have already made some friends." Surprised, Morgan exclaims, "Olivia, good grief I've only been in town for a couple of weeks and I wouldn't exactly call anyone I've met a friend, except of course you and Seth," "Well I'm sorry honey, but that is definitely not what we heard about your activities over the past couple of days. We were enlightened about your luncheon expedition yesterday by a good source and we were so happy to find out you are starting to enjoy the area and the people," Olivia says with a chuckle. "Boy word gets around quick in this town doesn't it? I assume by the smile you have plastered on your face you know I went to lunch with Brett. Do not get any ideas, Olivia, it was a very enjoyable lunch but that's all it was. He was nice enough to show me around the area." "Seth told me you went to Botero's for lunch. You probably don't know this but Botero's isn't open for lunch which means Brett set the lunch up for both of you," grins Olivia.

Before I can say anything back to her, I suddenly feel someone breathing down the back of my neck; I look over my shoulder and who is standing there but Brett. Olivia laughs, "Hey there, were your ears burning, we were just talking about you?" "It was all good too, I'm sure. Were you talking nice about me Olivia or was Morgan the culprit of this dialogue?"

Smiling I turn around and before I realize it, his arms are wrapped around me and he plasters his lips against mine. Amazingly enough, given such an unexpected embrace, I slide my arms around him, and I kiss him in return. It is for a moment, like no one else is there. Olivia clears her throat and suddenly reality steps in and breaks us apart.

After the awkwardness, everyone seems to talk at once, but Brett being the powerful personality manages to penetrate our chatter. "Well, what a nice Hello, can we do that again," laughs

Brett. I regain my composure and speak up, "Brett, it's great to see you, I've wanted to find you today so I could tell you what a great time I had yesterday. I hope there is a chance for me to thank Mrs. Botero as well." "It was my pleasure Morgan, he said with a swooping bow which tickled me. The Boteros' are family friends and I wanted you to experience some of the finer places we have here in the Millersville area. I knew so far, your exposure was just with the Hotel and the Tavern, plus I may have had an ulterior motive. It gave me a reason to spend more time with you. Leaning down toward me Brett whispers in my ear, "Since I have done nothing but think about you most of my waking moments." I can feel myself blushing and a warm feeling washes through me.

Trying not to seem overly affected by the sensuous smell which clings to him, I smile and grab Olivia's arm. Olivia laughs, "Enough you two, do you want me to leave so you can continue whatever this is between you?" "Oh God no, I blurt out, if anyone is leaving it's me."

All of sudden Brett looks at Olivia then turns, looks at me and smirking says, "I will save you the ladies the trouble, I'm already late for an appointment so just continue on with your walk and I'll catch you both later." He makes an about face and heads down Main Street. Under my breath, I whisper, "just like that uh." Olivia starts cracking up, Morgan if I didn't know better, I would say you think a little more about Brett than you admit. "No, I don't. I think this is just a passing fling. Olivia, my track record with men is not anything to be written home about believe me." I can't afford to let Brett distract me, though I do seem to be subject to impulsive behavior when I see him. "Listen I need to get going, can we catch up with each other later?" Olivia looks a little worried but responds, "Sure Morgan, Seth and I will be going out to the tavern later, so if you can, stop by."

I work my way back to the Hotel. Going up the steps, Edmond appears on the landing, "Hey Morgan, did you have a good day in Millersville or were you out causing trouble?" "Who me, you should know better than Edmond. I was just hanging out with Olivia. She invited me out to the tavern later to have a drink with Seth and herself." Edmond appearing somewhat irritated looks at me, "I don't know why you are trying to hide what you were really doing. I saw you with Brett. Don't you know you are asking for trouble hanging out with him?" "Mind your own business Edmond, I know what I am doing. It's time for me to head upstairs and change especially if I'm going to meet Olivia later."

Heading upstairs, I can't get out of my mind what Edmond said about Brett. What could he mean, and how does having lunch with Brett constitute hanging out with him? How would Edmond know about the feelings I am trying to ignore for Brett? I can't let my sudden weakness for Brett deter me, however, maybe I need to find out a little more about Brett, the tavern owner.

Nick & Coach (Past)

Nick, up early, finds himself aimlessly driving around Millersville trying to figure out what is going on with his life while waiting for Jonathan's call. Between Misty, Coach and all the rumors going around about Misty's family, he really didn't know what he was going to do. His own family was starting to question his relationship with Misty and what their plans were for the future. College pressures were affecting them as a couple and Coach's irritating attitude was starting to become a problem he felt needed to be addressed. How many athletes from Millersville were being touted by Big 10 schools like he was, and Coach was treating him like he had the plague. It was time for him to confront what was going on with Coach and put all the doubts he had about going to Michigan to rest. Misty's family problems were becoming a burden. They were going to college and things change once that happens whether they wanted to admit it or not.

Whitney was a whole other problem, she was calling constantly and the things she was saying about Misty and how her Dad was causing trouble with the Electric Company were starting to bother him more than he wanted to admit. He always knew her Dad was onto something with the testing he was doing with the rods and the stray electric current was a real issue. Misty wasn't being open about her Dad, but rumors were circulating throughout the County giving a lot of people pause. No one was fully aware of the impact it was going to have on the utility companies if he could prove the peril stray electrical currents were bringing to the residents of the area. No matter what he knew about her family, his love for Misty had always overcome any issues which may have arisen.

School was letting out, and Nick was preparing to see if he could talk to Coach. Michigan's coach had called the house yesterday wanting to talk to him, but he had missed the call. The coach had left a message that he would try to reach him again on Friday. Coach Baron tried to hide his annoyance when he saw Nick leaning against his doorframe and instead put a smile on his face. "Hey Nick, what's up? I'm surprised to see you here today. I thought you were spending the day over at Misty's place helping on the farm," remarked Coach. Nick tried to be nonchalant about his reason for being there and said, "They weren't ready for me yet so I thought I would take a chance and stop by to talk to you. I missed a call from the Michigan Coach yesterday. He left a message he would call back on Friday. Somehow, I think you know more about this than you are letting on and if you do, I want you to be honest with me. I deserve to know if there is something serious holding up this scholarship." Nick said worriedly.

Coach looked away for a minute and to Nick it seemed like he was deciding on something. "Nick, I've been trying to resolve in my mind how to handle what I'm about to tell you. It's been plaguing me for weeks and I realize how unfair it has been for you not understanding my attitude. You know how much the Michigan coaches have been working with you and your family concerning your financial packet and your ability to stay focused next year. I am the one who has been concerned about your relationship with Misty affecting your ability to stay focused next year. Going to a Big 10 school is a huge nut to crack coming from a small school like Millersville, I have the utmost confidence in you except for one area." Nick felt himself getting irritated and was trying not to be on the defensive. "You don't think I can handle what will be required of me? As close as you have been to me and her for that matter, you didn't think it was something you could have talked to us about?" "Nick, you are jumping to conclusions, no one is saying anything bad about Misty. I realize your dreams are materializing but I also know how much a part of your life Misty is." "Misty's my girlfriend, but she's not going to change my mind about going to Michigan. She wants me to go almost more than I want to go."

"Coach, Misty and I love each other. We have talked about the changes which will be necessary in our relationship with us going to different colleges. We understand it will mean a lot of adjustments for both of us and time away from each other, but we both are committed to supporting one another in the pursuit of our dreams and ambitions. You are speculating about all of this, and our relationship is something you know nothing about. There are a lot of athletes who could use your attention, Coach. Instead of worrying about my life why don't you focus your time in cultivating your upcoming players." He was angry now.

"We will survive our college separation, so if you have been debating on whether to continue to support me in receiving the scholarship, I hope you hear me today. You have nothing to worry about with my focus or my desire to do well in my future. Coach, I need to go now! There is something I need to do before it's too late. All of this speculation about my scholarship needs to end." Nick proceeded toward the exit with a determined gate and walked to his car. He sat inside for a long time with so many feelings racing through his mind. He punched the steering wheel. He knew the feeling most prevalent in all his thoughts was his desire to leave and play football for Michigan.

He needed to talk with Misty, but he decided it would be better to cool down somewhat before talking with her. Deep down inside he knew some of what Coach said was true because he had been thinking those exact same things. Misty and he had sworn to each other they would stay together through college but that was when they both thought they were going to Michigan. Now, only Nick was going to be heading to Michigan in the fall. Misty would be leaving for the University of Arizona for school due to her financial status. They had talked about the chance they wouldn't be going to college together but they both had hopes

Misty's financial status would change. Unfortunately, that was not going to happen, Nick would be heading in different directions next fall. Nick knew it would be hard to keep up his relationship with Misty. The football schedule he was going to be subjected to and Misty's academic schedule would make seeing each difficult.

Leaving Coach's office, he decides driving around may clear his mind and then he would be able to talk with Misty with a level head. He calls Misty to let her know he will stop by to spend some time with her in an hour or so. Shortly after he began driving, he found himself heading to the lake. It was a lake of ample size to accommodate a good number of kids and yet was secluded from the road. It is where he and his friends gathered for parties on the weekend. Tonight though, he decides the tributary in a sequestered part of the lake is a perfect place to contemplate his present circumstances and try to relax before he goes to see Misty. It is the part of the lake where he and Misty go sometimes to park and be alone.

As Nick navigated the single lane dirt road and parked, he saw someone swimming toward the edge. Who would be in the water right now? The water was still cool due to the nights below average temperature. Walking toward the water, he tries to see who it is when suddenly he hears Whitney laughing. Walking up out of the water was Whitney grinning from ear to ear. "Nick you look so funny standing there with your mouth hanging open, haven't you ever seen someone swimming naked before?" laughed Whitney. "Whitney, what the hell are you doing swimming with no clothes? Get over here and get in the car so I can turn on the heat for you." "I have to tell you Nick, it is the most exhilarating feeling ever, and you should try it sometime." "Come on Whitney, get in the car, it might be late spring, but the water has got to be cold and you are swimming stark naked. Seriously, have you lost your mind? "Now that you mention it, I am feeling a little chilly, so I think getting into your car for some warmth is not such a bad idea." Nick leans over and opens the door for her, but not before handing her a blanket he had in his back seat. "Put this around you before you get into my car, I don't need Misty finding out you were sitting here naked." said Nick. "Really Nick, you have a naked woman in your car, and you are worried about your girlfriend," Whitney remarked sarcastically. "You know Whitney, you should be ashamed of yourself, she's your best friend or at least that's what she thinks. What do you think she'll have to say to you if she finds out you were out here running around naked?" Looking around Nick asks, "is there anyone else here with you, or were you swimming naked alone?" "I was waiting for you", murmured Whitney. "Me? How did you even know I was going to be out here?" demanded Nick. "Misty called me Nick and mentioned you had called after seeing Coach and sounded stressed. She was concerned because you told her you would see her later. I know you and this is where you come when you are bothered about something. All this debate about Michigan is worrying you right?" "Whitney, it is not something you need to think about, much less get involved in. It is between Misty and me." "You know Nick, I've been trying to get you to pay attention to me for weeks, hanging by your locker, spending more time with Misty so I could get to see you more." "Whitney, now I know you have lost your mind, why in hell would you do that when you know I love Misty. Or is that it? You can't stand that Misty is dating me. We all know how competitive you are with her."

As Nick was talking, Whitney was sliding over next to him when she slipped the blanket draped around her off her shoulders and it fell onto the seat. "Nick, I have done nothing but think about how we would be together. The images which travel through my mind are so intense I can feel myself getting aroused and I can't ignore the desire I feel for you. There is nothing I want more than to feel you inside of me, sending me to the place I've dreamed of you taking me for so long. Sometimes I can feel you hard, pulsating in my hand. I can feel when I stroke you, a tremor which excites me so much. God Nick, you are all I think about." "Whitney you are talking crazy, why are you saying all this stuff," moans Nick. He was feeling himself starting to get aroused, and it was a feeling he didn't want to have right now with Whitney and it was beginning to frighten him. "I'm saying this Nick because it's the truth, I want you more than anything I've ever wanted in my entire life. You are everything to me and I've had to watch you from a distance while you put your arms around Misty and kiss her by your locker, passing each other and smiling that smile, the meaning of which only the two of you know. Do you know how it devastates me seeing you two together? Please see me, Nick, I love you and I want to give all of myself to you. Misty will never know. Think of it as two best friends giving to each other what they need." "Really Whitney, do you think it would be that easy for me?"

While she was talking, Whitney slid back on the seat and opened her legs. He shuttered and a wave of lustful wanting finally overcame him, and he surrendered to the force of it. He pulled her naked body against him and kissed her, his tongue in motion sliding deep into her throat. One hand caressed her breasts, while fingers of the other moved inside her. The words, "Is that what you were hoping for, Whitney?" fell unbridled from his lips. Whitney leaned into him, then working his belt loose, she slid naked under him. Nick groaned as he felt Whitney's breasts swelling beneath his touch. Their breaths were coming quicker now. Whitney opened her legs against his thighs, and he entered her. Nick lost his grip on reality and the consequences of this moment as they caught each breath moving and moaning in the ecstasy of climax. Nick, finally gaining back his senses moved to release her, his eyes giving away that he was now thinking of Misty. Whitney still wrapped in euphoria reached to keep him there.

Whitney was lying across him naked, lightly snoring. Now all Nick can think of is what the hell Misty must be thinking since he was supposed to be at her house to see her and he was late. He nudged Whitney trying to get her to wake up and move. "Come on Whitney, I've got to go!" "Oh Nick, can't we just lie here a little longer before you go," she whined. "No, we are not going to lie here for longer! I need to get to Misty." Whitney began to cry, Nick feeling guilty about all that happened, knowing he had not only allowed it to happen, but encouraged it, said softly "Whitney, sometimes I do think of you when I shouldn't, but Misty would be devastated if something happened between us. Tonight, was a mistake. You and I should not have been together. I want to be with Misty. I have always wanted Misty."

Whitney sat straight up and with as much control as she could muster looked at Nick and said, "Are you kidding me, after the sex we just had you are worried about getting to Misty. I hate to tell you this, Nick, but your relationship with Misty is soon to be irrevocably changed because after tonight we aren't going to be able to stay away from each other." "You don't know what you are talking about Whitney, so move over and buckle up, I'm dropping you off. I'm going over to pick up Misty. I'm already late. From now on Whitney, stay away from Misty. I don't trust you not to tell her everything." "You can keep thinking that Nick, but there is no chance in hell I'm going to give up on you and having you for the rest of my life. You just don't get it do you? I love you

94

and that love has been growing ever since I met you the first day of high school. You wouldn't even look my way, even before you started dating Misty you couldn't keep your eyes off of her," cried Whitney.

Gathering herself together, knowing she had put herself on shaky ground she said, "Nick, don't you worry about it, this is going to be our little secret." *At least until the moment is right, and then I just might have to let the cat out of the bag as they say, she said silently to herself.*

Misty and Whitney (Past)

Prom night was in two days! Everyone in school was buzzing with last minute preparations starting with the junior class gathering decorations for the venue to all the girls trying to get appointments to get their hair done and find out what beach house they were all going to for the weekend. Misty and Whitney were prom dress shopping again and Whitney was getting irritated because she couldn't find just the "right "dress. "Misty, why is it every dress I try on is either is too big or too small, can you tell me," whined Whitney. "I swear if I didn't know better, I might think the universe is trying to stop me from going to the Prom." "Really Whitney, quit being so dramatic," sighed Misty. "I already told you if no one asked you to the Prom, you could go with Nick and me and still have a great time. I know it's not what you want to do, but there is no way in hell, Nick and I are going to let you miss your senior prom, so let's keep looking for a dress. I know you will find one you just love but if not, we'll run over to over to Delaware and see if we can find something at the Mall," said Misty.

While Misty was talking, Whitney was thinking about the plan she had designed, very soon she thought as they were leaving for the Mall. As they were walking to the car, Whitney leaned over to Misty and with a smug look on her face, said "I know I will go to Prom and it won't be with you and Nick." "Oh really, you're that sure of yourself, are you? Come on spill it out, did someone ask you or are you just being your normal self and holding out telling me about it. Because if you are, it's bullshit, so you had better come clean and tell me what you are getting at," demanded Misty. "Don't get yourself all twisted up, Misty," laughed Whitney. "I'm just saying I won't be sitting home that's all. Let's see about finding me a dress and stop talking about whether or not I have a date."

Finally, after spending an inordinate amount of time trying on dress after dress, Whitney finally found one and Misty was thankful the dress shopping trip was over. Whitney's need for a dress had now been satisfied and Misty's thoughts turned to Nick. She had not heard from him since he called her after seeing Coach to delay his coming to see her. He said his father had asked him to go to Philadelphia early the next morning to help him deliver supplies to a customer, and he would call her as soon as he returned. On top of not being able to talk to Nick, Whitney was behaving as if she was on top of the world but her attitude toward Misty was nothing short of smug. She couldn't put her finger on it, but Whitney was acting like she had some kind of secret she wasn't willing to share with Misty yet.

Brett (Present)

I've been back in my hometown now for three weeks and people are getting used to seeing me walk through town. It's been encouraging to see the townspeople smile and wave, although sometimes tentatively in the way people do when they aren't sure whether they should. Maybe this is a sign they are getting used to seeing me.

As much as I try to focus on the photos I take, Brett's face continually distracts me. I meet the guy three weeks ago, have lunch with him and now I can do nothing but think of him. It is time to find out a little more about Brett, the bar owner. It is getting close to happy hour at the Tavern and probably will be a good time to head over there. Olivia told me earlier Brett usually worked the night shift, especially on Thursday night.

Walking into the bar, I quickly scan to see if there is anyone I might recognize from the past and who do I see sitting at the bar but Whitney. Figuring now is as good a time as any to face her, I move toward her and before even voicing a word, she turns and says, "Hey Morgan that is your name, right?" Surprised I say, "Yes, and you're Whitney, Nick's wife." "No, I'm Whitney and Nick's my husband. I get so tired of hearing myself being described as Nick's wife I could scream. Nick is everybody's friend, but no one really knows what a selfish bastard he can be. Life according to Nick is what he likes to say. By the way, are you married?" asks Whitney suddenly. "Who me?" nervously laughing, "No I'm not married. I never felt the need to get married, I can take care of myself. It's great for some people but not for me." "Wow, I never thought of it that way, I didn't think about anything else other than having a boyfriend going to the Prom and getting married. Those were my priorities and look where they have gotten me," rambles Whitney. "I know now it wasn't what I was thinking about back then because if so, I wouldn't have done certain things." murmurs Whitney.

Trying to get away from the conversation I appear to be preoccupied and finally Whitney notices. "Looking for someone or are you just trying to get away from me, that's what everyone else does when I start bashing Nick." declares Whitney sarcastically. "No there definitely aren't too many people I could be looking for since I'm new in town, however, Olivia and Seth are nice people. Do you see them anywhere?" I say scanning the room. "They are always here but I'm not in their circle of friends, they are Nick's friends." gripes Whitney. Thankfully I hear my name being called from across the bar, "Hey Morgan over here!"

Looking toward the other side of the bar I see Olivia and Seth waving me over. "Whitney, it's been nice talking with you, but I think I'll wander over and talk with Olivia and Seth. Maybe I'll see you around town, I plan on staying for a while," I say warmly. As I walk away from Whitney toward my new friends a moment of melancholy passes over me. Whitney and I had been such great friends, but terrible events and time ruined the relationship we could have had.

Shrugging off the bad feeling, cheerfully I say, "Hey you guys how are you? It's great seeing you both, what a day it has been." "We have been looking out for you," said Olivia. "We were wondering where you were." "Oh, I've been exploring the area, checking out all the farmland that you have here. I rode out of town a couple of miles and turned on this side road, called Jenkins Lane. There is an older farm there, but it doesn't seem like a working one since I didn't see many livestock around." "You were by the Jenkins Farm, our friend Jonathan's place. They've slowly been scaling down for a while and have been selling off most of their animals." Seth said quietly. "Yes, that's true." Olivia said. "Jonathan did seem though to have a new outlook on life when we saw him the other day."

"Morgan, Jonathan Jenkins has been a dear friend of ours who went to high school with us and he has recently fallen on bad times. His parents owned the farm you went by, but after the events of 20 years ago and his dad's passing, Jonathan's interest in working the farm practically ceased. The farm has been deteriorating since then," Olivia volunteered. "Their family, and in a way the town, hasn't been the same since those events of 20 years ago."

"What events?" I ask. Listening to Olivia and Seth makes me realize how much twenty years ago had affected more than just my family. My parents and the farm were such an integral part of Millersville that those events had affected the whole town and the town endured a disturbing aftermath.

Lost in my attention to the conversation, I don't see Brett coming toward me until I feel him lean down and whisper in my ear, "Hello beautiful, nice to see you again." When I turn to look up at him, he kisses me so sweetly I feel myself leaning against him. Olivia looks at both of us and grinning says, "Hey Brett, what are you doing over here flirting when you should be running this busy bar." "Olivia, I've got this place humming like a top, so I can spend all the time I want paying attention to my special customers," laughs Brett. "Special customers huh. I think the special customer you have is seated right in front of you, the one you just planted your lips on," quips Olivia. "Whoa, you guys, don't get carried away, it was just a little kiss." Meanwhile, I think what it would be like if we were alone and how I could lose myself in that kiss. Brett looks at me and smiles so devilishly I feel like he must have read my mind. I find myself smiling back and I know there will be added ending to this. "So, Morgan, were you exploring today around our illustrious town?" inquired Brett. "Yes, as a matter of fact, I took a ride out of town a couple of miles and turned on a country road where I saw this old farm and it turns out Seth and Olivia knows the owner. Apparently, their friend Jonathan owns it, right Olivia?"

Looking at Brett I see a sudden shadow pass over his face. It happened so quickly if I hadn't been looking at him right at that moment, I would have missed it. I get an uneasy feeling and decide I must find out what caused the shadow.

Finding myself having a good time hanging out with Seth and Olivia, I don't want to leave the bar. The look on Brett's face has me wondering what is driving the attraction which he obviously has for me. *Is it out of curiosity for the new girl in town or is it something else entirely?* What I wonder too is if he has had any connection to the past events of my life. As much as I am starting to feel something for him, I need to find out more about him. "Brett do you have time to sit down and socialize a little while?" quips Olivia. "I most certainly have time Olivia," he answers looking at Morgan.

"Morgan, I have wanted to spend more time together with you, but life as a bar owner leaves very little time for personal things so I haven't been able to leave the bar much over the past few days." Blushing, I smile up at him and he leans down and whispers, "I want to get to know you better." "Well maybe times are changing, and we will see a new Brett," Olivia says with a grin. Gazing at Brett, I wonder what has changed for him, my own ego thinks maybe it's me. There hasn't been anyone in my life either, however it wasn't something I was going to share with any of my newfound friends. There is definitely some chemistry between Brett and me and I want to spend more time with him. I want to determine if there is any connection between Jonathan and Brett but right now, I just want to be with him. I can't believe the feelings which have found me but now is not the time to wonder just pursue!

Jonathan (Present)

It's a warm day, something we don't see much in January, and Jonathan views it as a blessing. He is walking around the farm looking at all of the devastation among the buildings. Today he is going to work again on getting some of the farm cleaned up. Somehow, he says to himself, I am going to figure out a way to slowly rebuild the farm. He remembers what his Dad always said, "Never look at the whole farm and what you have to do because in life you can only farm one acre at a time."

With that thought in mind, Jonathan decides he is going to start cleaning up the place. He gets on the phone and calls the local recycle company to have a dumpster scheduled to arrive the next day. A friend who owns a backhoe was going to be coming by to help clean things up. Tom Fraser was going to be coming out to re-inspect the property in two weeks, so he needed to get as much done as possible. He could get it cleaned up enough to have the investors rethink their offers and if nothing else, that was the least he could do for himself and Misty. In the past he couldn't resolve his negative feelings about Misty leaving the area. Now he had begun to understand what she must have been feeling and why she felt like her world was unraveling. Jonathan marveled now about the strength his little sister possessed at such a young age. To leave her home and never look back is something he knew deep down inside he never could do. His feelings of being trapped had become a detriment to the farm and were now why he had to scramble to try to make its value high to the investors.

For now, he realizes he will need to start small, so he decides to begin in the shop where his Dad did most of his work. The door creaks when it opens from the rusty hinges and the smell penetrates the air is a damp and moldy odor which only enhances the feeling of neglect Jonathan is feeling. He knows throughout the cleaning of the farm he will also be cleaning up his own life and new things will be happening.

If Misty was here, she would be taking this on with such gusto and would have it organized in no time. It was times like this he wished she would come back home, and he could tell her how sorry he is about so many things. He knows though now is not the time to start berating himself about Misty. He needed to get moving and make some headway on the re-establishment of the farm.

At that moment, he envisions milking again and having different pedigree cows breeding more and more of the same pedigree. Reality barges in though, and he realizes it is best to just start small and get it cleaned up.

A New Home (Present)

Heading over to the diner to get breakfast I begin to think about moving from the Hotel. I think it is time I seriously think about finding something a little more permanent. I look up Olivia's number and give her a call. "Hey Olivia, this is Morgan, how are you today?" "Morgan it is great to hear from you, what's going on?" Olivia asks cheerfully. "Well, I was wondering if you would have time to take me over to look at your neighbor's house and maybe talk to someone about renting the place." "Well, of course I do, especially if this means you are going to stay in Millersville for a while. Meet me at my house. The rental is right next door to mine. We will go in and check it out." "Great, give me your address and I will see you in a little while."

The day was overcast but I suddenly feel lighthearted I had decided to stay in Millersville. This was what I had envisioned many of those years I was away, coming back and staying. I notice though an uneasy feeling lurks in the back of my mind, but I can't put my finger on it. I brush it away and leave for Olivia's.

"Damn Olivia, it is a shame this couple had to separate, but it looks like my lucky day. If it is Ok, I can move in here right away since I really don't have much stuff with me, and this is furnished." Olivia smiles, "You crack me up, not long ago you were telling us you weren't going to be staying around, now you can't wait to move in. Go figure." "I know, I know, but who could resist the charm of this little town," I laugh. "Plus, I'm just getting to know Seth and you so that's reason enough for me to stay." "Really, it doesn't have anything to do with a certain tavern owner?" smirks Olivia. "Well maybe a little bit but that's between the two of us, we wouldn't want him to get too cocky with all this adoration," I say with a wink. Olivia smiles, "It would be nice to see you two getting to know each other better. Brett has not had the best luck with women over the years, not for the lack of trying, but there never seemed to be the "one" who caught his heart. Somehow, I think there is something brewing between the two of you which neither of you realize," laughs Olivia. "Don't get ahead of yourself, Olivia, we are just friends." "Sure, that's what you might think, but Seth and I have already decided you are just what the doctor ordered for Mr. Brett Compton," grins Olivia. "Ok, if you guys say so, but right now I'm excited to get moved in, so I'm going to head back to the Hotel and pack my things. I'll catch up to you later."

On my way back to the Hotel, I stop by the food store to pick up some essentials to get me through tonight. Getting out of my car, I glance around the parking lot, still on the alert for anyone who might recognize me, and I see an elderly couple sitting in their car. Realizing I'm staring, I look away but not before the older gentleman glances over at me.

My mind had all of a sudden slipped back in time to a conversation I had with my Dad. He was struggling to come up with a plan to help a couple who lived a short distance away from the farm. The health of his wife had become increasingly poor. They had exhausted most of the accepted avenues of treatment, but nothing seemed to extinguish the debilitating symptoms she was dealing with on a daily basis. My Dad went over to their house every week to see how she was doing and to continue to work with the electromagnetic fields surrounding their house.

The husband's health was perfect, but he also didn't spend very much time in the house because most of the time he spent at a vinyl lettering business they owned. All of these thoughts are swirling in my head while I'm trying not to stare at him. He ends up going into the store and then leaving. I decide I need to find out what happened to his wife, because the woman with him is definitely not her. The best place to find out something is probably to stop at the Diner and see if Susie Mitchell is working, I think to myself. There is no better time than now to see if I can find out something more about the couple, besides I am getting hungry.

Leaving the store and getting to the diner was a matter of minutes. The parking lot was actually full which makes me happy because nothing will please me more than to see Millersville survive. There are too many small towns which look like ghost towns and Millersville is not going to be one of them. The thought was almost my demand to the powers which have the responsibility of its future. I hear Susie as I walk in, before I can even see her. Luckily, she's working the counter, so I slide onto a stool, catch her eye and wave. "Hey you stayed, that's great" chimed Susie. "Yes, I did, I just found a more permanent place to live while I'm here, so I'll be leaving the Hotel" I laugh. "Thank God for small favors, I just met you a couple of weeks ago and I couldn't stand the fact you were staying at the Hotel." "I will miss Edmond. You know Edmond?" Susie exclaimed. "Susie, how could you even be anywhere near the Hotel and not know Edmond. He has been very nice to me and has given me some insight into the town since I'm new to the area." "I'm just glad you are staying and getting out of the Hotel. So, what can I get you today? We have a great chicken pot pie on special today and most of the customers who have had it have said it's great!" "Well plate it up for me because I'm starving and when you get a minute, I would like to talk to you about something." "Sure, give me a few minutes, I'm about to go on my break and I can come out and sit for a minute in one of the booths. Why don't you find an empty one and we will spend a few minutes talking?" "I'm not going anywhere, so take your time and I'll go get a booth," I reply as I hop down from the stool at the counter.

Soon, Susie walks over to my booth and sits down. "I only have a few minutes, but I really wanted to get to talk with you."

"There is something about you which seems so familiar, yet I can't place why when I know you are new to the area." Susie explains. "But I know how that can be. Sometimes people look so familiar and you think you know them, but you don't. They just remind you of someone, and then you struggle with who they remind you of. Believe me I get it," I smile. Susie, I need to ask you something about a couple I saw at the food store earlier today. It was very eerie. He was staring at me and somehow, I felt a connection to him, but I don't know how that would be. I guess that's why I would like to know who this couple might be." "Morgan, it might be hard for me to figure out who you saw. If you could let me know what make of car they were driving, it might help. A lot of the older generation comes in here to eat because we have a mini-meal which is cheap." "I wish I had the nerve to talk to them, but I could only stare back at them. "Well, if you don't have anywhere to be right now, dinner is about to start and maybe we will be lucky, and they will come in tonight. Then you will have a chance to talk with them or at least find out who they are. So, what would you like for dinner? You might as well eat while you wait," Thinking for a minute, I say, "I'll go ahead and have the special with an iced tea if you don't mind."

As I sit and wait for Susie to get my food, I try to remember the man's face and why it struck such a feeling in me. He must have thought he knew me the way he was staring but I don't see how that can be possible when I just got back into town. "Hey

Morgan, are you OK, you look like you are a million miles away," asks a concerned Susie as she set down my dinner." "Just thinking, that's all," I say. The aromas which were wafting up from the plate in front of me were making my mouth water, so I decided to dig in and put my worries away for now. Eating my dinner, I think back to the summer before I left and how devastated I had been with the events which transpired.

I snapped back to the present when Susie worked her way over to my table and smiling, said "Morgan how is your meal? I know you are just dying to have some homemade pie. You wouldn't know this, but we are known for our pie and I recommend the coconut custard." Laughing, I say, "Susie, this chicken pot pie was fabulous, and I don't think I have room left for pie, but I definitely will take it to go if that's ok." "Why, of course, Morgan, I'll go and get it ready for you." Just as Susie turns around to go back toward the counter, the door rings as a new patron comes in. I turn my head and watch as an older couple walks in and waits to be seated. It's the man from the food store parking lot. He sees me, smiles and nods and then Susie is in front of them. I hear her say, "Mr. & Mrs. Ottinger. How are you both doing? Did it get around Millersville we were serving chicken pot pie? I know you love our chicken pot pie so let me seat you in your favorite booth."

When I hear Susie say their name, it all comes back to me. Mr. Ottinger is not with the woman I remember as his wife, but he definitely is the neighbor my Dad had been trying to help. Something must have happened to the other Mrs. Ottinger and I need to get Susie's attention and see if she can answer my questions without revealing to her who I really am. The diner is busy with the dinner crowd now, so I am just patiently waited for Susie to slow down enough to stop by my booth. At one point when she walks by, I ask her to go ahead and bring me the piece of pie and a coffee.

Finally, the diner is becoming empty and the Ottingers have left but not before stopping by my booth and asking if I was enjoying my time in Millersville. Somehow, I feel Mr. Ottinger knew me. Susie has finished cleaning up and now, after taking her apron off, is headed over to my table to sit down for a few minutes. "Morgan, do you mind if I join you for a few minutes?" "Of course, Susie, get off your feet and relax, I'm not in any big hurry," I smile.

Trying not to seem too obvious with wanting to know the story behind the Ottingers, I conversationally say, "Susie, you've worked here a long time, haven't you?" Laughing, but with some sadness in her eyes she says "Yeah, ever since high school. It was just a summer job at first but before I knew it, I had been working here for 5 years, then 10 and suddenly 20 years has passed me by. The money is good enough and I guess now it's just too easy to stay. But enough about me, what do you do and what has brought you to Millersville?" "Oh me, well I'm a freelance photographer and I decided to take a road trip. It brought me to this area. Millersville has some beautiful farm country, so I have decided to stay awhile and do a piece on the area."

Taking a chance, I change the subject, "You seem to know the older couple who came in a little while ago very well." "Oh, the Ottingers, yeah I've known them since I was a little girl. Well Mr. Ottinger, anyway," says Susie. The first Mrs. Ottinger passed away about 15 years ago. She died in her mid-forties, but they never really knew from what. She just was always sick, and Mr. Ottinger tried everything to help her get well. There was a local farmer who was working with them. It had something to do with electromagnetic fields and is something which is way over my head." "There are a lot of environmental people rumbling about the effects of EMF fields," I respond. Susie looked like she was getting ready to say more but apparently decided against it.

I decide I have taken up enough of Susie's time, so I reach over, give her a quick hug, thank her for being so friendly and welcoming and say, "Well, it looks like you are wanting to get finished so you can go home, and I need to figure out when I can move into the house I'm renting from Seth and Olivia's neighbor", "Ok,

Susie grins. Please make sure you stop in again, I enjoyed talking with you." "I will, Susie."

I slide out of the booth, turn back and wave as I open the door. Leaving the diner, I decide to take a chance and go to the local cemetery to see if I can find the gravestone of the 1st Mrs. Ottinger. I want to see the date when she exactly died.

When I arrive, I sit for a while in my car gathering up the courage to begin my search. Walking through the cemetery makes me very uneasy. There are so many names of people I recognize as being families my Dad knew. My eyes tear up. Many are graves of people who died because of the towers. The dates are blurring in my tears. Why couldn't someone see what was happening with so many people dying so young? Seeing these gravestones makes me realize how many years have passed while I have been away trying to find the courage to come back.

As I wander around the cemetery, I notice a caretaker who looks as though his legs are giving him pain as he meanders along maintaining a discreet distance behind me. Turning back toward him, I wave him over. "Sir, I'm here looking for a friend's mother's grave and I was wondering if you would be so kind as to help me." "Well sure Miss, who was your friend's mother?" "Mrs. Ottinger was her name. I told my friend if I ever came upon Millersville in my travels, I would somehow find a way to visit her Mother." "Well young lady, I think this is your lucky day, because it was just yesterday I was near Mrs. Ottinger, God rest her soul. Follow me and I will take you over to her so you can pay your respects." As we are walking over toward the grave, the caretaker takes a few sideway glances at me making me just a little nervous. There doesn't seem to be any recognition just curiosity, so I relax and follow him to the grave. When we arrive, the caretaker leaves me and goes along his way.

Looking down at the grave I realize the dates closely coincide with what Susie said. She must have died the fall of that year and it suddenly strikes me this was what drove my Dad even further into finding out what the electric company was going to do about the stray current. Remembering the frustration and despair which haunted my Dad when he would come home from the Ottingers struggling with the realization he couldn't help her, once again becomes so real to me after all these years. I sob for all the time lost and the humiliation which must have consumed my Dad during those years of trying to prove the electric company's complicity in the health issues consuming the area.

Dad (Past)

I went to look for him that day. Dark clouds skated across the sky. There was a storm brewing. Usually, I could find him in the barn checking on the cows or out in the pasture fixing a broken fence, I shouted his name and when there was no answer. I mounted the tractor and took off to the back pasture to look for him.

He was not anywhere I could find him. Finally, I headed for the house. Worried, I ran in the back door, and headed straight for the kitchen where I knew my mother would be preparing dinner. There he was my steadfast and hardy father sitting with his head in his hands and my Mom kneeling beside him. His hands, slightly gnarled from years of hard work, trembled as she held them, and tears of anguish wet his lined and aging face. Looking at him, I knew he understood he was losing the battle he had been fighting for over 20 years. It all started with the cows being sick all the time and milk prices falling year after year. Dad felt something had to change to make the life of the farmer more successful or all of the farms in the area would be out of business in the next several years.

After hearing the information from Dr. Sebastian during the music concerts, he realized there was something he could do to possibly help prevent the demise of the farming community. He spent time visiting farm after farm, talking with the farmers about the issues they were facing and then coming back and working with Dr. Sebastian to come up with a solution to their problems. The determination was the farmers could add a combination of charcoal and limestone to their feed and spread over their plants to ensure the food chain would be free of damaging enzymes which were contributed by the electromagnetic fields which were generated by the stray current.

Finally, the farming community understood and started changing their practices and utilizing the program Dad and Dr. Sebastian had formulated. With the cooperation of the farming community, there became a hint of suspicion this same theory would be applicable to people. He became fixated with checking people and it was a constant conversation with him. No matter what was being discussed it always came back to the effect of the electromagnetic fields. Longtime friends were struggling to understand the change they saw in Dad while feeling sorry for our Mother.

Milk production went down and in turn the farm wasn't as profitable which infuriated Jonathan. Too much time was being spent on "fixing" everyone and the farm was on the receiving end of the neglect. Things around the house were being neglected because he always had to leave to go help someone. It broke my heart to see my Mom so upset and torn between her loyalty to her husband and the desire to see her son become a successful farmer. It became a juggling act for her, with my Dad she would listen and be sympathetic to his complaints about the disbelief people were showing. She would help him on the farm and try to be supportive while listening to Jonathan rant about what Dad was doing and how he was going to ruin the farm. I don't know how she stayed as calm as she did for as long as she did and still manage to be a good Mother and wife.

Jonathan

It's not hard to understand why Jonathan turned into such a bitter man. Growing up with him was usually a roller coaster of emotion. His entire life was spent getting ready to farm on his own. Following Dad around, mimicking his every move with the animals, spending every waking moment out in the fields and in the barn was his training ground for becoming a farmer like Dad.

He was much older than me and sometimes wanted to try act like a father to me instead of just a big brother. I spent most of my time trying to get his attention by doing things to irritate him so he would take a minute and give me his attention. When it came to our normal family dynamics, he became the Jonathan I didn't see eye to eye with most of the time. His temperament would change, and I couldn't reach him anymore. This transformation happened more frequently and the role he relished as an overbearing and criticizing brother was the starring role he wanted. Unfortunately for me, he excelled at the role and became Nick's worst critic. He continuously informed me Nick was no good for me and I was settling for a guy who would eventually break my heart. Even after all the time, or should I say years Nick and I were together, he still could barely stand to be in the same room with Nick. His disparagement of my relationship with Nick had shattered what small amount of respect I had for him. The constant badgering and threats of repercussion became very unsettling for me and the uneasiness I felt also impacted Nick. My brother's attitude toward life was infuriating and after my mother died it seemed pointless to try to salvage any kind of bond we might have had before. By the time I left the area our relationship had been reduced to practically nothing.

Sometimes I lie awake at night and imagine how different my Dad's philosophies and beliefs would be accepted today. Now so many people have embraced alternative medicine, homeopathic remedies and eating healthier to increase their longevity on this earth. The theory of electromagnetic fields destroying our environment wouldn't be viewed as crazy.

Brett, Morgan, Seth & Olivia (Present)

It was a busy morning in Millersville and there seemed to be a lot of traffic on Main Street. As a result, Brett sat through two series of the traffic light in the middle of town. Again, he felt a wave of tenderness. Just thinking about her now, it was all he could do to stay focused on the road and it kept him from noticing the light turning green until he heard a horn blow behind him. Moving forward he decides to take a little ride over to Seth's and Olivia's to see if their new neighbor has moved in yet. Right now, all he can think about is spending time with Morgan talking and learning about the things which are important to her. He knew there was more to Morgan than she was letting on and then there was a burning need for her in him.

Moving in was going to take a matter of a few minutes since I didn't have much with me. Olivia is waving to me from her kitchen window giving me hand signals which are supposed to tell me she will be out in a minute. The house I am moving into is very quaint. It has nice landscaping around the front and the entrance and is very welcoming. I find myself smiling broadly and feeling very contented for the first time in many years. It is good to walk through a front door and feel you are where you belong.

Right at this moment, I see Brett in my mind's eye and know there is going to be more to deal with in that arena. Olivia pops her head in the door with a bouquet of flowers and with a big smile says, "Welcome, Morgan. We are so happy you are going to be our new neighbor. Just think, we will be able to have coffee in the morning out on your cute patio and there will be so many nights Seth and I can come over and hang out, she says happily." Laughing I take the flowers from her and start rummaging through the cabinets to see if I can come up with a vase. Giving up on the vase, I settle for a mayonnaise jar which is sitting clean in the cabinet. "Olivia, I can't wait to wake up here tomorrow and be able to walk out and enjoy the outside without all of the noise of Main Street. I have you and Seth to thank for all of this. You are definitely both welcome here whenever you want to come over." "Oh, I wouldn't go that far, Morgan, it seems to me you were in the right place at the right time and had a need for a place to stay. Seth and I are glad we could help out and we are very pleased you are here. The Hotel was not a place for you to stay long term. As far as I know this house is available indefinitely," declares Olivia. "Let's go outside and look around. I'm pretty sure they had a patio setup in their backyard. "Don't look now but that appears to be Brett's truck turning the corner and heading this way." Seth tells them. "What the hell, does he have a beacon on me I don't know about? It seems like during the last couple of days he's been everywhere." "Oh Morgan, you should be flattered, he doesn't usually spend this kind of time getting to know someone," smiles Olivia.

As usual a smart retort is on the tip of my tongue. I realize though this kind of reaction is normal for me in response to any attention paid to me by a man. I really am glad to see him. "Oh Olivia, it's really a nice surprise he's here."

Brett sees Seth, and Olivia and Morgan standing in the side yard talking and wonders if he's the subject of the conversation. Shaking his head, he says to himself, "*Dude get a grip on yourself, and are you so hooked on her you think she feels the same way.*" As he pulls in, he can't help but smile to himself. Opening the car door, he whistles and as they turn their heads toward him, he sees Morgan's face light up and the smile turns his heart to liquid. In that moment, he knows...this is it. His search is over. He has fallen for her. He feels so gloriously happy he wants to shout it from the rooftops, but instead he smoothly saunters over to them, and tips his ball cap, saying, "Ladies, how are both of you gorgeous women doing today? "Hey Seth, what's up?" laughs Brett tipping his hat again. "Just keeping the company of two loosely wrapped but beautiful women. Of course, one of them being my wife, I might be a little biased. You know how it goes. After all she is my best friend and the love of my life," he declares, as he pulls her close to him. "Ok everybody enough! What I really want to do is help Morgan get settled into her new digs." declares Brett. Laughing, I look at Brett, "Really how much do you think I have to move in, remember I just arrived a few weeks ago. But if staying to give me a little company in my new home is part of your helpful personality then I graciously accept."

Seth and Olivia take their leave and let me know they are available if I need anything. Brett takes my arm and walks me into my new home. Once in the door, he turns me toward him and with the sweetest touch of his lip's whispers, "I've been waiting all day to do that." Trying to act as detached as ever, I move away from him, but he gently pulls me close to him. "Seeing you when I pulled in well, it made me smile." Then gathering me even closer he says, "I saw my Mother today, which in itself can be somewhat trying on my mind." "Tell me, Brett," I ask. "Today she was reminiscing about my stepfather and my memories of him are much different than hers."

Totally uncharacteristic of me, I wrap my arms around his neck, and tuck my head close to his cheek. "Your voice changes when you talk about your stepfather. Is there something about him you don't like, because that's what it sounds like to me, I say softly?" Brett turns his face away but not before I see a look in his eyes I recognize well since it is the same gaze my eyes have when I am thinking of my own past. But it is gone as quickly as it came. "Nothing for you to worry your pretty head about, its old news anyway," proclaims Brett. I raise my eyebrows and look intently at him but instead decide to let it go. "Ok, if you say so, but I know that look and it's one full of hurt and anger so whenever you want to talk about it, I'm a good listener." "Thanks, Morgan, but I'm fine, but I appreciate your caring about me." As he's talking, he's moving me over to couch so we can sit down. Sitting there next to him, I rest my head against his shoulder and close my eyes for just a moment. "Sleepy?" he whispers?" "No, just need to rest my eyes and your shoulder seems a comfy place," I whisper in return. Before I know what is happening, he has turned me around so suddenly I am laying on the couch his body resting next to me, his face displaying an impish grin. "Now Morgan, don't get nervous, just lie here and relax. I've decided I will ravish your body later, because right now I just want to close my eyes and have you close to me, so rest and get some of the needed sleep I see in your eyes."

Nick (Present)

Nick was annoyed! He couldn't stop thinking about the friend Seth and Olivia had met at the bar, this Morgan woman. Something about her was bugging him and the more he thought about her, the more agitated he became. Whitney had been moaning and groaning about how she saw her at the Hotel with Edmond and me plus complaining about Morgan talking down to her. There is something about this woman which makes me think of Misty and for the life of me I can't figure out what it is. I have determined she was the woman crossing the street a couple of Saturdays ago and I remembered then how I was thinking about Misty. It would be impossible for this woman to have so many similarities as Misty but there it is. She reminds me of Misty, not in looks but virtually everything else, all the way down to the way she sits, holds her head, and flashes her eyes. There has got to be a way for me to find out more about her and that is from one person, Olivia. She is the only person who has developed any kind of relationship with Morgan. Olivia can be difficult when pressed so I will talk to Seth first and feel out the territory before I make any kind of declaration.

Seth always stops out to the Tavern for lunch on Tuesdays so I'm going to make a point of stopping there to see him and try to figure out what the deal is with this Morgan woman. He leaned back in his chair and for the first time in a very long time he thought about Misty. He could picture them with their children laughing and loving. Just as fast as he thought about Misty, the image of the woman Morgan came to his mind. "What the hell is going on with me, I need to settle down. Maybe seeing Seth will help." Talking to his best friend was usually what he needed, so this time shouldn't be any different than before.

His daydreaming was interrupted by the ringing of his phone. "Nick Darlington here." It was Seth. "Hey Nick, are you busy for lunch? I thought we could grab a bite to eat and catch up. I haven't seen you since we were all at the Tavern after your game." "Seth, you must have ESP because I was just thinking about coming out to the Tavern today to see if I could catch you. I know you always have lunch there today," Nick laughed. "It just so happens I am free through the afternoon, so we won't have to rush through lunch." "Great Nick, I'll meet you at the Tavern at noon."

The rest of the morning was quiet, and he was able to concentrate and get some of the paperwork done that had been sitting on his desk. Close to noon, he left the office and headed over to the Tavern. Walking into the dimly lit bar after being in the bright sunlight, his eyes needed a second to adjust. Who does he see sitting at the bar right in front of him but the woman he had just been thinking about? He decides right then he is going to find more out about this woman, so he saunters up toward her and notices there is an empty stool next to her. "Hey it's Morgan, right? Is this stool being saved for anyone or can I have a seat next to you," asked Nick. I looked so startled I think Nick thought for a second I was going to say no, however, I answer quietly "Whatever, there seems to be an empty stool sitting there so if you want to sit down, go ahead."

Even though I really don't want him to sit down, he swings his leg over the stool, leans his elbows on the bar and turns toward me. "Tell me, Morgan, how are things at your new home?" I hesitated, wondering if it is wise to engage in conversation with him.

Looking closely at him I can see the lines around his eyes, the downward turn of his mouth and the anxiety which he is trying so hard to hide. For a minute I remember the young man he was and how much potential we both had if we had stayed together, but reality snapped into focus and I smiled. "It's good, Olivia provided a helping hand and since there wasn't a whole lot to move, I think I can start calling it home." "Well, I want to let you know you couldn't have picked a nicer place to come and stay. Millersville is a unique town. It has been where my family has lived and called home for a very long time. Most of the people who live in this area have been living here for what seems like decades and they are all good people." "It seems that way. Edmond, of course, was the first person I met when arriving in town. Now I have gotten to know Olivia, Seth, Brett, Susie Mitchell, and of course, you and Whitney." Nick becomes very still and looks at me, "you know there is something about the way you just said that which seems so familiar, almost like I've heard your voice before," Nick said with a searching look on his face.

I know the next few minutes are going to be very important for me. Somehow, I need to be sure Nick doesn't think any more about my comment. "Nick, Olivia and Seth talk about you so much when I'm with them I feel like I know you," I said smiling. Seth saves me from saying anything else, when he walks up beside us. "Funny seeing you here Morgan since I saw you this morning in your kitchen with Olivia. Is this guy harassing you or what?" laughs Seth. "No, he is just informing me how nice of a town Millersville is, but I told him I knew already because of the nice people I've met, especially my new neighbors." I said smiling at Seth.

While talking to Seth, I glance at Nick and he appears to be lost in thought. With a tap on his arm, I say, "Well Nick it looks like you are going to need another stool for your lunch companion, so I will vacate mine." Standing up, I look at Seth and quickly say, "Hey have a seat, I need to run some errands and pick up some stuff for the house, so enjoy your lunch you two."

Turning away from them I have to concentrate to keep myself from running for the door. Interacting with Nick so closely made me very uneasy and sad at the same time. I need to go home and figure out what my next move is going to be. Having these unexpected moments with Nick are very unnerving. There was a definite moment when I felt some kind of connection with him and it just reinforced the fact I need to stay away from Nick. Something tells me he is getting curious about my being in Millersville.

While Seth and Nick were enjoying their lunch, Nick was trying to keep himself from drilling Seth with questions about Morgan, wanting the conversation to just lead there without him appearing too interested, though after having the short interaction with her today, he realizes more than ever there is something more to Morgan Kiernan than anyone knew.

NICK (Past)

Driving erratically Nick somehow got home and leaned his head on his steering wheel. Swarming around in his head are visions of Whitney's body glistening with the intensity of their lovemaking. Leaning back in his seat he tries to bring Misty's image into his mind but fails miserably. All he can think about is how good Whitney felt when he touched her. Now just remembering the sounds coming from her throat were enough to push him over the edge. He looked down and it was evident he was thinking about her, how she tasted and felt had given him an erection. Shaking his head vehemently, he knew he had to talk to Misty and try to obliterate the image of Whitney from his mind. Suddenly he couldn't get out of his car fast enough. Running into the house, practically knocking down his Mother, he ran to the phone and dialed Misty's number. After several attempts at getting the right number, he hears Misty's voice, "Hello, you've reached Misty, you know what to do. I'll call you when I return." Banging down the receiver he swears loudly and turns to head down the hall to his bedroom. Concerned his Mother looks on and anxiously wonders what is going on between him and Misty. Remembering as parents they had agreed to let the two of them figure it out, knowing the prospect of college looming ahead was putting stress on them, she turned back to the book she had been reading before Nick so unceremoniously entered the house.

The next day sitting at Whitney's house, Misty was trying to bring Whitney down to earth. She was going on about this guy she had met and how intense their relationship had become in such a short time. Skeptical about her recollection of the events Misty drifted off and wondered what Nick was doing right now. Feeling a little apprehensive she shoved any uneasy thoughts away and focused back on Whitney. "So, could this wonderful guy you are so ecstatic over possibly take you to the Prom.? Nothing would please me more since going to the Prom is all you have talked and worried about for weeks now. So, my advice to you is to make sure even if nothing else goes on with this guy, you get him to take you to the Prom. If that happens then you and your new guy can double date with Nick and me." Arrogantly Whitney responded, "Lucky for me, there is no doubt he will take me to the Prom. You'll see this guy is right for me and I feel like I've been waiting all my life for him. Isn't that crazy?" "You really think he's going to ask you or should I say agree to go with you to the Prom. You just met him, didn't you?" Misty said exasperated. Smiling devilishly Whitney said, "Misty, you are going to be totally surprised about my Prom date and I hope you find a way to be happy for me." Feeling a little peeved at Whitney Misty decided it was time to leave and try to connect with Nick. "Whitney, I'm out of here, I hope everything works out for you and let me know if you want to hook up with Nick and me for the prom. "

Meanwhile Nick continues to try to rid his mind of Whitney and replace the distracting image of her with the image of Misty. He was desperate to experience again the desire and joy Misty's image always made him feel. His instincts though, would not release him from the memory of Whitney's passion and her body glistening with the aftermath of their sex. At the same time waiting for Misty to either call or just show up was driving him crazy. Hours passed and the image of Misty replaced the memory of Whitney. Now, fear of Misty finding out, losing her, and what the devastation would mean for him overwhelmed Nick. He became more distressed and wondered out loud, "What am I going to do? How can I manage to hide this? What if Whitney tells her? Misty was the love of his life and somehow Whitney had twisted her way into his being. Now, it felt like the beginning of a struggle for which he was not prepared.

Jonathan and Nick (Present)

It is early. Jonathan can tell by the light outside the window and the early dawn colors illuminating his bedroom window. Remembering then there was not going to be any cows waiting to be milked this morning. Today was a new day. There had been an awakening in him which would make his family proud. More often now he thought about Misty, there had to be a way to locate her. This change which overcame him was definitely something he wanted to share with Misty and finding her was all he could think about. It was time he started to work his way back into the community.

In Millersville there was a strong web of threads which weaved itself among the prominent members of the area. These were the people he needed to talk to because someone was going to be the link he needed, to lead him to Misty's whereabouts. Misty's disappearance was somehow connected to the community and it was those townspeople who might be privy to where she might have gone. So, it was time to get up and start the day, nothing was going to get accomplished lying around. Today's work was going to be all about finding Misty. Thinking back about her life, he realized the only person he knew, who would have any information about her, was Nick Darlington. Over the years, he had heard about Nick Darlington and his contributions to the community. Although he appreciated what the man had done for his hometown, he knew deep down it was just an act. His opinion of Nick was less than stellar. He knew how much Misty had loved Nick, but he never knew what happened between them, due in part to his own selfishness. Rumors were flying throughout Millersville that summer, and he chose to ignore what he was hearing. He never believed what everyone was saying about Whitney and Nick, but Misty became so distant then now looking back he knew it was all true. His heart felt leaden when he thought about his sister and wished he could have the chance to tell her how sorry he was for not being there for her.

In an instance, his stomach starting churning and he knew this was not going to be easy for him. Figuring the best place to start was the diner, he jumped in his car and headed over there. Driving there, a multitude of memories ran rampant through his mind. Little did he know she was just a couple of miles away, moving into a house which meant she was staying in Millersville for a while.

Walking in was like stepping back in time, never did he think he would be eating here again. His childhood had been so entwined with this diner, from walking here after basketball, and football games to picking up Misty after her cheerleading. Susie Mitchell and her perky attitude and the constant movement of the counter customers, the smell of coffee, the chatter of the short order cooks, the waitresses, the loud clanking of dishes and the low buzz of chatter were all of the familiar sounds and smells assaulting him as he walked through the door.

Anticipating the chance of knowing most of the customers, he settled in an empty booth. Sure enough, there was Susie Mitchell with the biggest smile adorning her face. Sitting in the booth, he looked around. There were so many familiar faces, he found himself wondering which one of them knew something about Misty's whereabouts.

Unexpectedly Tom Fraser walked up to the booth. "Hey Jonathan, how are you? I was expecting to hear from you this week and found myself wondering why you hadn't called me, especially after our last conversation," Tom said with a forced smile. "Funny you should say that Tom, I think our last conversation was you were going to re-evaluate the investors who were interested and get back to me. Go back to the bank and sit tight because I am realizing my family farm is worth a lot more than you are proposing." Abruptly, Tom walked away not knowing his small, minded attitude was just another boost in Jonathan's determination to keep going and find Misty. Just as Jonathan looked up, Susie was heading his way, "Hey you, it's so good to see you. Where have you been? You know your omelet has been sitting back there just waiting for you to show up." Jonathan laughed. "Well, you need to bring it on out here because I'm getting very hungry." Susie gave her brightest smile and said, got it, Jonathan, it's coming right up."

As he leaned back in the booth, he found himself smiling and finally understanding the power of family, friends, the familiarity of Millersville and the people in the community. Enjoying his food, he tried not to constantly look around, but it was hard not look at all the customers, the people who he had known all of his life who now seemed more interesting than they ever had before.

Lost in thought, he didn't see or hear the person walking up to his table and before he could get his wits about him, Nick Darlington was asking him if he could sit down for a minute. Inherently he despised Nick Darlington but any information he could glean from him concerning his sister was worth his being civil. "Jonathan, do you have a minute? I won't keep you long." "Sure Nick, have a seat." Looking across the table at Nick, he realized how miserable he appeared. For a moment he felt a sense of elation but quickly let it go. "Well, Nick, this is quite a surprise. What is on your mind?" In a quiet voice Nick began, "There is no way to start this conversation Jonathan. Unfortunately, I've realized my destiny in life isn't what I thought it would be. Never in a million years did I think you would be the person to whom I would need to disclose any portion of myself. However, seeing you today so unexpectedly have made me realize there is so much to say and clear up about the past which has affected both of us."

The sounds of cars driving past the diner's windows were loudly ringing in his ears as he waited for the explosion brewing within Jonathan. He knew in his heart Jonathan was the last person to whom he wanted to bare his soul. He was prepared however to hear whatever insults would come his way. Jonathan became very still, and Nick prepared himself for the onslaught of anger rapidly brewing within Jonathan. "Nick, do you really think I want to hear your life's woes, I have enough problems of my own. You and I have nothing to talk about, our conversations ran out twenty years ago and whatever you have to say now, I'm not interested in hearing," Shaking his head, Nick looked intensely at Jonathan and said, "Please just listen, something has come to my attention which might have something to do with Misty." Jonathan started and stared at Nick, "Jonathan, listen to me. I think Misty might be here in Millersville.

There was a long pause. Do you hear me?" "There is a woman who suddenly arrived here a few weeks ago and there is something about her which reminds me so strongly of Misty I just can't shake it. You are the only other person I know who would see the same thing I have seen." "What are you talking about? I don't think you should even utter Misty's name after what you did to her," retorted Jonathan. "Jonathan, I know you can't stand the sight of me, but you need to listen. There is a woman who has just located here or something and as God as my witness she reminds me of Misty," pleaded Nick. "What the hell do you mean or something? Is she living here or just passing through?

So, she reminds you of Misty. I'm sure with the guilt you are carrying around there are many times you imagine you've seen Misty a lot over the last several years, Jonathan said sarcastically." "I know, Jonathan, it seems crazy, but ever since I talked to Tom Fraser about the sale of your family farm, I've been haunted with images of Misty." "You are kidding me, right? Tom Fraser is my banker, and do you want to tell me the reason he would be talking to you? Can you honestly tell me why this is? Were you talking with him about me and my farm, or are you going to come up with some kind of crazy story about how you are on the board of the bank and this is how you were having a conversation with Tom Fraser about 'My Farm'? "No what is crazy, Tom was the one who brought up Misty and it made me seriously reflect on where she went and why she never made any kind of contact with anyone. You are her brother and if there was someone she would reach out to, it should have been you, don't you think?" "No, I don't think so Nick, and if I had heard from her, telling you wouldn't be high on my "to do list," declared Jonathan. "Yeah, whatever Jonathan, regardless of what you think about me, this woman resembles Misty, and I don't think it's a coincidence." Nick said vehemently.

"Ok, Nick, I'll keep that in mind, but any time you want to vacate my table so I can finish eating, will be fine with me."

Leaving Jonathan to his breakfast, Nick decided it was time to go elsewhere to find out something more about Morgan.

Misty Nick and Whitney (Past)

Hours passed and Nick still had not connected with Misty and the trepidation he felt about talking to her was causing him to feel sick. Never in a million years did he think he would have had that kind of encounter with Whitney. He still can't believe he actually had sex with her and worst of all he can't stop replaying it in his mind. In the distance, he can hear the phone ringing, and with something close to terror waits for his Mom to yell it is Misty on the phone. "Hey Nick, are you up there?" Misty is on the phone, pick it up and I'll hang up down here," hollers his Mom. "Ok, I got it" and he hears the click of the downstairs phone. "Hey Misty, what's going on?" asked Nick trying to sound normal. "Nick, I should be asking you what's going on, I haven't heard from you in a couple of days. I kept thinking you were going to stop around or call, and then when I didn't see or hear from you, I got worried. Then worry became anger and I swore calling you was out of the question, but yet here I am." "Misty, there was no need to worry about me. I was just recovering from my trip to Philadelphia with my dad," Nick answered nervously.

"Ok, but you know the Prom is Friday, and we need to decide who we are going to go with and what we are doing on the weekend, said Misty. Whitney has been doing a lot of bragging about her date and how surprised I'm going to be, which to be honest is really irritating me. It's not like I'm not used to all of Whitney's drama, but this time she seems smug and almost giddy." sighed Misty. "Don't worry about Whitney, Misty. She always talks too much and thinks the most miniscule thing is as big of a deal to us as it is to her, but we both know it's just the way she is," said Nick.

In the distance, Nick can hear a car door slam. Getting his mind back to Misty, he says, "Why don't you head on over here and we can spend some time together? My Mom is making sloppy joes and I'm sure she would love to have you eat with us." "Sure, I can head on over and maybe then we can figure out what we are doing this weekend. It's our Senior Prom Nick, and I want it to be one we will never forget." said Misty.

Meanwhile, Whitney was downstairs making small talk with Nick's Mom and as Nick walks toward the steps, he can't believe his ears. The car door had been hers. From the sense of panic, he careened as he got halfway down the steps. He could see Whitney sitting on the couch in the family room. She had a smile on her face. He knew beneath that smile, she was plotting something, and Nick felt sick wondering what it was.

Getting to the bottom step, he managed a smile, and walked into the room. "Hey Whitney, what brings you by, looking for Misty? She's not here right now but is on her way over and we are heading out." So maybe you should be on your way too and I'll tell Misty to reach out to you later, OK?" Overhearing Nick say they were going out, his Mom spoke up and said, "I thought you two were staying in tonight and eating dinner here. Did something change from 10 minutes ago? Whitney moved over on the couch, and with the voice of a temptress she patted the couch and said, Nick come over and sit down here with me. We can wait for Misty together, won't that be nice." Nick shook his head quickly so Whitney was the only one who could see it, and said, "No I think I'm good right here, I have a bird's eye view of the street, so I'll be able to see Misty coming." He saw her smirk and knew right then he needed to keep Whitney away from spending any time with Misty. In what seemed like an eternity, he saw Misty pull onto the street. "Whitney, why don't you get ready to head out," he said quickly. "Misty and I haven't seen each other in a couple of days, and I would like to spend time with her..." **alone".** Oh no Nick, I think I'm going to stay right here since having Misty here has set the stage just right for my announcement," Whitney said with a smirk.

Nick felt the sweat beading on his brow and his heart beating faster as he began to try to figure out how he was going to manipulate the conversation which was about to ensue right in his living room. Berating himself as to why he let the past 48 hours happen, he heard Misty's car door slam. Turning toward Whitney he tried to warn her not to do something stupid. Laughing out loud, Whitney jumped up to get to the door to let Misty in. She moved so fast that Nick was one step behind her. When the door opened, it looked to Misty like they both were there together greeting her. Seeing the two of them together, Whitney with a big smile on her face and Nick with something akin to panic made Misty very apprehensive. Shrugging away the dreadful feeling, she smiled and said "Hey Whitney, fancy seeing you here. I thought you were working today with your Mom." "Yeah, well I got finished early and wanted to stop over and see Nick. You know I haven't seen either of you guys for a couple of days," said Whitney. "So, you came over to Nick's, why didn't you just call me, and we could have hung out?" "Come on Misty, it's not a big deal, I just wanted to stop by," shirked Whitney. "Don't' give me that shit, Whitney, why did you really come over here?" "You have been acting so weird lately, like you have some big secret. The comments you are making about the Prom and how you have a date which will surprise me are all very strange, Whitney." Nick, do you know anything about this? Why is she just standing there with such a self-satisfied look on her face?" cried Misty. "I don't know Misty, please don't get upset, she just stopped by here for a minute." Whitney moved toward the couch, and motioned Misty to sit down. "Misty, why don't you come sit so we can have a conversation. I have so much I want to talk to you about and Nick should be part of the conversation since he is so much a part of what I want to tell you." Nick now panic stricken moves toward Whitney and says, "Really Whitney, don't you think it's about time for you to leave, I need to talk to Misty," "No Nick, I think it's time we share with Misty what has been going on over the last couple of days," "Misty, why don't you ask Nick what he's been doing lately, since obviously he hasn't been with you?"

You know Whitney I trust Nick so much I don't need to know what he has been doing the last few days. Why are you still here? We asked you to leave," "Well Misty, there is a first time for everything, so if I were you, I would find out what has been going on because if Nick doesn't want to tell you, I will happily oblige."

Nick looked at Misty and saw doubt cross her eyes. He knew then he was going to have to find a way out of this mess if he was going to have any chance of keeping Misty. Nothing mattered now but finding a way to explain what had happened with Whitney. He needed Whitney to leave so he could talk to Misty without Whitney's chirping in the background.

"Whitney, I'm not kidding you need to go. Misty and I need to talk, and our conversation does not include you, so please do us both a favor and leave," shouted Nick." Whitney picked herself up and as arrogantly as she could, turned and looked at Misty, laughing. "You are so naïve, all the talks you had with me about Nick and you waiting to have sex. The sappy looks you two would give each other when you were at school made me sick. I knew Nick wanted something different though. I could feel it whenever I was around the two of you."

"Whitney, what are you saying, I think you should do what Nick suggested, and leave," cried Misty. "Oh no, I'm just getting started. I had enough of the two of you being goody two shoes, so I decided to take matters into my own hands, smirked Whitney. "What do you mean, Whitney?" screamed Misty. Feeling sick to her stomach, Misty looked at Nick wanting him to say something but instead he stood there like he was frozen. Not wanting to share her first time with Whitney, Misty moved to stand with Nick and grabbed his hand. We really don't think it's any of your business, but Nick and I aren't as 'goody too shoes' as you think. So, whatever you want to say about us and how we are together needs to end.

Whitney decided it was time right now to tell Misty everything. "Misty, Nick and I spent several hours together down at the lake the other day, and you can be guaranteed he wasn't worried about where you were. His mind and body were occupied with someone else. After being with me, I'm sure he realizes who he wants to be with now. I'm sure you have never given him the experience I did," laughed Whitney.

Feeling as though the air had been sucked out of her, Misty, stunned and trying to keep herself together looked up at Nick for some kind of denial. She saw his eyes fill with tears as he whispered, "I'm sorry Misty." Trying not to cry in front of Whitney, Misty pleaded, "Nick, please tell me this isn't true. Were the two of you together that way, "Oh God", please tell me this isn't true?" Nick lowered his head and tears streamed down his face, but he was silent. "I love you so much how could you do this to me, to us, Misty sobbed." Turning away, Misty tried to hold her head up and without looking at Whitney's smug expression, she looked at Nick her pain and sorrow changing to rage. "I have to leave, I have to leave, the sight of you, *Oh My God*. I can't stand the sight of either one of you right now! Neither one of you ever call me again or stop around the farm. You will never be welcome there again. Whitney glared at her with an expression filled with arrogance. "Now Misty you know who my mystery man is and why I couldn't tell you about him."

With that last comment, Misty turned and walked toward the door. Nick, afraid he would never see her again, grabbed her arm and broke down. "Please Misty, he begged. I am sorry, so sorry. Please don't leave. Please give me a chance to make this up to you." Misty snatched her arm from him, slammed the door behind her, ran to her car and drove toward the farm. She had barely managed to keep herself from collapsing in front of them. Now she was sobbing. Between the sobs, her fist hit the steering wheel. Sorrow and anger were interwoven now. If she had turned back to look, she would have seen Nick standing in the street watching her leave with Whitney standing behind him, a grin on her face.

Feeling Whitney behind him, Nick quickly turned around. Whitney fell back. "Hey what are you doing Nick, you almost knocked me over." cried Whitney. "I should do more than knock you over, Whitney. Telling Misty about us was your whole plan since you found out Misty was coming here this afternoon, wasn't it? Outraged, he continued, it's why you stopped here to begin with to see if you could get Misty here with both of us so you could destroy our relationship." "Destroy, is this what you think I was doing? You are so wrong. It was for you I did this. Misty needed to know she isn't right for you and your happiness is only going to be complete with me. Don't you understand, Nick, I love you. Misty can't have you, it's not in the plan," whimpered Whitney. "What Plan? Whitney, what are you babbling about? You just ruined my life, and you are telling me it was all part of a plan. Have you lost your mind?" exclaimed Nick.

Turning away from Whitney, he trudged back into the house wondering what the hell he is going to do to get Misty to forgive him. Seeing his Mom coming toward him with a look he was very familiar with, he put his hand up and said, "Don't Mom, I really can't deal with anything else right now." "Well, you are going to have to do this, get that girl out of here and make sure she knows she is not welcome at our home, ever!" With that she went through the swinging door to the kitchen and Nick knew not to follow her. Seeing the swinging door moving back and forth seemed to match time with his rapidly beating heart.

Moving to the phone, he hesitated but knew he needed to call Misty. Except what was he going to say? What could possibly make Misty believe anything he had to tell her? Short of just downright begging for her to forgive him, he was at a loss. So instead of calling her, he put the phone down. Deciding to take a ride, he yells to his Mom he is leaving. She poked her head around the kitchen door and said quietly, "Nick, do what is right and go see her. You owe her that much." Walking to the door, he turned and shook his head. Getting into his car, he thought about what his Mom said and knew she was right. Misty had never done anything in their relationship to have this happen. He had no excuse, none.

Pulling up in front of Misty's house, Nick sat in the car and tried to get the nerve up to go to the door. Just as he opened the car door, Jonathan came out of the house and walked toward him. "Hey Nick, what brings you by today. Misty doesn't seem like she is accepting visitors right now so you might want to hit the road, and Nick, don't bother coming back here, I don't think Misty wants to have any kind of conversation with you after what I overheard her tell Mom. I told her when she was a freshman and all she could do was talk about Nick Darlington, you weren't any damn good. Well, it's taken four years, but I knew you wouldn't let me down. You are a real piece of shit, you know" controlling himself from knocking him flat.

Nick couldn't find the words to rebuke Jonathan because right then everything he said Nick felt was true. In that moment he knew he had lost Misty. Her pride wouldn't let her come out to see him then and seeing her in the future would have to be from a distance. Her passion went both ways, and he knew she could love passionately, and her disdain could be as strong.

Trying not to let Jonathan see how upset he was he got back into his car and left.

Jack Callahan (Past)

Recently my parents had found out there were going to be several large electrical towers installed off of a main road in our county. The area was not heavily populated but the few residents who did live in the area had started a petition. Their premise was the amount of stray current which would emanate from the towers would eventually be detrimental to humans and animals. A report filed with the county zoning board and the DEP stated the following: "Thus we can now define "stray current" as the continuous flow of any current, other than momentary fault current, over the earth, metallic piping, building steel, into houses and farms, etc. which is thus objectionable and undesirable to the continued good health of humans and animals."

All along my Dad knew there was enough stray current existing to cause health issues among animals and people. He knew initially it was affecting the cows on the farm but also knew the cow epidemic would have a parallel existence with humans. All of this information related directly back to the electrical companies who made money due to this procedure. He knew there was data but with the lack of money and resources it was hard to find.

Waking up early one morning shortly after my parents became aware of the installation of new towers, I overheard my parents talking about Jack Callahan. Knowing I shouldn't be eavesdropping, I opened my closet door. Hiding there when I was a kid, I found I could open up a small trap door and see into my parent's room. Kneeling down into the closet I could hear my parents very clearly. My Dad was telling my Mom he had seen Jack following him when he was going over to the Ottinger's. My Mom was very upset Jack was trying to secretly watch what he was doing. I could hear my Dad persuading her there was nothing to worry about. Jack Callahan, he assured her, had been coming over to the farm once a week just to ride with him. He explained to her Jack's interest was purely based on Jack's desire to see how the dowsing rods worked when Dad was using them with people. "Ok Carl, if you are sure." I heard Mom say. "I am sure." he said. "Then I won't worry, Carl." she reassured him. Satisfied, without a sound I left my closet and closed the door.

Meanwhile, Jack Callahan was sitting on his back porch trying to figure out a way to get the Jenkins's man to give him access to his methods. He believed Jenkins was monitoring the electrical currents to determine how much stray current was emanating from the high-tension towers in the area. Headquarters was getting concerned about the influence Jenkins had on the residents of the area. The last thing they wanted the townspeople to know was this area had been targeted for an analysis of how much stray current was being filtered into the environment. Knowing the towers proximity to the neighborhoods scattered throughout the countryside affected the company's plan to saturate the area, they wanted to experiment with the towers' power to provide stronger wattage and thought they were in an area where the community would be less likely to notice.

Understanding most of the residents were part of the farming community, the company felt they wouldn't be a threat to the plan. Ironically, it was someone who was part of the farming community who was sounding the bell and somehow Callahan needed to figure out how to silence the noise before the electric company increased its involvement. The phone calls from the company were becoming more frequent and trying to put them off was becoming more difficult.

In the middle of his thoughts, the phone rang. It was his supervisor, Don Wharton. After a brief conversation about golf, Don told Jack, in no uncertain terms, the company wanted Jenkins shut down with whatever means were necessary. Jack hung up the phone hardly believing what Don had implied. "Whatever means were necessary?" The words sent a shiver of fear through him. Jack Callahan had come to respect what Jenkins was doing with the community. Jenkins had a real understanding of what the residents who lived near the towers were facing. Callahan knew without testing the area stray current was emanating from the towers because the attention the Company was giving to the project was a strong indication of how important it was. The message from the company now seemed to be to silence Jenkins no matter what. This was not an avenue he wanted to head down but the situation was spirally out of control.

Jack was so caught up in his thoughts he didn't realize his doorbell was ringing. Jumping up he hurried to the door and opened it to see his old army buddy Charlie Kemp standing there. Charlie still thought he was in the army, and wherever he was, his eyes were constantly scanning the area around him. Charlie also worked for the electric company, but in a separate division. Suddenly he had an idea he could use Charlie's services in trying to solve the Jenkins problem before it escalated. Jack knew Charlie's loyalty to him was solid because of their time in the war. Jack was sure with some heavy persuasion; Jenkins would give up his pursuit of the electromagnetic field. Little did Jack know it was the electric company who had sent Charlie to visit him that day.

My parents were considered good people and throughout their lives always acted in an upstanding way. When Dad began working with the rods and claiming there was stray current hurting people, his reputation suffered. Jack Callahan continued to portray himself as a friend, but his visits were becoming more frequent and the conversations were developing into interrogation. Dad was so wrapped up in his findings he barely noticed how agitated Jack was becoming during the conversations.

One day when Jack stopped in, he wasn't alone, the gentleman who came with him was introduced as Jack's good friend,

Charlie. He was large in stature. His shoulders were so broad they blocked the sunlight when he was in the room. His demeanor was aggressive, and he constantly wore a scowl. His relationship with Jack was authoritative and it was obvious who was in charge. He scanned the area watching everyone while seeming disinterested in what he was observing. That day I remember as being one with a black cloud looming over it. Nothing seemed to go right with the farm. A cow went down with a twisted stomach, others got out and were wandering around near the major highway which was at the end of our road. Having to deal with visitors was annoying Mom. Jack was always asking so many questions and looking back on it now, I think Mom knew he was gathering information to report back to the electric company.

If it became known the stray current was directly related to illness in the community surrounding the big towers, the electric company would lose millions of dollars in court hearings and fines. It became obvious "Charlie" was more than just a friend to Jack and things were definitely not as they seemed. Never in a million years would I have ever believed my parent's lives might be in danger. Every time this "Charlie" would show up with Jack I would feel a sense of foreboding but never really understood why Dad didn't seem to be bothered. So, I just considered it my imagination.

Not to make excuses for my actions at the time, but I was seventeen years old and about to launch into a whole other chapter of my life with college looming closely in my future. Eventually Jack dropped some of the pretense which had been meant to ingratiate himself to us, and the effect his actions had on my parents was very painful to watch. Instead of the feigned friendship of the past, he became very belligerent with my Dad, demanding answers about the dowsing rods. His demeanor changed so drastically my Mom begged my Dad not to let Jack on the property anymore. Dad never had a problem telling salesmen to take a hike so when his action was so fatalistic, Mom became concerned Dad was so distracted by the details of his work he was unable to recognize something was going to happen, and our lives may actually be in some kind of danger. When she spoke of this with Dad, he would just brush it off and tell her it was all in her imagination.

What he never spoke of to any of us was he finally believed all the years of trying to monitor the stray current and its effect was truly a broader problem than he ever imagined. It became obvious the evidence obtained from all the families suffering needed to be safeguarded. Jack Callahan was definitely not going to get any more information from any of us, least of all my Dad.

I did not know it then but later in my life it would become my mission to find the truth in all of the research my Dad did and the terrible cost it had to my family. With all the research available online I have finally found data supporting his claim from all those years ago. There is and has been a monetary drive to the existence stray current in our environment. Research has been done by experts all across the country and that information will prove what has been said all along.

Again, the utilities and related corporations have placed the "health" and functioning of the transformer above the welfare of the humans and animals. The savings in costs equate to additional profits to the Electric Company and other utilities and showed their indifference and insensitive to the safety of humans and animals.

Later when Jack was sitting down the road from the Jenkins farm waiting to see if there was anything suspicious going on and biding his time there, his mind wandered back to the war and the beginning of his relationship with Charlie. The war was nothing he had ever experienced before. Seeing the soldiers running into the enemy with nothing but their Country's freedom on their minds had made such an impact on his personality. He knew he had found his place serving his fellow man in fighting for his country and this is how he met Charlie. They fought side by side in the war and the number of times Charlie put his life in jeopardy made Jack a fan. Then the time came when Charlie's enthusiasm with the war saved Jack.

Brett and Elizabeth (Present)

Brett is finishing up with the bar duties and spending way too much time trying to persuade Jillian, his best bartender, to stop complaining about the new girl and to give her a chance. With that behind him, he decides to make a visit to his Mother. Knowing he shouldn't show up unannounced, due to her insistence on proper etiquette, he decides to go anyway. He needs to talk to her. It has to be face to face. She had always been extremely difficult to live with. Her obsession of having the best of everything and being part of all the social events of the area drove him crazy. Every time he had any kind of issue in school, she would go on and on about what would people think, knowing her son was not perfect. Those times would hurt him. It was a sensitivity he still carried, even now.

One incident, though there were many, he remembered of her anger was a time when Jack and she were not invited to the Christmas party of one of the founding families in Millersville. Her anger lasted for days. She would rant and rave about how they were not good enough anyway. This was the one thing Jack and Brett had in common and there were times when they would complain and laugh about her tirades. She was so obsessed with Jack continuing to work for the electric company because of the position and status it provided them. Now she has grown older and Jack is gone, he wonders if it was all about the money. There was never a time when he can remember her not spending lavishly on whatever took her fancy.

Because he had the bar, Brett had been able to have expensive things, with sensible spending while keeping his business successfully running. However, his mother's constant badgering of him to be the best, to do the right thing, and to have the perfect life might be, if he thought more about it, why he was so attracted to Morgan. She had all the traits he loved and those his mother loathed. The more he thought about it, he needed to talk to his mother and tell her how he felt about Morgan. He was preparing himself for the tirade which was about to fall around him. This was going to be the first time he knew he was going to go against his Mother's wishes. Morgan Kiernan was not the woman his Mother would think was best for him.

Suddenly he felt something dripping down his back and knew as he got closer to his Mother's house, he was breaking out in beads of sweat. Walking around the side of the house stepping among his mother's flowers, he waits to hear her yell, "Brett, will you please watch where you are walking." But hears nothing! As he steps on the back step and opens the back door, he again waited to hear his Mother's voice. "Brett, please don't let the backdoor bang, it gives me such a headache." Again, nothing. He quickens his step. Keeping the door from banging he walks into the house.

"Mom, are you home?" Listening, he realizes the house is eerily quiet.

Wandering through the rooms, he wonders why the house has always looked like it was not lived in. His Mother kept their house so immaculate as a kid, Brett never wanted to have his friends stop by. He was always so concerned they would make a mess, and his Mother would become angry. The only friend who ever stopped by was Seth. Seth had an understanding with his Mother. Brett proceeded to sit down on the couch no one ever used for lying down and rarely used for sitting. Thinking about a bunch of cartoon characters lounging on his Mother's couch made him laugh aloud.

Still wondering where Mother is, he lays back his head and thinks of Morgan. He smiles to himself knowing how happy she has made him. He hears he sound of footsteps on the stone entrance and as the door opens a bluster of wind blows some leaves into the foyer. "Damn, he hears his Mother say, "Why can't the lawn care service do its job and clean up the leaves. I do dislike people who don't do their jobs." "Mother are you talking to yourself?" laughs Brett and he quickly rises from the couch. "Oh my God Brett, Is everything alright? You never stop here unannounced. You know how that annoys me." "It is good to see you, Mother." He wants to hug her but knowing his Mother he just smiles at her and pats her on her shoulder. "Mother, it is so good to see you, have you done something different with your hair, you are looking very beautiful today," "Don't try to butter me up, Brett, what are you doing here? You never come here uninvited". "Well, there is a first time for everything. I want to talk to you, and I wanted to come unannounced so you couldn't cancel the visit like you always do," he remarks. "Don't talk to me like that, Brett, you know better," scolds his Mother. "No Mother, you are the one who shouldn't be talking to me like that," grins Brett. His Mother walks into the living room and sits down. "Well after all this ridiculous chatter, what do you need to talk to me about today?" "No Mother, I don't need, I want to talk to you." "Really Brett, I don't like your tone of voice and please don't forget I am your Mother". "Well, you are right Mother, but I don't think it's me who needs to remember, but you." Smiling devilishly, he continues. So how about we start this visit over and you tell me how happy you are to see me today." His Mother stares down at the floor for what seems like an eternity. Finally, she lifts her head and with a smile, although somewhat forced, says "Brett, how nice it is to see you. When did you get here, I hope you haven't been waiting long?" "No Mother, I just stopped over a few minutes ago and it is also great to see you as well," grins Brett. "Why don't we go in and sit down? I want to talk to you about something." He sits down across from his Mother.

After some small talk, he manages to formulate how he is going to tell her about Morgan, so without further delay, he says,

"Mother, I've met someone, and she is wonderful. I would like to bring her around to meet you sometime soon." "Well, what a surprise, I didn't expect you to tell me something like that. When did you meet this girl, and does she have a name?" "Yes Mother, she does. Her name is Morgan Kiernan and she's new in town. I met her at the Tavern." "The Tavern, oh she's one of those. I should have figured that would be where you would meet someone. "Are you kidding me right now, Mother, I do own the place and I work there. As for Morgan, I met her through Seth and Olivia. "Oh, how is Seth, he should be scolded for not coming around to see me." "I thought that would change your attitude when you found out she is a friend of Seth's, Mother. You always did have a soft spot for Seth. When can I bring her around to see you?" After a few seconds, she looks at Brett and says, "I'm sorry, honey, but I'm going to be leaving on vacation next week and I won't be back for a month or so. Do you think you could get here this week sometime otherwise it's going to have to wait?" "Annoyed Brett retorts, "When were you going to let me know you were leaving for a month?" "I'm telling you now, Brett, what are you getting irritated about?" "Oh, I don't know, Mother, maybe it's because I stopped here uninvited and therefore, if I hadn't stopped you may have never told me you were going on an extended vacation."

Brett gets up from the chair, walks over to the fireplace mantel and leans on it. Looking over at his Mother sitting so stiffly in her chair, he wonders how she could be his Mother. As quickly as the thought materialized it left because he knew deep down her indifference was a cover for invisible and deeper scars she bore. "Later this week will be fine, I will check with Morgan and see if she has an afternoon free to come over. I will let you know soon. How does that sound?" "Well Brett, I am looking forward to meeting your friend and I'm sure we will have a nice visit. How about we make it lunch, I haven't entertained for quite a while and it would be nice to get out my fancy dishes again." "Mother don't feel as though you have to do lunch, we can come over afterward," said Brett. "No, No, I want to do this, so no argument." "Ok, Mother, I'll let you know what day we can come over."

He looked down at his watch and stood up to leave. "It's been nice visiting with you, but I have to get back to the Tavern. We are expecting a big crowd tonight because the Philadelphia Eagles are playing." Giving his Mother a quick kiss on the cheek, he left through the front door. As he was walking to his car, he glanced back at the house and his Mother was standing at the window. He waved quickly. She smiled and turned away.

The Cemetery (Present)

Going to the cemetery to see her parent's grave had been weighing heavily on Misty ever since she had gone there to find the grave of Mrs. Ottinger. She had wanted to visit their grave then but knew this trip to the cemetery was for an immediate mission and she wanted to wait. Seeing her parents would be a special dedicated time for her. She would do it later, she told herself then.

This morning she woke thinking of them. *I miss them so*, she said to herself. *It is still hard to believe they are gone. I know it will be hard, but I am going to the cemetery today to see them.* Determined, she showered, dressed, got in her car and drove toward the cemetery. Driving there she wonders how she will be able to gather up the courage to stand at their grave. She is afraid she won't be able to remember where in the cemetery they are buried. Swallowing hard, a lump forming in her throat, her voice barely audible, she whispers, *these two people were the most important people in my life, two people who I love, admire and who supported me in whatever I did. They are my mother and father.* Barely able to focus on the road, tears wet her face. This is much harder than I thought it was going to be, she admitted as she sees the entrance to the cemetery. Pulling into the parking area it is so quiet she can almost hear her heartbeat. She sits there for a moment. Assembling herself she moves to get out of the car, then hesitates. "What is this going to accomplish?" she chides herself. Morgan, get out of the car! She demands of herself and begins her journey into the cemetery to find them. While she is walking, she wonders how many times Jonathan may have found himself staring down at their headstones, she doubted very often. Looking around, so many familiar names adorn the gravestones which just enhance the feeling of dread welling up inside of her.

Suddenly she recognizes a row of stones, and there seems to be a splash of color in front of what she thinks is their headstone. She quickens her pace. She is practically running when she finally stops and looks down at her parents' final resting place. Fresh flowers are propped up against the stone. Instinctively, she kneels, touches the stone which bears their names and begins to weep. At first it is a quiet, almost silent crying, then from somewhere down deep begins a sobbing made of loss and sorrow which echoes through every fiber of her body. Tears well and stream down her face in a flow of buried anguish as she gently slides her fingers across their names and wraps her arms around the stone.

She hears a snap of leaves behind her and with tears still streaming down her cheeks, she turns around and standing there is Jonathan, a bouquet of flowers clutched in his hand. Startled, and staring at her in confusion, she realizes to him she appears to be a stranger. "Jonathan, it's me, Misty," she declares. "No,'" he shouts. "You can't be. My sister is gone, No one has heard from her in 20 years." Walking slowly toward him she answers "I know Jonathan. It is me. I promise." Jonathan takes a step backward, his head shaking, his hands raised in disbelief. "Jonathan, I grew up on the farm with you, our Father and Mother were Carl and Janet Jenkins." Speaking rapidly, Misty continues... "Your birthday is Flag Day. You are nine years older than me. We used to ride four wheelers through the pasture. You took me on your motorcycle when you had to babysit me. Jonathan, please stop looking at me like that, you look as though you've seen a ghost," she cries. He grabs her arm and pulls her close to him. He stares at her face. Intuitively she gently touches his face and quietly says, "Jonathan it's really me, I've come back home." Jonathan looks at her incredulously and his mouth is trembling. He's holding onto her and chanting, "Oh my God, it can't be, oh my God, it can't be." She wraps her arms around her big brother and cradles him until he calms down.

They sit there in front of their parents' graves weeping with sorrow and then laughing at the absurdity of it all. They speak of the good memories, of their mother's music, running through fields of crops, their dad's dedication to the farm. Finally, they make their way out of the cemetery after deciding the two of them would go to the farm where it all began.

Jack and Charlie (Past)

Jack and Charlie arrived at the farm and headed out to the barn to see if they could find my Dad. It was milking time, so Jack was sure Jenkins was taking care of his animals. Walking into the barn, Charlie scanned his surroundings with a focused eye trying to figure out how he could deter this farmer from the path he was headed down. Charlie's actions were starting to alarm Jack, and he felt like he needed to warn Jenkins. His threatening diatribe was worrying him because if he didn't fulfill the company directive to shut this man down, he was going to lose his job. He needed to have this resolved before the Company sent in re-enforcements. Nothing good was going to come of the situation. Jack was sure Jenkins was onto something, and there was no way he would be able to fight the power of the electric company.

They found Jenkins in one of the pens helping a cow birth her calf. The calf was twisted, and the mother couldn't expel her, so Jenkins had a rope tied around the calf's hoof trying to pull her from the Mother. Charlie was so fascinated by the process for a minute, he forgot why he was there. Jenkins, with the cow's placenta wrapped around his arm, looked up and said "Jack you are just in time. I need some extra pulling to get this one out. It's being stubborn." Jack got behind Jenkins and wrapped his arms around his waist. "I'm going to count to three and on three we are going to pull as hard as we can," Jenkins instructed. "Don't listen to the sounds the Mother will make we just need to get the calf out and breathing. OK?" Jenkins was right, the noise the Mother made was a low moaning which seemed almost musical in its tone almost as if she was calling to the calf. Suddenly the calf was free, and Jenkins and Jack almost fell back but Charlie stopped them from falling. Righting himself, Jack couldn't stop looking at the calf and was in awe at the way Jenkins was stroking the calf and talking softly to the Mother. Finally finding his voice he said, "Carl, that was phenomenal, I have never in my entire life witnessed, let alone participated in something so beautiful. Thank you for this experience." Jenkins got cleaned up and came around to where Jack and Charlie were standing. "Carl, let me introduce you to my ex-Army buddy, Charlie. He served with me in Vietnam and was considered one of the best soldiers in my unit," said Jack. "What did you do in the war, Charlie?" asked Jenkins. "I was a sniper," said Charlie with a smile which never reached his eyes.

The Aftermath (Past)

The next day arrived and Misty was not feeling much better. Whitney had decided her time to share her little secret about she and Nick with her was yesterday. Misty lay on the bed wondering how she could have been so naïve to think her and Nick would be together forever. Seeing Whitney's smug face while she was devastating Misty's life played over and over in her mind. Nick's pathetic attempt for forgiveness had been enough to make her feel physically sick. At first, she felt sorry for herself and then she became angry she had missed all the signs. Whitney hanging around his locker, her secretiveness about the Prom date, Nick's disdain for Whitney, which thinking back on it was probably a diversion.

The sudden confession was as if they were lying in ambush anticipating Misty's arrival. Well, Misty was shocked, that's for sure. Her heart felt as though it was breaking in two. She couldn't believe just a few days ago, she had slept with Nick and they were talking about their future, when they wanted to get engaged, where they wanted to live, how many kids they wanted to have. The whole time he knew what he had done with Whitney. Then suddenly she thought, "Oh my God, the Prom! How am I going to face everyone at school?"

It was obvious Nick was the mysterious Prom date. Tears welled in her eyes again. "How could he do this to us? This is our senior prom!" she sobbed. "We were going to be so busy getting ready to leave for college, our Prom weekend was going to be so special. Tears soaked her pillow. She didn't hear Jonathan knock on the door. Not getting a response he had walked into the room. "What the hell are you crying about, Misty?" questioned Jonathan. "Don't tell me, let me guess, its deadbeat Nick, right? I don't know why you are wasting your time with him." "Leave me alone, Jonathan. I don't need your opinion right now," she sobbed. "Don't be ridiculous, stop your crying. I know what happened or at least I can figure it out. Nick showed up here yesterday practically begging me to let him in to see you. I told him to take a hike and you never wanted to see him again." She sat straight up in bed, her words choking in a scream, "Nick was here yesterday? Why didn't you let him in to see me, Jonathan? I needed to see him and hear what he had to say. Don't you get it, stay out of my life! You are always trying to control it, but you never want to be supportive. Now I'll never know what really happened." she yelled. "Are you kidding me right now? You are acting like this because of that guy? It was an exclamation as much as a question. "I know what happened, he cheated on you and then he had the nerve to come here and try to make it ok. Well, I wasn't having any part of his bullshit," said Jonathan. "You don't know how bad it is for me, Jonathan. He cheated on me with Whitney, my best friend," she yelled at Jonathan. "Do you know what this means, the love of my life slept with my best friend. Whitney has been my friend forever, we were always together. Jonathan, even you cared for her. Don't deny it. So, don't tell me I shouldn't be devastated because of this, her voice choking into tears again. I'm not going to my Senior Prom, but my best friend is going, with guess who, MY BOYFRIEND," she cried. She laid her head in her hands and her voice changed. "I don't know, Jonathan, how I am supposed to feel?" she lamented.

Jonathan moving closer to her, looking into her eyes, which were now filling once again with tears, said in a determined but gentle voice, "You need to grow up, Misty and realize Nick is not good enough for you." His tone now beginning to show resentment he continued, "He's got a great football future and don't think he wasn't getting pressure to end things with you. You were becoming a liability." "A liability? What are you talking about?" exclaimed Misty. "Misty, Coach has been trying to tell Nick for months to keep his distance from you. He felt Michigan would frown on his being seriously involved in a romantic relationship. Everyone is afraid it will affect his commitment to football." said Jonathan, in a calmer tone of voice. "That's not true, and how would you know?" Misty questioned him. "Misty, the concern for relationships clouding athlete's minds is well known in sports," Jonathan responded.

Whitney and Nick (Present)

It was almost the middle of the season for Nick's Midget football team. Today Nick is running crazy with the entire player's information. All of it has to be submitted to the league before the middle of the season. The team was undefeated, and he didn't need some political bureaucracy impacting the lives of these young teenage boys, who had worked their asses off to get as far as they had. There was always some league representative who wanted to manipulate the league standings. Many of the other team officials were jealous such a small town like Millersville could put together a championship team. In past years there had been a losing team year after year, but ironically when Nick started coaching the boys, things began to turn around. The players looked up to Nick as if he was a hero. Whitney couldn't get over how they worshipped him.

All those years ago, Nick was all she could think about. Music reminded her of him, commercials were about him, and everything that went on in her life had something to do with Nick. Now she couldn't stand the sight of him. Somewhere along the way she realized the hurt and humiliation she had caused Misty was the feeling she was experiencing. Nick was hardly ever home and when he was any communication with him rarely existed. He was distant, pre-occupied, and disinterested in any intimacy between them.

Somehow Misty was all she could think of these days and she couldn't understand why. Misty left after high school and went to college. She has never come back, and most people have forgotten her, but not Whitney. Misty haunted her dreams. She missed her over the years when she went shopping, to the beach, to the movies. She often found herself wanting to call her when anything good or bad happened, and sometimes for no reason at all. Unfortunately, she also found her way into Whitney's bedroom. Sometimes she felt like she could not stand to be in Nick's company one more minute. His arrogance, in the past, turned her on. His confidence in himself was one of the traits she wanted to be part of her life. However, what she discovered was underneath his impudence lived a very insecure man.

Shaking off her melancholy, she headed to the make her boys' football game. One thing good about Nick was he knew football. Having played at Michigan made him an idol in Millersville. Unfortunately for Whitney, her existence became very insignificant during football season

Abigail (Present)

I wanted to stop and see Seth and Olivia but there are a few cars in front of their house, and I don't want to interrupt their company. As I drive by, I see Brett standing outside which is enough to change my mind about not stopping. Getting out of the car, I take a moment to look at Brett. He is busy talking with someone I don't recognize. His look is so intent I wonder if something is wrong. I haven't known him long, but I do know him well enough to recognize the look on his face as alarming. I park the car and moving slowly, I wander up to where he is standing, trying not to invade their conversation but lingering just behind Brett so he can feel my presence. Standing there I hear Brett's anguished voice explaining to the woman he is talking to Seth and Olivia's granddaughter has taken a turn for the worse. I move so I am in Brett's view "Morgan, I'm so happy to see you, where have you been?' Brett exclaims. "Oh here and there, but I've been so busy setting up my new home, you know, Brett, right over there," I laugh. The woman Brett is talking to looks toward the house Morgan is renting. "Oh, you are living over there?" asks the woman. "Yes, I just moved in a few days ago. The owners are neighbors of Seth and Olivia and suddenly found a reason they couldn't stay in their house for a while. It's a win-win situation," replies Brett. "Brett, are you going to introduce me to your new acquaintance?" I laugh again. "Oh my gosh, Morgan, I am so sorry, this is Marcia, she is a friend of my Mother. She is visiting with my Mother right now. She knows Seth and Olivia and wanted to stop by and see them. Things are a little rough for them right now. Most of the people here are friends who know of their struggle." "Really, well I may be a new friend, but may I know too what is going on so I can help Olivia. She has done so much for me since I came here." "I think its Olivia's place to tell you what is going on but let's go in and see them. I know they will be happy to see you and it should be their place to tell you what is going on," said Brett. "It was nice to meet you Marcia, hopefully we will see each other again," Morgan says, as they turn toward the house.

Walking into their house, Brett grabs my hand. He looks down at me and smiles. I return the squeeze so he will keep holding my hand. I immediately see Olivia sitting on the couch. Her eyes are puffy and red. I move quickly over to the couch and find a spot next to her. "Olivia, what is the matter? I had no idea you and Seth were struggling with something. Talk to me, I know I haven't been part of your life for long, but I'm here for you," I implore. Olivia turns toward me and reaches for me. She hugs me, saying "I am so glad you are here." When everyone leaves, I will tell you what is going on," her voice cracks as she speaks.

Most of the people visiting Seth and Olivia are starting to leave, but the one person who is hanging around, is Marcia, Brett's mother's friend. The thought briefly went through my mind, Charlie, Jack Callahan's friend had a wife whose name was Marcia. I wonder if they are one in the same. Sitting quietly next to Olivia, I study the room to see how many are still there.

Suddenly, the back door slams, and Nick comes walking through the kitchen. "Oh Olivia, I just heard and wanted to make sure I came right over." Bending down to hug Olivia, Nick murmurs, "Oh darling, I'm so sorry, I thought she was doing better. Whitney is with the boys, so she couldn't make it, but she asked me to let you know her thoughts are with you." Casting a sidelong glance at Morgan, Nick tries to smile.

Finally, the last few people have left, and Marcia is off in the corner talking to Brett. Looking first at Nick then glancing at Olivia, I say, "Please would someone enlighten me as to what is going on?" Olivia grabs my hand, "Morgan, I didn't want to burden you with this when you were so new in town and Seth and I had just gotten to know you. Believe me, we were going to tell you because you have become such a good friend." "Our granddaughter, Abigail, has leukemia, and the doctors have just updated her condition to critical," Olivia starts to cry, and tears begin streaming down her cheeks. "Oh my God, Olivia, I had no idea," I breathe. "Has she been sick for a while? "Yes and no, she was diagnosed about five years ago. Seth is talking with Nick but turns at the sound of his wife's voice. "You know, Olivia, I think you are right. "Nick, it was the fall of the year you started coaching football. I know it was because you couldn't come and help them move that weekend. "As I remember it was not long after they moved in the house, Abigail began to feel ill, maybe 3 or 4 months. She got really sick about a year later." Olivia continues, "Abigail has a rare blood disease and there have been numerous hospitalizations, however, over the past couple of years she has been doing better."

"Our daughter and her husband bought a house in Spring Lake. Seth and I were uneasy about it, but they assured us it was the right property to buy. Our trepidation about the property has proven true because Abigail started getting ill shortly after they moved there." Seth shook his head, "Olivia, you can't blame the house for Abigail's illness." Tearing up again Olivia responds vehemently. "Tell me why she has been so sick and not getting any better. They take her on these long vacations, and she rebounds. But after she comes home, she becomes ill again. What is wrong with the house which makes her sick all the time?"

"Olivia, where in Spring Lake did they buy?" I ask. "You wouldn't know where it is Morgan, but if you want, have Brett take you there one day. "Brett, come over here," Olivia requests. Brett poses in a gentlemanly bow, "at your service, my lady." "Oh Brett, you always make me smile even when things are not so great," sighs Olivia. "Will you tell Morgan where Cissy lives? She probably isn't going to recognize the road, but maybe when you get some free time you can take her out there. The geography of the area is perfect for photographing." Olivia smiles, "Actually, you know Morgan, and I think it was one of the areas Seth told you to visit for your photography. So, you could get some good photographs. Their address is 140 Old Tower Road."

Out of the corner of my eye, I see Nick looking over at me. I decide it is time for me to leave. Leaning over to Olivia, I give her a tight hug and whisper to her, "Please call me Olivia if you need anything, to talk or just a shoulder to lean on. It doesn't matter when, day or night." Taking my hand, Brett walks with me to the door. "Wait for me, I'll walk you over to your house." Moving back into the living room I hear Brett say, to Seth and Olivia, "Take it easy you two. Stop in the bar later, dinner will be on me. There is no reason for you to have to cook, Olivia." Seth shrugs his shoulders and says, "Thanks, Brett, we'll see, I don't know if either of us wants to be social right now." Not really knowing what to say, Brett smiles, gives Olivia a hug, and shakes Seth's hand. "It's ok, I understand. Do whatever feels right to you both."

I can feel Brett glancing at me as we walk over to my house. I wish I could know what he is thinking right now. My mind was going a mile a minute when Olivia was telling me where her daughter's family was living. I'm almost sure that road runs directly under the oldest towers in the county. The technology is ancient, those towers must be emanating stray current. "Hey where are you," smiles Brett. "You look like you are a million miles away." "Yes, I'm afraid I was, but I just can't stop thinking about their granddaughter. The anxiety of seeing your daughter and your granddaughter in so much distress must be heartbreaking, I just can't imagine it."

Standing on my stoop together, Brett gathers my face in his hands and looks at me. Wrapping my arms around his waist, I lean into him. Hugging her back, Brett continues, "I wish I could stay with you Morgan, but I need to get to the bar because tonight's going to be busy. It is Eagles night." He looks intently at her, and says, "Please call me if you need me." "Thank you, Brett. I am alright now. It is going to be a good night for your business and hopefully Seth and Olivia will be up to coming out for dinner. It was so nice of you to say dinner was on you," and I hug him.

Putting his arms around her, he leans down and touches his lips to hers. His arms wrap around her and closing her eyes she feels herself melting into the pleasure. Reluctantly she steps back and reminds him he needs to get to the Tavern. "Brett, it is past time you headed to the Tavern. It is the Eagles playoffs after all. I'll be right here looking forward to your call." He hesitated for a moment wanting to stay with her. "You are right Morgan. I will call you as soon as I can."

Driving back to the bar, Brett begins talking to himself, "*Why are you acting like some lovesick idiot?*" He asks himself. "*Because you are in love with her,*" his heart says. Shaking his head, he pulls into his parking spot just a little too fast and a couple of customers jump out of the way. "Whoa, Brett, slow down dude." They move on and go into the bar. Brett goes in through the back door and checks the kitchen making sure everything is in order. Walking through the swinging door to the bar area, he hears laughter and glasses clinking. A cacophony of hello's and "Hey, Brett," ring through the bar. "*This is why I chose this life*, he reminds himself. *There is nothing like the comradery of people hanging out enjoying each other' company, football and the familiarity of the bar. The tavern has been a mainstay in Millersville for many decades and I am glad I have been able to keep the Tavern thriving.*"

Morgan & Jonathan (Present)

Morgan had barely walked in her front door when she decided she needed to go see Jonathan, without delay. Her empathy for Seth and Olivia is overwhelming, and she says out loud, "Somehow there has got to be evidence in Dad's container which will prove what the electric company has been hiding about the towers in our county. Now again, it strikes close to home! I can't just stand by and not do anything this time. All of this and more validates Dad was right about the towers. This is scary to me because this means the towers are still killing people. How many other families are experiencing health problems and are being treated incorrectly? I must go to the farm and talk to Jonathan. He may know where the container is hidden. Maybe he knows of other families which are struggling."

Grabbing her car keys, she jumps in her car and heads over to the farm. As she passes Seth and Olivia's, she is so lost in her thoughts she doesn't notice Nick standing on their step looking after her as she drives down the road. The more time he was around her, he couldn't shake the feeling he knew her. It made it even worse time he saw her, he thought of Misty. The last time he saw Misty was at her Mom's funeral, and then he only caught a glimpse of her because she was being shielded by Jonathan like he wanted to make sure Nick didn't try to talk to her.

Over twenty years have passed, and Nick has never heard anything about her. At first, he tried to find a way to contact her, but she had made it practically impossible. Every time he saw any of their friends from high school he would ask if they had heard from her. No one ever had. After a while he started to look pathetic to them, plus he couldn't be open about it because of Whitney. She would have gone off the deep end if she knew he was even trying to find her. Eventually it just didn't become worth doing anymore.

Thinking back to that time, Nick could feel himself getting angry. Life had not been fair then, now Whitney hates him, and it seems like all he can think about is Misty. *"This all started when Morgan showed up. I really need to find a way to talk to her one on one, find out where she is from and how she wound up in Millersville. It is strange too every time I am around her, I feel some kind of intangible connection between us."*

Pulling into the farm, Morgan stops the car, gets out and looks around. Weeds are growing out in the yard and a couple of windows are broken in the milk house. Old buckets and empty feed bags lie by the empty calf stalls. Tractors are sitting quiet and hay wagons are sitting lopsided because of soft tires. Before she can take in any more of the devastated landscape, Jonathan comes out of the back door of the house. "Misty, I'm so glad you are here. There hasn't been a minute in the day I haven't replayed seeing you at the cemetery. Never in a million years did I think when I went there for my weekly visit, I would be seeing my sister," smiles Jonathan. Laughing I reach for him and we hug tightly. "I know, it keeps replaying in my mind as well." I look at Jonathan and say quietly. "What happened here? It appears as if you just threw your hands up and said the hell with it. I don't want to think that so please tell me I'm wrong," I say softly. "Nothing I can say will make a difference now or change what it looks like. I know how bad it is. I look at it every day and wonder what the hell happened, now though, things are changing. I've gotten a dumpster and have been cleaning out Dad's shop," Jonathan responds. "Really, did you find any kind of decorative container in his shop?" I asked eagerly. "A container? What are you talking about? He had all kinds of boxes out there. What would you want with a box, Misty?" "He told me years ago Jonathan, the information he collected about the electric company was put into the container his father had made. He knew we would remember it because he was constantly writing in those stupid notebooks. I didn't understand or care then, but now it means a lot more. I keep thinking about how important it was to him that I remember them. Dad was a healthy man Jonathan, and he is found dead in a corn field. Haven't you ever thought it was suspicious? I don't know what you think, Jonathan, but over the years it has haunted me." "The only container I ever saw Dad work with was the one which had his paperwork on the farm and the cows," Jonathan said thoughtfully. "You know Jonathan, the little notebooks he would keep in his shirt pocket which had all the breeding dates in them. Where is the container he kept them in now, Jonathan?" "Why Misty? What difference it is going to make if we find it? What has changed for you? I know you came back but why is it now after all these years?" "What's changed? I couldn't take it any longer, lately here was all I could think about I kept thinking about Mom's sickness and how her continued decline affected Dad. It was almost as if every time the illness took fragments of Mom it took pieces of him as well. I kept in touch with what was going on in Millersville through the internet. I read the articles about the investigations regarding the excessive illness and death in Millersville."

"During one of those updates, I saw the farm was for sale. I need to tell you Jonathan, it devastated me. It was then I realized it was time for me to stop being a coward, come back to see you and face the past. For years I kept saying to myself, let the past stay in the past. It was hard, Jonathan, not having talked to you for so many years, I didn't know what to think. You were selling the farm. I didn't know why." "Oh Misty, you have no idea. Health agencies have finally been investigating the serious health conditions and deaths over the years which have plagued the citizens of Millersville. I tried to ignore all the rumors floating around the area, but it's not been easy. They remind me of Mom's illness and Dad's work with the dowsing rods in his investigation of the diseases and deaths. I think this is part of the reason why I just stopped everything, plus, milk prices have not gone up in years. There is no way dairy farmers are able to withstand the price of milk spiraling down. If you aren't milking over 500 cows, there is no way a farmer can make a living. It wasn't worth staying in it anymore. I know it sounds so cowardly, but Misty all we ever heard was how crazy Dad was and then there were the electric company goons hanging around here."

Focusing on Jonathan and changing the subject. I smile at him. "You and I can do this, you know. We can find those notes and discover why the notes were so important to Dad. We can find out what happened to him."

"Jonathan, we have a new lease on life, and we are going to figure out what has happened to all the people who have been struggling with their health or have died," I exclaim. "Tell me who else you remember was having serious health problems during the time I wasn't here. I have always thought there had to be more to all Dad was doing but I've never heard you admit the electric company had goons." Jonathan half laughs, "Yeah that's what Mom used to call Jack and Charlie especially when they started to hang around, as if they thought we didn't know what they were up to." "I'm still not sure what they were doing but I left, so tell me, how long did they stay around here?" "Well, Jack stayed and settled here. He ended up having somewhat of a friendship with

Dad, but as you know, before she died Mom never could warm up to either he or his wife. Charlie was the one who made us wary. He would constantly ride by the farm. Dad would be working out in the shop or in the field and suddenly Charlie would be there," said Jonathan. "What would he say? Why would he be sneaking up on him? I have to tell you, Jonathan, the more I hear from you, something just isn't right," I sigh. "Don't worry about it now Misty, they are gone. Charlie hasn't been around here since Dad died. He left the area suddenly, right after the funeral. Jack I heard he left his wife."

Trying not to look concerned about what Jonathan just said, I try to steer him back to the earlier conversation about anyone being sick over the years. I take a chance and decide to tell him about Seth and Olivia's granddaughter. "Jonathan, did you know Cissy's daughter, Abigail is in the hospital right now in critical condition?" "No, I didn't, what happened? Last time I saw Seth and Olivia was at the bar and they seemed fine." "Apparently, she has been sick for a while, but they have been able to manage it. Now, she has taken a turn for the worse and the whole family is terribly worried. Before I came over here, I stopped to see them." I answer. "Misty, you know them pretty well, then? "When I first got back in town, I needed to get my bearings and I figured the best place to do that was to go to the Tavern. They were there and started to talk to me and we have become good friends. Of course, they don't know who I really am, and I don't want them to know yet, ok? To them, I'm Morgan, a photographer traveling around the county." I declare.

"Oh my, Misty it's so good to have you back here again. You have no idea how hard it has been for me over the past few years." Looking around, I just shake my head and say, "You don't have to explain this to me, Jonathan. No one is blaming you for what happened here. Now I'm home we are going to put this back at least to what it needs to be to get the most money from the bank. You are trying to sell, aren't you? It's been going downhill for several years." "It's time, Misty, I have to sell," explains Jonathan. Tears welling up in my eyes, I turn toward him. "I know, but this our family home, I say just beyond a whisper through the lump in my throat. What will you do after the farm is sold?" "I don't know, but it doesn't matter Misty, I will be fine. It's time for me to move on and find something else to do. Besides I'm not selling the house. The land is what they are interested in."

"Well before the property is sold, I've got to find the container Dad left here. I don't know if he hid it in the house or if it is sitting out in broad daylight." "Misty, what is the deal with this box? Do you think Dad put money away in it or are you looking for something else? Don't tell me you think there is something in there which has to do with his pre-occupation with effects of the stray currents from the electric towers. If you do, I don't want anything to do with looking for the damn thing. All that stuff died when

Dad died. None of it caused us any happiness and I really don't want to go there anymore," Jonathan said emphatically.

Exasperated with the conversation, Misty said, "Jonathan, I believe now, and have always suspected Dad was murdered. It has taken years of remembering those days on the farm. I don't believe Dad just dropped dead in a cornfield. I have come back to find the evidence of what I believe is the truth. So, you and I are going to find out exactly what happened to Dad the day he died. This is why I need to find his container. He told me he had hidden it in a safe place. He told me it was important we find it if anything ever happened to him. I left before he told me where it was hidden. Jonathan, it is somewhere on this farm and we have to find it," I declare.

"You know, Misty, all anyone has to do is look at you closely and anyone who knows you from the past will figure out who you are. If you are thinking no one knows you are snooping around, I think you are sorely mistaken", says Jonathan. "That's not true, I've stayed away from all the people from the past. The only person I've been remotely close to is Susie and Nick, and he is and has always been too wrapped up in himself to even notice a resemblance. Although, I will admit at times it's been a little too close for comfort. The last thing I need right now is to have him asking a bunch of questions." "Well, I think you are flirting with disaster, so if I were you, I would stay away from Nick," warns

Jonathan. "Chances are if he gets too close to you again, he will figure it out, and then you are going to have a whole other problem on your hands." Jonathan tentatively smiled at me.

Leaving Jonathan's, I feel better than I have since coming back home. The finding of the container our Dad left was now going to be a priority. Both of us committed ourselves to finding more evidence of the health issues occurring around the towers. I have been away, and Jonathan has been wrapped up in his own problems, so neither of us has paid much attention in these last years to deaths around the county. I need to find someone who has been living here all this time and would be willing to talk to me. The first person who comes to my mind is Susie Mitchell. Now I think about it, I am getting a little hungry, so I turn my car toward the diner.

Morgan and Whitney (Present)

Walking into the diner, who do I see sitting at the counter, but Whitney. Trying to avoid eye contact with her, I move quickly to an empty booth. Sitting down, I notice there aren't too many patrons here meaning Susie will hopefully have some free time to sit and talk with me. How am I going to get the information I need from Susie? I wonder. I overhear Whitney talking to the person sitting next to her. Apparently, Nick's team is having their championship game later. Her tone of voice when she was talking about Nick, leads me to believe things might be a little rocky with them. The disdain for Nick is obvious in her body language and her attitude about the game. Tilting my head down and looking at a menu, I try not to think too much about what I am hearing, because Nick and Whitney's problems is the last thing I want to be concerned about.

Whitney suddenly looks around the diner and sees me sitting there. Getting up, she meanders over to where I am sitting, stops and looks down at me. "Well, look who it is? It's Morgan, right?" queries Whitney. I look up at Whitney and I have a fleeting thought of just saying, "*Hey Whitney, how's the last 20 years been with the love of my life? Have you enjoyed it and, oh my, are you miserable now?*" Instead, I smile and say, "Hey Whitney, it's nice to see you again. Yeah, I just stopped here to get a bite to eat. I'm supposed to be going to Nick's championship game but I' not in any hurry to get there," she responds. "Oh, well please don't let me hold you up from getting there." "How long are you going to be in our town, Morgan," asks Whitney. "Rumor is you are just passing through, but you have been here for a few weeks. What is so interesting here in Millersville?" asks Whitney. "Driving around the county has given me a lot of material to photograph, so I have decided to stay for a while and see what other things I can find to photograph. "Really, well I don't know what you are up to, but I can guarantee it isn't photography, so take this as a warning. You are not welcome here in Millersville. I have a feeling you are trying to tip the equilibrium we have achieved here. If your intentions are what I think they are, I'm telling you now, you should leave and never look back." I didn't see that coming. Startled I am silent for a moment. Gathering my thoughts, I hear myself say, "Wherever did you get the notion I was here for some devious reason? I'm telling you now, you are way off base. If you want, you may see the pictures I've taken of your beautiful area," I say. "No, I'm not interested. However, I'm telling you again and this is coming from more than just me. You are not welcome here. Nick has already been wondering for weeks about what you are doing here. "You are making no sense Whitney. I will tell you again, I'm only passing through."

Suddenly, I want to tell her, scream at her, she ruined my life, and her betrayal of me is the catalyst to all which is happening now. Coming back to this town where everyone knows your name, has become the truth. I know my time of hiding is almost over. "Whitney, there is nothing I'm doing which will have any impact on whatever it is you are rambling on about. I am here to take some nice pictures for my documentary about country life in the Northeast," I said. "Whatever, Morgan, I know something else is going on and right now I really don't care. My relationship with Nick is appalling. I know deep in my heart my whole marriage is and always has been a sham. Do you want to know why? Misty Jenkins, that's why. However, if I didn't know better, I might think you have a spell cast over my husband, because he's starting to act just like he did twenty years ago," cried Whitney. "Whitney, I am sorry about your relationship with Nick, but I have no spell cast over him."

Getting up and leaving her and moving as quickly as possible, I wonder why I decided to come back here. Knowing this was accelerating to an end, I had to figure out what I was going to do. Just as I moved toward the door, Susie motioned to me to come and sit up at the counter. Watching Whitney out of the corner of my eye, I see her say a few things to some of the patrons and then leave through the door accentuating her departure with a loud slam.

"Please excuse her rudeness, Morgan. She has been like this for the last twenty years," Susie said as she came around the counter to sit down next to me. "Been like what?" I ask. "Miserable, sad, unhappy, drunk, and in love with a husband who has loved someone else for a very long time," said Susie.

Trying not to have this strain of conversation continue, I ask her about her day, the diner's history and what keeps the place going after so many years. Fortunately, those were exactly the right things to ask because Susie could not stop talking about the diner and the town.

After a few minutes of this, I turn to her and say, "I'm doing this photography piece on the area, and a lot of the places which have caught my interest are right here near Millersville. The problem is almost every time I snap a picture there is an electrical tower in the background. I never realized how many towers I took pictures of until I developed all the photos." "Tell me about it, those towers are disgraceful!" laments Susie. Stunned, I look at her and her face bares an expression of disgust and maybe just a little bit of fear. "What in the world do you mean Susie?" I asked. Quietly lowering her head so she could talk softly, she turns toward me and says, "People die around those towers, Morgan, no one wants to admit it but it's true." "What on earth do you mean, people die because of the towers?" I ask. "Not because of the actual towers, she continues "it's because of the electric which is falling from the sky. It makes people sick, and they don't get better. Some people don't want to stay in their homes because every time they are there, they feel sick," declares Susie. "If it is this bad, why don't they move," I ask, knowing exactly why. "You wouldn't know, Morgan, but the people in this area can't afford to up and leave. Most of them are living on their families' homestead, a place that has been in their family for years," she cries. "Now Seth and Olivia, you probably don't know them, but their granddaughter is terribly sick. Her family lives right near some of the oldest towers in the area and if you ask me their granddaughter would get better if they would move. Those towers are so old, and the electric company is still running power through them. Many say studies show most of the power escapes, causing illness in those who live nearby. Morgan, do you know what stray electrical current can do someone's health? It sneaks up quietly, reeks its havoc inside the body and then leaves and moves to the next person and no one can ever figure out why they become so sick. But I'm telling you it's been killing people for years." Sitting there listening to Susie, I feel sick knowing once more my Dad was right. It is somewhat of a relief hearing what she said because I knew all along it was bad. Now though there is no one to fight the battle. In the beginning when Dad began actively working to discover the issues, the electric company worried about his interest, but they appeared to be little more than a nuisance, or so it seemed at the time. Finding myself getting upset, I leave to go home and think about what Susie has said. This is what I need to prove Dad was right.

Driving home I remember the look in Brett's eyes when he left me at my house. I find my heart open to whatever might come. I know from the feeling which slides down my spine when I am nestled in his arms, the elation embraces me when I am with him, I am in with love him. The thought of him looking at me with disappointment because I have hidden my identity from him weighs heavy on me now. After much soul searching, I finally understand my history with Nick has been catastrophic both to Nick and to me. I reluctantly decide I need to tell Nick who I really am. Then, I may finally be free of the lingering effects of the memories of him.

Arriving home, exhausted from the events of the day, I decide to make myself a cup of tea and relax in comfort on my couch. I begin to think about the time when we realized something was seriously wrong with Mom. The memories were clear as I lay there. There were days when she wouldn't come out of her bedroom. I tried talking with my Dad about it, but he seemed to be preoccupied with what was going on with everyone else. Jonathan and I realized it was getting worse when she couldn't find her way home one day from town. Nick was trying to be supportive, but his attention was on his own dilemmas. Every day before heading off to school, I would make sure she was up and dressed for the day.

One morning when I was walking into their bedroom, I saw her sitting on the edge of the bed wringing her hands. Moving toward her, I said "Mom, are you ready to come downstairs?" As I got closer, I realized she didn't have her shirt buttoned. Laughing nervously, I said, "Going rogue today?" She looked at me with confusion in her eyes, "Misty, I don't know how to button it." Recovering from the shock of what she said, I laughed, "What are you all thumbs this morning? Let me help you." Taking control of the situation, I buttoned up her shirt, making sure her hair was brushed and walked with her downstairs. Once we were downstairs in the kitchen and the normal hustle and bustle was happening, she seemed to snap out of it and return to normal.

Looking out the door toward the barn, I saw a car pull in. Jack Callahan had arrived which meant Dad wasn't going to be in for a while. Seeing Jonathan walk across the yard with the milk buckets, I leaned out the door and yelled, "Hey Jonathan, can you come in soon. I have to leave for school and Mom needs some company." Telling Jonathan Mom needed some company was my way of letting him know she was having a rough day. A few minutes later, he made his way up to the house and I left to get to school. Each day there was something else she couldn't do or remember to do. My Dad was getting frustrated with her, his patience had never been very good and with her increasing confusion he had become even more frustrated.

Approaching the farm later that day after school, I saw Jonathan walking across the road with buckets of milk to feed the calves. Miraculously he was helping me with my chores so gratitude would be first when I talked to him. More than anything though, I needed to talk to him about Mom's illness because that's what it had become, an illness. Pulling into the driveway, I yelled over to Jonathan, "Hey, when you are finished feeding my calves, do you think you could spare me a minute before you go back to the barn." Making a face at me, Jonathan chuckled and said, "You've got that right, your calves, which you should be feeding, but you know it will cost you, right! Stopping beside him, I leaned out of the truck and said with a grin. "Somehow I think you were told to do this by Dad because I know how much you hate feeding calves." Smiling devilishly, Jonathan said, "Misty, what did you want to talk to me about, you need to get to it because Dad is waiting for me in the barn and you know how it will turn out if I'm not there when he is ready." I took a deep breath, "Jonathan, you know Mom is getting worse, don't you? She is forgetting more and more and now, it has affected things which come naturally, things she has done for most of her life." Jonathan looked at me like I had lost my mind, "Misty, what are you talking about, she's been a little forgetful, and once in a while we all are forgetful." Shaking my head, "No Jonathan, this is more than that. It's starting to really worry me. She is sleeping a lot and when she is awake, she is so distant, like she is somewhere else. So no, I don't think it's normal and when I think about it, I've realized the exact thing Dad is so worried about affecting other people, may have affected our Mother."

Getting out of the truck and moving toward him, I touched his arm, "Jonathan, please step back and look, things are not right, she is struggling and why? Tell me why? She can't remember basic things, Jonathan. She thinks you are milking at night when you milk during the day. She thinks Dad has hired all these crazy people to build their house, when their house is already built. Why are you ignoring this? She is sick and I believe it might have to do with the towers. They may be in the distance, but I believe they may have had some impact on our Mother's health. Every electrical current which isn't captured into the lines for power are still live. What do you think happens to those currents?"

"He started to walk away but then turned and shaking his head said, "Misty, I don't know what happens, but I surely don't think they can cause what you are claiming. You know, you are sounding just like Dad and this should be worrying you more than Mom forgetting a few things." By the time I could give him a piece of my mind, Dad was yelling from the shop, "What are you two doing, there's work to be done so get a move on." I fell asleep then.

Nick and Whitney (Present)

It seemed unusual for Nick to be home so soon after the game. Usually, he went to the Tavern and ended up closing the place. Whitney turned over feigning sleep when she felt the mattress settle under Nick's weight. Lying there quietly, listening to the rhythm of his breathing was making Whitney's heartbeat increase. This was just a repeat of every time Nick came home too late. His mantra now was the same. "You know, Whitney I realize you are awake, so if you have something to say it now. If not, turn over and go to sleep and we will talk about it in the morning. I am going to go to sleep," declare Nick. "Sometimes I don't know why I care and stay awake because it never makes me feel any better. Especially when you always tell me how 'Everyone was asking about you. They wanted to know where you were.' I am tired of your excuses when you stay out too late. I don't care if you are hanging out with all your buddies. The excuses you have made over the years, Nick, are now falling on deaf ears. Do you honestly think I buy that shit?" Nick sat up and looking directly at her. "You know Whitney, you're never wrong about anything are you? I want to discuss certain things about our life and you just brush it off as if there isn't any reason why I should be interested. I ask you how the boys are doing in school and you act like it's none of my business. I ask you how we are doing financially, because YOU are in control of everything, and I get the normal,

"Everything's just fine, you just worry about all the work you have to do and let me worry about our finances."

He was getting more and more exasperated and was standing now. "What the hell, are you so self-centered you can't see the wrong in all of this? Take a minute and look in the mirror, do you think who looks back at you is a good wife?" he ranted, his voice rising. Nick now began to pace, intermittently running his fingers from the front to the back of his hair. "You are so righteous, Nick, are you aware how judgmental you are about everything, I do and what I don't do?" Whitney shot back. "Do you realize how much you criticize, lecture and nag me? It is as if I can't do anything right in your eyes. Sometimes I wonder if I would be better off without you," Whitney moaned. She sat up and moved closer to the edge of the bed. Nick now pacing began to rant again. "You want to blame me for everything which has gone wrong in our life, the lack of sex we have, the time we spend together is not enough for you. Why is it we don't do anything together? Why don't we socialize?" Without pausing, he continued. "The list goes on and on of all the things which dissatisfy you, Whitney. So how in the world do you think I would want to have sex with you? Bitch during the day, sex at night, if this is what you want to call it, because that is what it is. Do you realize I don't want to spend time with you if all you do is bitch and complain? My patience is wearing thin, Whitney."

It was Whitney's turn now. "Every time I try to talk to you Nick, there is always some kind of issue. You know, this has been going on for most of our marriage. You have no problem criticizing me but when I point out something about you, you respond with defiance. What you can't see is the attitude you have with everybody makes it hard to be around you. I don't know, maybe I would be happier to be on my own. It might be what would help me thrive and become a human being again." cried Whitney, her head bowed. Memories rose then from somewhere deep, and tears fell from her eyes. "I can't repair all the damage I did before we got married," she whispered. "No Whitney, you can never repair it, and neither can I. It has always haunted our marriage. He sat down now beside her. In a gentler tone he continued. "You have so much drama, Whitney. Do you hear yourself? Half of the time you are drunk and stumbling through life." "Oh my god, are you kidding me?" Whitney exclaimed. "You have never really loved me. Your dreams are dotted with Misty. Some nights you say her name in your sleep. I think sometimes you even look at the boys and wonder what they would like if Misty was their Mother. Remember you were the one who consummated this union."

"Time and recollection have taken a toll on us, Nick, but Misty is gone, and she's been gone for over twenty years. Let her go! It is devastating us and if we are ever going to have a chance to salvage what love we have left, you need to leave her in the past." railed Whitney. "Whitney, it is true, I do think about her and now it's become more important to me to find out where she is. Go back to sleep, we will talk about this in the morning," he muttered as he grabbed a pillow and left the bedroom.

Brett (Present)

Olivia and Seth decide they really need to eat, so they are going to take up Brett's offer about going to the Tavern and getting a bite even though it is late. Walking into the bar, they scan for a seat. Looking to the other side of the bar they see two available, so they head over to sit down. Shortly after they order their beers, they see Brett come out of the kitchen's swinging door. Seeing the two of them sitting there in his bar and knowing what they were going through brought tears to Brett's eyes. They had wanted to come where they were the most comfortable and be among friends. "Look at this, my two most favorite people sitting at my illustrious bar," yells Brett. Sauntering over to them he says, "All kidding aside, it's does my heart good seeing the two of you come in here tonight after all you experienced today." "Thanks Brett. It means a lot to us. We were pacing around our house after everybody left and Olivia wanted to go out. So here we are. This place brings comfort to our scattered world, so this is where we want to be with one of our best friends," says Seth.

"Did you see Morgan before you left your house?" asks Brett. "Actually, we did see her, but it was her taillights heading down the road," Olivia answers. "I must confess Olivia, the feelings I am developing for her have sometimes overwhelmed me. I can't stop thinking about her. Every time I drive downtown, I'm looking for her walking down the sidewalk. I have never felt this way about someone, I honestly feel empty when she is not around," murmurs Brett. Olivia tilts her head to the side, puts her hand on Brett's and says, "Well if you don't know what it is, you are clueless about love. Those are the same feelings I have when Seth is not around. The love I feel for him makes me feel empty when he is not with me. What does this tell you, Brett? You are falling in love with her and you need to tell her before she decides to leave the area," directs Olivia.

Brett laid his hands over his face. Rubbing them back and forth like he is trying to wake up from some kind of dream, he inquires of Olivia, "what is wrong with me? I'm having trouble sleeping, eating and damn, sometimes I think I can't breathe when I'm around her. She exasperates me to a level of senseless I can't believe," explains Brett. "Maybe she's the one, Brett. We've never seen you like this before. Please don't waste any more time. Tell her how you feel. You might be surprised at the response you get from her, because we think she is as crazy about you," laughs Olivia. "What if she really is just passing through?" moans Brett. "Listen, Brett, I know when a woman is falling in love and no one is going to tell me Morgan is not, at the very least, falling in love with you. It's time you act on your impulses because this might be the one and you don't want to let this moment escape. In all the time I have spent with her, there has been very little time the conversation hasn't been steered toward you, Brett." "You should act on this Brett, and do it quick," remarks Seth. "We all know there is something mysterious about Morgan, but it's time to put that aside and encourage her to stay in the area and become a permanent fixture here.

The Tavern (Present)

Brett works during the morning hours, but wants to leave the Tavern before the lunch crowd comes in. Nothing is more important than the plan he has for the day. Morgan is going to go with him to see his Mother. It has been on his mind for a few days and it is time now to take the plunge and have his Mother meet her. Leaving the Tavern, he sees a lot of his customers pulling into the parking lot. College football is being broadcast today, and the big game is going to be between Michigan and Ohio State.

Stopping for a minute, he realizes this means Nick will probably be at the Tavern and possibly Seth and Olivia. It is time. No, it is more than that, everyone needs to know Morgan is more than just a passing figure moving through our town. He decides after the two of them visit with his Mother, he is going to take Morgan back to the Tavern. Smiling to himself, he heads home to change clothes. This visit requires a fresh shirt and a bottle of wine to break the ice with his Mother and Morgan.

On the other side of town, Morgan is trying to get home so she can regroup. Her emotions are now disorganized and disheveled, and she needs to get home to relax for a little while. After the lunch crowd gets settled in, Brett is coming to take her to his Mother's house. *What in the hell is he thinking?* She thinks as she shakes her head. Waving off the melancholy she feels after talking with Susie, she runs upstairs, throws on a dress, shakes out her reddish curls, puts on lip gloss and decides come hell or high water, she is going to be her natural self. *"It is time I become more transparent to the people I care about,"* she thinks.

Sitting down on the sofa for a minute, she leans back remembering all the days and nights she dreamed about what it would be like to come back home. Everyday has been so much more than she ever anticipated. Jonathan's joy in seeing her again has given her courage. No matter what happens with the farm, Jonathan has promised her together they will find out what their father had discovered and why his death had been such a mystery. Going to Brett's Mother's house is the first step in merging her old life with the new life she has created. In this moment, it will be a blending of the past and present here in Millersville. Visiting her today also seems like a first step in establishing a relationship with Brett. She has the feeling from Brett's attitude when speaking about his mother, their interaction with each other is always somewhat strained. This visit should prove to be very interesting to say the least, and I am ready she declares to herself as she rises from the sofa.

The Tavern was getting loud and raucous. It seemed like everyone was out today to watch college football. The high school game was last night, and the Millersville Wildcats won again. Certain so called football experts in town would say the success of the high school football team was attributable to Nick. His coaching of the younger players through the midget program had helped develop talented players who came up to play at the high school level. So many people still talk about his college career at Michigan. He had become a hometown hero and hero worship had gone to his head.

Most of the people at the bar were locals and every kind of greeting was heard over the loud TV and jukebox as Nick walked around the bar to sit with Seth and Olivia. "Hey Nick, we were wondering when you were going to work your way around to us," laughed Olivia. "Popular, aren't you?" said Seth. "Ok you guys, that's enough. Can't you let a guy enjoy all the accolades of a winning season," bragged Nick. "Sure, we can but you aren't the coach of the winning team, are you?" said Seth. "Maybe not officially, but they are using a lot the plays I designed for them. I know I'm not their coach but it's because of me they are winning," brags Nick, again. Laughing Olivia asks Seth, "Do you think this bar is big enough for all the accolades we are hearing right now." "Ok, ok, I know it sounds cocky, but they are running a lot of the plays I knew when playing at Michigan and they are killing it with their passing game. Passing like they are, while only in high school is unheard of, so yes, I am very proud of what I have contributed. May we change the subject now, please," Nick begged. "Don't be so sensitive, we are just joking with you. We know how much you have done for the football program here," announces Olivia. Looking thoughtfully around the bar, Nick leaned close to Olivia, "It's a good thing Whitney can't hear this. Whitney can't stand anyone talking to me about the football program. Football and Whitney do not get along at all," Seth laughs, "Is this some kind of newsflash because we already read it." Nick flashes Seth a look. "It's just been bad lately, she is over the top with her complaining. She's drinking more now and suddenly she has this obsession with your new neighbor." "Morgan? Why in the world would she be obsessed with her, she doesn't even know her," questions Olivia. Nick thought carefully, somehow, he needed to express his questions about this new woman in town, but he was not sure how to put his feelings into words.

Looking at his best friends, he decides it is time to share his uneasiness about Morgan. "How well have you gotten to know your new neighbor?" Nick asked off handedly. Wondering where this remark came from, Seth looked at Olivia, "Olivia, I think you should answer Nick. You have spent a lot more time with Morgan than I have." "Nick, I'm not sure what you want to know. Morgan and I have talked quite a bit since she moved in next to us, before we met at the tavern a couple of times but that's really it. Why?" Hesitating, Nick looked at his friends, knowing what he was about to say might make them think he had lost his mind. "There is something about her that is familiar. When I am around her, I feel something," he said lowering his voice. "You feel something, Nick, like what, she hasn't even been close to you, remarks Seth. "I know, but when she is in a room where I am or here at the bar, there is an unexplainable dynamic in the air. It's hard to describe but it's real. The night we were all at your house, it was stronger than ever. You could almost see the air around her change," argued Nick. "This is crazy, you need to go home and see Whitney, get a reality check," laughed Seth. "There is something about her that's for sure, but it's nothing like you are describing," said Olivia. "We are not entirely sure of her story about why she is here, but it is something we are going to talk to her about in the next few days. Listen to Seth Nick, go home and forget about it." "You both will see I'm right, but for now I'm going home like you suggest, he answered. Turning to leave his friends, he thinks "*This isn't finished yet!*"

Elizabeth (Present)

Leaving to drive over to pick up Morgan, Brett is wondering what the next few hours are going to bring. His Mother seemed cheerful when he called her to confirm the visit. She sounded like she was looking forward to meeting Morgan, and this was enough to make Brett begin to sweat. Pulling up in front of Morgan's house, he taps the horn.

While waiting for Morgan to come out, Brett glances over to Seth's and Olivia's home, hoping they are enjoying themselves at the bar, where he had left them talking with Nick. There is something about Nick which has never sat well with Brett. He knew he was a good friend to Seth, so he tolerated him. Brett believes Nick Darlington has a mean side which hovers just beneath his friendly persona. Seth and Olivia think the world of him, and he respects them greatly, but still Nick bothers him.

Shaking himself out of his contemplation, he notices Morgan standing on the step, stretching to pull a dead flower out of her hanging pot. Seeing her reach up, he could almost picture gathering her in his arms. Moving to get out of the car, Brett sees Nick's wife Whitney drive by slowly looking at Morgan.

"Wipe the frown off your handsome face," I laugh. "What in the world were you thinking about which caused that look anyway?" "Nothing to concern yourself with, it's just a passing annoyance," smiles Brett. "Hop in and we will get on our way." "I just hope you aren't taking me somewhere dangerous, but then I know you wouldn't do that, right Brett?" I retort with just a slight touch of sarcasm. "Don't worry, she might seem unfriendly at first, but once you've been in her company a few times you will see right through the mask she wears." Leaning closer to him and crossing my eyes, I say with a chuckle, "Thank you for the reassurance, Brett, makes me feel so much better."

Pulling up to his Mother's house, he wonders what the hell he is doing. Seeing his Mother is never an even keeled event, but now bringing Morgan into the situation might do nothing but irritate his Mother, he thinks to himself.

While Brett is contemplating to himself the pitfalls of bringing Morgan to see his Mother, Morgan watches the landscape race by, "*This just might be the person I've needed to talk to all along. She may know something about what happened all those years ago.*" Pulling up to the house, I see the home Brett grew up in. It is a Victorian style house, white with dark green shutters and a long spacious front porch with rocking chairs. The front porch overlooks a meticulously maintained elegant front yard with perfectly manicured shrubbery, and a live Oak tree stands stately just to the side. What an awesome place to grow up in, I exclaim. "I honestly think of the tavern as my home, not this place," Brett discloses as if he read my mind. My stepfather never made it welcoming to me. Now I think back, I somehow think she was never very happy here. In hindsight I thought it was about her job, not anything personal. Since she decided to be on her own, I have seen another side of her I hope will be welcoming.

I want you to meet her because I think you might find her interesting. She has lived here in Millersville for quite a while. You know, Morgan, she might be able to give you some good locations to shoot for your photography project," Brett smiles. "Really, it would be wonderful if she could, because it seems I have exhausted the places other people have told me about. Millersville is such an interesting area to photograph with its farmhouses and fields, elegantly designed homes scattered in the countryside and a diverse array of shops and stores in town. But you know I never expected to see so many high-tension towers in such a small area. They dot most of the landscape I photograph. Oh and of course, I cannot forget this terrific and busy welcoming tavern where everyone gathers, I wink. I need new material anyway." "I guess it's time we went in to visit, she's probably wondering what we are doing out here," laughs Brett. Suddenly, I feel nervous yet excited. This might be the chance I have been waiting for. Brett had said his Mother has lived in Millersville for a long time.

As we walk up to the front door, I get the feeling of someone watching us. Tilting my head back I look at the curtains. If I didn't know any better, I would swear I see the curtains fluttering and for a split second I feel someone is looking at the two of us. Brett knocks on the door. Somehow even that makes me uneasy. Having to knock on your parent's door, what did this say about Brett's relationship with his Mother?

Lost for a moment in my thoughts, I am startled when I hear his Mother say, "You must be Morgan, please come in." Moving automatically, I walk into the house. I hear Brett say, "Mother, it's so good to see you. Morgan and I are excited to be here. What is that I smell, are you cooking my favorite chili?" "Brett, dear, of course, I made your favorite, what else would you want or expect," his mother grins. Looking over at Morgan, he wonders what she is thinking. Trying to keep his tone light, "You're right Mother, what in the world was I thinking, your chili has been my favorite since I was a child." he chuckles.

Brett's mother escorts us into the formal dining room where she has the table set with her best china for our lunch. I look over at Brett and the expression on his face seems to be one of apprehension. Smiling confidently at him, I decide to ease his concern. "Tell me, what do you use to season your chili? It smells delicious. I genuinely ask his mother. "Funny you should say that, because my chili is known for being excellent. Honestly, I haven't had any reason to make it for a long time until today. Today, I felt in the mood and as I said before its Brett's favorite." Sitting down next to Brett, I grab his hand and squeeze it trying to let him know I am happy to be here.

The lunch is uneventful, and I decide it is time to introduce the subject of my photography of the area and take the opportunity to casually mention the abundance of electrical towers in my photographs. Casually I begin. "It is a little unusual for me not to know what I should call you. Brett hasn't told me your first or last name. We have not met until today and it would be nice if we got to know each other. I just can't go around calling you Brett's Mother, so I'll officially introduce myself. My name is Morgan Kiernan." Taken slightly back, but recovering quickly, Brett's Mother responds as her upbringing had trained her. She smiles and says, "Well, it is nice to meet you, Morgan Kiernan, my name is Elizabeth Callahan." I cannot believe my ears, Callahan! Brett's Mother's name is Callahan! Could it be the same family as Jack Callahan? *"No, no, this just can't be, what are the chances it is the same family"*.

Trying to keep my face from revealing a sudden demeanor of distress, I smile and say "Well it is so nice to meet you. I have had a wonderful time getting to know the area better and Brett has been gracious enough to show me around." "Yes, Brett has a wonderful personality and is always accommodating to everyone. Sometimes this is his downfall, isn't it, Brett?" smiles Elizabeth.

Wondering where his Mother is going with this, he looks at Morgan, shrugs his shoulders and laughs uncomfortably. "May I call you Elizabeth? I ask "Of course, we are all adults here and you appear to have a kinship with my son, so a first name basis is perfect." "Well, you can be proud of your son, Elizabeth. He has welcomed me to Millersville. Also, I have been fortunate to meet his best friends, Seth and Olivia." "My dear Seth isn't he a wonderful man, and Olivia is so sweet," smiles Elizabeth. Taking a glance at Brett, I see a fleeting look of something dark, but Elizabeth is taking my hand and asking if I want to see the house. Brett excuses himself and says he has to make a phone call.

While the two of us are walking around Brett's family home, I wonder what was behind the look I saw fleetingly pass over Brett's face. Moving along through the house with Elizabeth, I try to envision Brett growing up in this house which seems so sterile and cold. Nothing is out of place. Every room is immaculately decorated with art and antiques. Suddenly, I realize Elizabeth is asking me a question. "I'm sorry, I was admiring your beautiful decorating, and what did you say?" "I was just wondering how long you have been in the area?" she asks again. "Not long, but there is so much to see here in Millersville, I will probably be here for quite a while." Just then, I hear Brett's footsteps on the stairs, and he walks into the room. "Mother, are you interrogating Morgan?" Brett laughs. "Morgan, I should have warned you about her, she is over the top, isn't that right Mother?" remarks

Brett. "The way you say that doesn't sound very nice, Brett." "Well Mother, you are over the top, but I love you in spite of yourself," and smiling turns to hug her. She abruptly steps aside, which startles me and his smile never reaches his eyes.

Quietly watching this exchange between the two of them, I decide there is more to Brett and his relationship with his Mother than meets the eye but that, I think to myself, is for another day. Remembering the reasons I am in Millersville, I quickly change my train of thought. I want to find a way to get Elizabeth to describe her early days.

Following Elizabeth and Brett back to the dining room, I manage to contain the excitement I'm beginning to feel. Maybe just maybe I might find more evidence regarding the electric company, the illnesses and deaths of those living near the towers and if Jack Callahan was her husband, his extraordinary and particular interest in my father's work.

"Elizabeth, when did you and Brett's Father move here? It must have been many years ago with all of the beautiful local art you have collected." I remark. The atmosphere suddenly turns ice cold, and the look which passes between Elizabeth and her son speaks volumes. Brett's father never lived here, my second husband, Jack lived here with me," states Elizabeth. "Oh my, I'm sorry, I just assumed Brett's father...*my voice trailing off.*" Brett puts his hands on my shoulders and whispers "Don't be sorry, there was no love lost between us." "Was?" I say quietly. Brett's Mother looks like she wants to take Brett's head off and maybe mine as well. "Brett, do you really think we should be talking about this right now. Morgan's visit should not be tainted with our family drama. Let us move out to the solarium, so I can show Morgan and you this rare strain of lily I just purchased," announces Elizabeth.

She rose from her chair, presses her skirt down with her fingers and begins a stately walk toward the door of the solarium. "My Mother has a fetish for rare flowers, and there is no price tag which is too steep. Isn't that right Mother?" "Morgan, Brett is trying to get me to confess, but there is no need. I love flowers. They bring such brightness to every day whether it is warm and sunny, or bleak and cold. Flowers give a burst of color which just cannot be replicated," smiles Elizabeth. When we approach the rare lily, I realize why she wanted it. It is beautiful and from a glance at her I see she is entranced by its distinctive beauty. I feel her grab my hand and I realize she wanted to share her enchantment with someone, anyone.

As quickly as she grabbed it, I feel my hand fall from hers. She turns and asks, "What have you found so interesting to photograph here in Millersville, Morgan? I haven't found the area to be very photogenic during the time I've lived here." I hesitate to respond to give myself time to formulate my thoughts, because it might be the only chance, I have to express them. "Elizabeth,

I have taken so many beautiful pictures, if I do say so myself. However, I've found in several different areas in the County there are large and intruding electrical towers dotting the landscape." Watching Elizabeth closely for a reaction, I see a slight, almost imperceptible squeezing of her hands. It is subtle, but just enough for me to detect it. I push forward. It's typical to see a spattering of towers when driving along our highways. Believe me, I've seen a lot of different landscapes in my travels, and towers have been visible, however, these towers are distracting in my photos," I continue. Waiting for her to respond, I remember the photographs I have taken. I shiver remembering the strange feeling of an invasive kind of energy when I was close, and a barely perceptible hum coming from them.

Brett moving toward his Mom and sliding close put his arm around her. Elizabeth smiles at Brett, while turning toward me and says, "Morgan, it's funny you should say that my husband, Jack talked about the towers in the area too. As a matter of fact, he seemed fascinated with them." Trying to hide my interest, I encourage her to keep telling me. "Really, he was intrigued by them. What was it about them that made him so interested?" The few seconds that pass waiting for her to answer, seem like a lifetime to me. I find myself holding my breath. Would this be what I needed to link the pieces together?"

Getting up from her chair, she walks over to the window and looks out at her yard, her flower gardens bursting with color. "You know, I'm not sure what his obsession was, all I know is he spent a lot of time talking to a farmer in the area. He used to tell me stories of his visits there and how the farmer was always using dowsing rods. I never understood why he was so interested in this farmer and what it had to do with the towers, but for a long time most of his waking hours were involved somehow with this farmer and those towers".

Taking a deep breath, I walk to stand close to Elizabeth and look out the window with her. Brett moves to stand beside me, and I can feel him looking over my head at his Mother. "Did you ever know the farmer's name?" I blurt. Brett jolted, and Elizabeth had an astonished look on her face at the question. Looking over at Brett, I raise my eyebrows questioning. "Mother, Morgan is asking you the name of the farmer Jack spent so much time with," explained Brett awkwardly. Impatiently Elizabeth spoke, "I didn't pay much attention to what Jack was doing at that time. There was nothing I could say or do which would get him to discuss his visits there. After a while I just didn't ask anymore. Quietly, in almost a whisper Brett responded, "Then there came the time when you didn't care anymore, Mother." Brett's words cause Elizabeth to unexpectedly drop her guard. "I know, she admitted. What you say is true, Brett. There was nothing I could say or do which would get him to talk about what he was doing, except for one day, she said remembering. I was here working with my flowers, and he came in very flustered. He was bursting with energy and excited to tell me something. Even though I had stopped caring about what he was doing, he was so compelling that day. I could not help myself, I needed to hear what it was which had brought home the man I had once loved who had become so disengaged in our life, so excited. Sitting down he finally talked to me about the farmer he had been visiting." "Really, it must have been an exciting day for him and maybe for you too. Did he tell you what happened?" I ask. "He did. I was so intrigued by his recounting of the event. It was amazing!" Brett looked unabashedly at his Mother. "Mother, I don't remember Jack ever talking about his job let alone the people he was seeing." "You're right Brett, he kept his job very private, but this day was different. I'm not sure how to explain how he was that day. It was so unlike him, and the event which took place that day changed Jack," declares Elizabeth. Elizabeth continuing explains. "Jack had gone over to the farmer's place to talk to him. When he got there, the farmer was pulling a calf from the mother. Apparently the Mother was struggling to deliver, when Jack got there the Farmer had his arm inserted into the cow's womb trying to turn the calf. According to Jack, when it did not work, he attempted to put the rope around the calf's hoof to give some leverage to pull," said Elizabeth. Brett moved to put his arm around me, almost as if he knew this was uncomfortable for me, how could he though? "The farmer was having some difficulty, according to Jack it's not the easiest thing to do pulling a calf." Laughing out loud Brett looks at me but Elizabeth didn't miss a beat. "He asked Jack to grab him around the waist to give him more strength and together they pulled until the calf was birthed. It was such a life altering experience for Jack it took him some time to tell me what had happened." Wobbling just slightly I bow my head, "This is an incredible story. Who was the farmer? I'm not sure why you are so interested in all of this Morgan, but if you need it for your photography, the farm where he spent so much time is not too far from here." Looking at Brett, she says "It's the Jenkins' farm on Jenkins Lane. You know where it is, don't you?" "Yeah, I do. The owner stops into the bar every now and then. He's a good friend of Seth and Olivia, his name is Jonathan," says Brett.

Somehow, I am able to maintain my composure during much of the conversation, but I find myself needing to sit down. Brett noticing my demeanor has changed move quickly to my side. "Morgan, what's wrong"? Brett asks, concerned. "I think my blood sugar has taken a drop." With his arm around me, we move to the couch. Elizabeth brings a glass of water over to me. "Here you go Morgan, drink this, you'll start to feel better in a few minutes. Do you have low blood sugar often?" Wondering how to keep from blurting out some crazy epithet about how the farmer was my father and Seth's friend is my brother, instead I say, "Not often, but when I do it comes on suddenly." "Smiling, well my dear we will fix it quickly. Brett there is some orange juice in the refrigerator, will you go and get Morgan a glass, please?"

Without Brett in the room, Elizabeth's posture changed somewhat. "Morgan, why don't you tell me what your intentions are with my son?" "My intentions? I don't have any intentions. Brett and I are friends. He's been very kind to me since I've been here in town." Laughing, Elizabeth mocks me, "kind to you, well I know my son and kindness is not what is on his mind." He is infatuated. I can see it in his eyes when he looks at you." I hear Brett's footsteps coming down the hall. Looking at Elizabeth, I quietly say. "You have it all wrong."

After leaving Brett's Mother's home, I beg to go home feigning a headache. Brett is very understanding, and I think he realized I needed time to wind down after the visit with his Mother. What he didn't know is I needed to get back to my house to think, in a few days I am going to the bank with Jonathan to talk to Tom Fraser. This will be the first time I will be functioning in the role of myself. My old self! Doing this was going to be a risk. If I wasn't ready for everybody to know I was back, I might not want to go. But I promised Jonathan I would help him with the bank, and this was the only way. We need to present a unified front and the only way to do that is to go in there as a family.

Elizabeth, after her meeting and conversation with Morgan tired and cloaked in memories, sank into what had been Jack's recliner. It was his favorite place to relax with a glass of vodka over ice resting on the end table next to him. Now it was her place to be. She had adopted it after his leaving, but without the vodka. She reaches for and then wraps the handmade quilt from the couch around her, closes her eyes and let herself wander in the memories. Jack was not home much. He spent a lot of time away from the house. She often wondered if he had spent those days with the farmer. She knew over the many months he spent there he had become friends with the man. Sometimes she could see Jack struggling with the relationship he had developed with the Jenkins farmer, and it was troubling to her. There were days when his moods were terrible, and now looking back she realized it was always after seeing his new friend.

Suddenly there came the fateful day he became communicative with me, and she finally understood the stress he had been experiencing. He could barely keep it together trying to tell her what had happened. Finally calming down enough to talk, he told her Mr. Jenkins had been found dead and she could not find any words to console him. Everything changed that day and every day after. Bringing herself out of her reverie, Elizabeth decides it is time to start packing. Thinking about the past made leaving for the next couple of months more enticing.

Whitney (Present)

Running late again, Whitney hurried out to the car yelling back toward the house for Nick to make sure the boys get to school on time. Jumping in, she complains to herself, "*If those boys are late to school one more time, they will get detention, so I really hope Nick gets them there on time.*" Driving, she decides to go into town the back way. She had not taken that way in years. Finding herself suddenly in front of the Jenkins farm she feels a sudden pang pass through her. Pulling over to the side of the road, she tries to breathe deeply to dissipate the feeling. Taking a minute, she looks around and suddenly feels the urge to cry.

The fields all around her were overgrown, and empty of the animals that would normally be grazing there. Looking toward the farmhouse, she feels a stinging in her eyes. This house was where she had spent so much of her youth and teenage years with Misty. Striking her hand against her steering wheel, she berated herself for all the pain she had caused Misty. She knows the events of that year led to what had now become her reality.

Misty left the area to go to college in Arizona and Whitney had not seen or talked to her since then. Nick ended up getting his scholarship with Michigan. He had a phenomenal football career at Michigan and was destined to go to the NFL. It was not to be. His destiny was forever changed on the last game of the season. Running a play action QB rollout against Michigan's arch football rival Ohio, he rolled out to throw a long pass to one of his favorite receivers. Coming from his blind side was one of Ohio's, All Star linebackers. People later cringed when retelling the event. After he came home it took him a long time to recover from what had happened.

A few years later Nick decided it was time to make his years at Michigan worthwhile and share his knowledge with the youth of Millersville. He thought maybe he would be able to send another talented player to the NFL and he made it his mantra to have the youth of Millersville succeed.

Straightening up, she drove up the road past Misty's house. Slowing down so she can see if anyone is outside, she sees a woman walk out of the back door. Taking her foot off the accelerator so the car begins coasting, she looks again and there is Morgan, the woman who had become friends with Seth and Olivia. She brings the car to a complete stop. She continues to look at the house, and before she can look away, Jonathan comes out and hugs Morgan. Whitney can't believe what she is seeing, how does Jonathan knows Morgan and why in God's name is he hugging her? Speeding up so she won't be noticed, Whitney drives off.

She is distracted with the thoughts of Morgan with Jonathan, and she doesn't see the truck pulling out. Suddenly she hears a horn blowing and the unexpected noise snatches her from her stupor. She swerves quickly to miss the truck. Shaken, she pulls over to the side of the road and leans her head back against the seat headrest, her hands still shaking. Her heart is racing, and she is close to tears. "What in the world was that woman doing at Jonathan Jenkins place?" She just arrived in Millersville a short time ago. How in the world would she know Jonathan?" After a few minutes pass and her heart stops racing she says to herself, *"I'm going to find out more about this new visitor to Millersville."* and begins her drive toward town again.

Nick (Present)

The boys are arguing as Nick gets into the car, irritated he looks at them in the rearview mirror. "Will you two stop your bickering, please? Every time I turn around you two are arguing. For once can you just put a lid on it, PLEASE!" After that expletive, the boys get very quiet for the rest of the ride to school. Pulling into the school drop off zone, Nick suddenly feels bad about barking at the boys. They aren't responsible for his bad mood. Turning around to look at them he says, "Have a good day at school. I'm sorry for yelling at you both." Smiling at their Dad, the boys get out and wander over to their friends.

Moving along behind the other carpool vehicles, Nick begins thinking back to his conversation with Seth and Olivia about Morgan. He can't shake the feeling there is something familiar about her. The conversation that day had not gone to his liking. Seth and Olivia seemed to think he was not thinking clearly when it came to their new friend, Morgan. Well, if he had to admit it to himself, he probably isn't thinking clearly. Nick believes in life you make your own luck, forge your own path. But the one thing he has never been able to resolve is Misty. Every time he is in the company of this woman, Morgan, he thinks about Misty. For a long time, Nick would catch himself looking for Misty whenever he was in town or at the local stores. When it finally became pitiful is when he stopped. He ceased beating himself up and tried to work on his marriage to Whitney. For a while, Whitney and he really seemed to be happy, but recently things had gone awry. Nick would not be happy to find out Whitney was also thinking about Morgan, who she was and what she was really doing in Millersville.

Jonathan (Present)

Waking up early as usual, Jonathan makes his downstairs to get coffee. Standing at the back door he looks for the first time in awe at the morning sky. The colors are vibrant and captivating. Then he remembers, 'Red sky in the morning, sailor's warning'. Walking down toward the farmyard, he looks again at the sky's myriad of red color and remembers how Mother Nature's beauty can sometimes be deceiving. Birds are chirping, small rodents are scurrying to their hovels ready to hunker down for sleep and the sounds of traffic in the distant are competing with nature's sounds in the early hours of the morning.

Jonathan wanders inside the empty milking parlor where the milk tank is looming among the concrete and glass milking lines like a steel giant, empty and cold. Standing quietly for a minute, Jonathan almost hears the sounds of the milking equipment pulsating, the milk swirling through the rubber lines up to the glass pipeline making the trip to the steel monster to then reside and cool. Then reality sets in. The cows are gone, and the everyday activities of farming were over. Shaking off the doom and gloom of his memories, he walked back to the house.

Today was going to be a good day, because Misty was back in his life. Even if she was somewhat tentative with establishing a solid relationship, she has come back and that must stand for something. He needs to talk to her to see if she will go to the bank for the meeting, he was going to have with Tom Fraser the next day. Tom Fraser hadn't produced the phone numbers of all of the investors, so the meeting was bound to have the outcome Tom Fraser was anticipating. The bank's view was Jonathan was just waiting for someone to buy the property so all his worries would be over. Little did he know, or anyone else for that matter, Misty was here, and she was the Tasmanian devil when it came to getting her way especially when it came to her family. So now it is time to reassess the bank's offer and with Misty in his corner who knows what could happen.

Smiling to himself, he found he was looking forward to the day. Lightening his step, he went in to get a shower and get ready for the day ahead. He was going to do some cleanup and go through Dad's shop. Misty was looking for a box, and Dad's shop, which is full of all kinds of tools, wood, and stuff is where he might have hidden whatever she is looking for, he thought.

Tomorrow was the big day for the bank visit with Misty. *"Wait until Tom Fraser gets to hear from my little sister,"* Jonathan thought, a hint of a smirk finding its way across his face. *"I've always said she had an intimidating way about her even when she was young girl, but now she has a lot of experiences and not all good ones. I think I might enjoy the bank meeting for the first time,"* he considered with a slight shiver of anticipation. But for now, *"I need to go out and see what I can find in Dad's shop. Misty is so sure her Dad put something for her in a container of some sort, so I need to help her find it. The first thing I need to do though is clean up some of the debris which has accumulated in and around the shop."* His gate was now quick and determined. To make it easier to find this mysterious container, Jonathan put on his work gloves, grabbed a wheelbarrow, a broom and dustpan and strode a determined gate to the shop.

Walking into the musty, dark, cobwebbed interior began to bring back memories. Sunlight was barely shining through the windows, reflecting off the tools stacked all around and the glistening of the sheet metal he had propped up against the wall. The image brought nothing but regret. How could I have left Dad's shop so cluttered and in such disarray? He had so much knowledge. I turned a blind eye to all he knew and stood for. His mood switched again. "It is now time though to push ahead now and find what Misty is looking for. It should be in here! Dad spent so much time in this shop the box Misty is looking for could be here, but then again, knowing Dad, he may have put it in a less obvious place, and where would not be this shop. But no matter where it is, I am going to help Misty find it," he said out loud in a determined voice.

He began to move things around and rummage through some of the old drawers where he had stacked against the wall. Spending about an hour looking for something which resembled a container, he begins to wonder if Misty was right about his Dad hiding something. Maneuvering his way through the rest of the shop, he decides he will come back later and spend more time in his search. As he is walking to the door, out of the corner of his eye, he sees a bright light reflecting off of a blade hanging up across from the window. Realizing the light is the sun reflecting off of the blade, he moves back from the door and turns around. He spots an envelope hanging from a hook in the ceiling. Getting a ladder, he climbs up to pull the envelope down. On the front of the envelope in his Dad's handwriting is Misty's name. Wanting to open it but knowing her name is on it, he slides it into his pants' pocket. Walking, and then running, Jonathan hurries back to the house, jumps in the truck and heads to Misty's house.

Morgan (Present)

Meanwhile, Morgan decides it might be worthwhile to take a ride to scope out some of the old towers and see if she can locate Cissy's house. Making sure everything is turned off, coffee machine, lights and alarm she walks out the front door. Pausing for a moment she remembers conversations with Seth about the alarm. Alarms were definitely not a part of her normal environment, but Seth was adamant about putting in the alarms, so she gave in. While driving out toward Cissy home, she makes sure she views the landscape very objectively.

I realize my history, the impact my dad had on me and the circumstances surrounding his death may have colored my vision. Driving through the countryside I remember the area where we always hung out when we were teenagers. It had been called the "Towers". Parties with alcohol and drugs ran rampant during the 80's and "Towers" was the place to enjoy all of those vices.

My mind travels back to that place and time. I slow my speed and my hand grips the steering wheel a little tighter. We were all there and I knew in my heart even then the towers looming above us as we were partying could not be a good thing. I was young then, I remind myself, and involved with the happenings and possibilities which are important to a teenage girl. If only I had paid attention to my instinct regarding the towers and supported Dad in his attempt to expose the danger, they were to the health of Millersville residents, maybe I could have made a difference. Those towers did not pass the quality controls during that time. Now, there is no possible way the towers are functioning up to the standards of today. Stray currents have to be emanating from them and infiltrating the environment.

Driving down the dirt road leading back to the towers, a myriad of memories floods her mind, and she thinks of Edmond. He had been there too. My gut tells me it is a possibility his continued decline of health could be attributed to the time he spent beneath those towers during much of his youth. She wonders how many of them have suffered sickness or died during her years away from Millersville, how many could be having health issues?

I realize now, over time, the burden of Dad's solitary dedication to disclose the truth and discover mitigation, diminished him little by little by with the realization the life in our beautiful county was knowingly being harmed and our livelihoods impaired.

Morgan slows her car and pulls off to the side of the road. Tears are spilling from her eyes from the remembering. In the memories though, she finds a strange strength. "Now it's time for me to find out what stray current is under these towers, because I truly believe it is the culprit of Abigail's illness. I know my dad was right. Too many people in this county are suffering and it's time for Jonathan and me to correct it. Twenty years ago, my father stirred the pot and the electric company responded. I believe the outcome was catastrophic for each of our family, she says out loud."

I drive further down the dirt lane wondering what the attraction was coming here to the towers so many years ago. Slowly getting out I looked up through the massive structure, staring at the coils and old transformers which were resting on what I believe to be a monster of death. I can faintly hear the crackle of current struggling to move through the antiquated wires.

Standing there quietly, the memories of my youth come flooding back again. Remembering Edmond, I know my deception to him wasn't fair. Reminiscing about riding around town in his truck and the music playing is now replaying in my mind. Even when I got my farmer's license my friends and I would still ride out there with him. Scanning the area, I wonder what the electric company is doing about this string of towers. It is obvious the functional viability of the towers is minimal at best. Knowing the bureaucracy of the electric company, it isn't high priority to pursue the declining condition of the towers in the County. So, they stand looming over me obviously still putting out current. I learned from my father the deteriorating quality of towers causes the stray current to infiltrate the atmosphere. I believe it is affecting Abigail. They have been living too close to the towers and Abigail's sickness is being fed by the currents which are falling from the old towers above me. Disgusted and determined I get back into my car and drive back to Millersville. I begin contemplating whether I should go and see Seth and Olivia, knowing if I do it will be very hard to explain. Jonathan is expecting me I remember, and I don't want to let him down now, we are planning on figuring out the game plan for the bank and Tom Fraser. Seeing Seth and Olivia will just have to wait a little while.

Whitney and Nick (Present)

Finally getting back home, Whitney wanders into the living room and sinks down on the couch. Leaning her head back, she closes her eyes and tries to make sense of what she saw at Jonathan Jenkins's farm. *"Morgan hasn't been in the area long enough to have become that familiar with Jonathan. It doesn't make sense."* It had been a long time since she felt she needed to talk to Nick, but right now, she couldn't wait for him to get home. She gets up from the couch and starts to pace. *"Where the hell is he? Why is he not responding to my messages?"*

Weary of pacing and wondering where her husband is Whitney moves to their bedroom to lie down and think. Lying there she realizes most of their relationship has never been good but admits the intimacy they experienced together in this room eclipsed that part of their marriage. Now things have changed, and she recognizes it is time for her to be true to herself and own up to her mistakes. Recently Nick had become very distant. She knows there is something going on which she should be concerned about but as bad as it sounds, she feels like she just doesn't care anymore. It is time now to face her guilt and make right what happened twenty years ago. She realizes too her marriage to Nick was a mistake from the beginning. Coming to this realization is in some way a relief.

Seeing Misty's face as she walked away had haunted her during her deepest sleep. Trying to justify her actions to Misty had fallen on deaf ears. The lies she told her best friend had been reprehensible. It did not make it right, but she had been a teenager then. There were no excuses today. She is a woman now. She shakes her head, rolls her eyes and thinks to herself, "grown, mature, right Whitney!"

"*I can't lie anymore!*" It is an instruction more than just a thought. She realizes she needs to tell Nick how unhappy she has been. Revitalized, she tries to call Nick again. It is important for her to know when he is going to come home so she has time to gather her thoughts. Nick's strong suit is his ability to think on his feet and she doesn't want to fall victim to his tongue twisting dialogue.

Meanwhile, Nick makes it through the long carpool line to drop the boys off. He decides the next time it is his turn to drop them off he is going to have to leave earlier. The line is so long. He had no idea the number of parents who dropped off their children at school. Driving back toward town, he decides to stop by the bank and see Tom Fraser. Parking was minimal at best and he needed to go around to the back of the bank to find a parking place. Just as he is getting out of his car, he hears a familiar voice. Looking up he sees Morgan walking with Jonathan Jenkins toward the front of the bank, Morgan's hands are moving in description as she is talking to Jonathan. "Misty, you need to open up this envelope before we go into the bank. There could be something in there you need to see, and something might change how you handle this meeting," implores Jonathan. "Jonathan, let's get this meeting over with and then I will open up the envelope," she answers. "No matter what is in there we still have the bank to deal with, so let's do it."

Nick hesitates for a moment and then he decides it would be advisable to get into the bank quickly. Just as he walks up to the bank door, he senses someone coming up behind him. Peering over his shoulder he sees Morgan with Jonathan trailing closely behind. "Hello Jonathan, he says, with a raised eyebrow. Morgan, what brings the two of you here, together? "Well, well, isn't it the favorite son of Millersville, Nick Darlington," smirks Jonathan. Morgan hearing the disdain in her brother's voice puts her hand out to Nick. Startled with her gesture, Nick begins to fumble with his keys, but shakes Morgan's hand quickly. "It's nice to see you again, Nick," smiles Morgan. Having trouble finding his voice, he nods and smiles. Holding the door for them, Nick watches as Jonathan puts his hand under Morgan's elbow to guide her through the lobby of the bank. His eyes and his mind were not in-sync with what he was seeing. After two or three people bumped into him as he was standing there dumbfounded, he made his way into the bank.

Nick is trying not to be discovered paying too much attention to Morgan and Jonathan. It is almost impossible for him to comprehend the notion they are here together. However, this is exactly what it appears to be. Moving closer to where they are standing, he overhears Jonathan ask if Tom Fraser is in and if so, to please tell him Jonathan Jenkins is here to see him. He sees Morgan looking at him out of the corner of her eye and wanting her to know he saw her, he smiles devilishly. She immediately averts her eyes, and at that moment, Tom Fraser strides into the lobby. "Jonathan, it's great to see you finally. Come on into my office so we can talk." Misty grabs Jonathan's arm to stop him for a moment. Looking directly into his eyes, she smiles at her brother, "Remember stay strong, I'm going to be right beside you." As they moved to follow Fraser back to his office, Misty takes a backward glance into the lobby and finds Nick watching with them with a look of confusion and slight displeasure.

Tom opens his office door and stands aside to let Jonathan enter. He closes the door before Misty can follow. Misty opens the door and steps inside. Tom, visibly annoyed, instructs Misty. "I'm sorry but this is a private meeting. Pointing back toward the area where they had come from, he continued, "The lobby is back down the hall toward the front of the bank. I'm sure someone there will make you comfortable." Jonathan laughs, "Tom, she's with me. Let me introduce you to my sister, Misty." Standing there with the doorknob still in his hand, Tom struggled to find his voice.

With a look of utter amazement, he stared at Misty. "You can't be Misty Jenkins. She left Millersville twenty years ago." Not wanting to say much right then, Misty looks at Jonathan for support. "Well Tom, I was as surprised as you are now when I saw her, but this is my sister, Misty. She has come back to Millersville." Tom, trying to find his voice, could do nothing more than mutter, "Why now"? "Well, now that is funny Tom because I said the same thing why now? You know, it doesn't really matter to me why she's back because she is and here, we are," grins Jonathan. Glancing at Misty, Tom, attempts a smile back at Jonathan, and failing terribly, responds "Yes she is".

"So where does this put our negotiations, Jonathan?" Realizing this is her opening, Misty smiles, moves toward Tom and puts her hand out for him to shake. "Tom, it's very nice to meet you. I'm sure you have heard a lot about my leaving Millersville, since it seems to be the elephant in the room. However, I am here today to support Jonathan in the negotiations for our family farm," pronounces Misty. "Really, I hate to tell you, but you might be a little late to the party, because these negotiations are over. The deal is about to come to the table, declares Tom. Isn't that right, Jonathan?" "Well, Tom, things have changed. Misty is here now, and the negotiations are being reopened."

Nick is still in the bank lobby stunned. He just witnessed Morgan and Jonathan Jenkins walking with Tom Fraser to his office. Realizing he is standing stupidly watching a now empty hallway, he turns to leave the bank. Checking his phone, he sees Whitney has tried to call him several times. As much as he doesn't want to call her, he decides it would be smart to get home.

Whitney, in the meantime, is trying to decide whether to stay at home and wait or ride into town to see if she can find him in one of his many haunts. Weighing all the options, she decides the mature thing to do would be to wait. The decision was accompanied with a solid stomp of her boot abruptly followed by a lingering grimace. Patience was not one of her better traits, but she would wait.

Brett (Present)

The lunch crowd at the Tavern is light for a Friday, it is fine with Brett because he needs to get some paperwork done which has been neglected over the last few weeks. His mind has been preoccupied with the new woman in town, Morgan. He had overheard some of his patrons talking about how they saw her here and there. Today he decides he is going to work in his business and try not to think about Morgan. He hasn't spoken to her or seen her since the visit with his Mother. Thinking back on that day Brett, remembering how interested Morgan had seemed when his Mother was talking about Jack's farmer friend, closes his eyes. He envisions his Mother's image and recalls seeing the difficulty of remembering as she recited those last few months with Jack. His mind moves to Morgan's face at the moment his Mother called the farmer by name. She looked like she had seen a ghost.

Opening his eyes, he tries to get back to work, but he can't stop thinking about Morgan's reactions he noticed in that instance and in other situations. Deciding he isn't getting anything done, he gets up and goes out to the bar area. Scanning the patrons, his eyes light on Seth and Olivia. He works his way over to them, wondering if they have had any good news about their granddaughter. "Hey, you two, what are you up to today? No good I'm sure if I know the two of you," he laughs. "Hey Brett, what's going on today, it seems so quiet in here. Seth stood up to shake

Brett's hand while laughing, "Don't listen to her, she's being difficult today, aren't you Olivia." "How are you guys doing?" asks Brett. "You both look tired and I hope this doesn't mean what I think it might, how is Cissy doing?" "Actually, Brett, she is doing ok. Abigail is holding her own right now and if, in the next few days she keeps getting stronger, they will be bringing her home. After that, we're not sure what will happen. We are praying there will be some kind of miracle," Olivia answered quietly. "Well, this is good to hear. She's a little fighter and I know Cissy is giving her all kinds of Mommy love and that has to be helping her," smiles Brett. "Enough about us, what have you been doing? We haven't seen you for a few days. Have you spent any time with Morgan?" asks Olivia. Seth rolling his eyes, says, "Brett, you don't have to answer that question. It is none of her business or mine either for that matter." He pulls a chair closer and sits down with them, Brett shakes his head. "It's ok; I need to talk to you two anyway."

"A couple of days ago I took Morgan to meet Mother," explains Brett. "You took her to see your Mother, Brett? How did it go?" exclaims Seth. "Damn Seth don't act like it is the worst thing I could have done, and for your information it went fine. Mother was on her best behavior and Morgan, well she was fine," declared Brett. Hearing a hint of hesitation in Brett's voice makes Olivia wonder exactly what actually went on during the visit with Elizabeth. Even though there was a chance she might make Brett uncomfortable, she dove right in. "Brett, we know you too well and your last comment leaves the door wide open so details Brett, details." Brett made a split-second decision to confide in the Seth and Olivia. They were his best friends and know enough about his family dynamics to understand what he was about to tell them.

Scanning the bar for any issues which may have arisen, he caught the eye of his bartender, Jillian. Motioning her over, he leans over the bar and whispers in her ear. "I have some things I need to go over with these guys, so can you do your best to see we aren't disturbed." Smiling at Brett, Jillian nods her head and replies, "You got it boss!" Walking over to one of the tables which border the edge of the bar, he motions Seth and Olivia to follow him. After Seth and Olivia's drinks are refreshed and Brett gets water, they sit down.

Looking at his two best friends, Brett realizes he has wanted to tell them his thoughts for a few days now. A sense of relief comes over him which is so strong he hesitates for a minute before he speaks. "I know you two have been worried about me lately, even with all the concerns you have about Cissy and Abigail. Olivia, smiling endearingly at Brett, reaches over and takes his hand in hers. "Brett, no matter what we always have time for you." "I know, Olivia. It has always been that way." Seth was sitting back listening to the two of them. "Really Brett, is this some earth-shattering announcement, because if it isn't the two of you are making a big deal out of nothing. Just spill it, Brett! Do you love her or not?" Laughing, Brett high fives Seth and says, "I think you've got it!" With a smile big enough to light the bar, Olivia hugs Brett. "Finally! You are admitting you love her! Tell us all about it!" Shaking his head, Brett bows his head in admission. "You have no idea, I have had a ton of bricks fall on me and I have no idea what to do. Her life is a play, and I don't know if I have a permanent role. At times I feel so empowered and it's all because of Morgan. The visit we had with Mother was something I had dreaded but ironically, she and Morgan were able to relate to each other about Jack. The story Mother told Morgan was a story I believe my Mother has been keeping silent about for years. Why? I do not know. However, that day she was as animated I have ever seen her."

Staring at Brett while he was talking, Olivia thought about the past few weeks with Morgan. The images were coming together. Her interest in the town, the reaction she had when she found out about Abigail's sickness and where Cissy lived. Now Brett is telling them about the visit with his mother. Knowing Elizabeth, it amazed her she was "animated" when telling a story about Jack and Morgan's level of interest in the in the story baffled Olivia.

Nick (Present)

Traffic was crazy in town today and pedestrians were everywhere, using the crosswalks which were just installed this past year. One needed to pay attention when driving in town now because pedestrians have the right of way and at any given moment, they may walk out in front of you. This is what happens to Nick while he is distracted driving home. Slamming on his brakes in front of the post office to avoid a pedestrian, he realizes he needs to get his act together before facing Whitney at home.

An uneasy feeling comes over him. What am I going to be up against when I arrive home, he thinks? Whitney can be a worthy adversary when she is pushed and realizing his actions of late haven't been the best, she is going to be a rollercoaster of emotions. Nearing the entrance to his neighborhood, he pulls over to collect his thoughts. Memories of the past flood his mind, Misty smiling at him as he walked her to her locker, Misty laughing at all of his quirky comments, Misty's eyes when she wanted more than a kiss. Suddenly and unexpectedly his thoughts of Misty were interrupted, and flashbacks of Whitney replaced them. He saw Whitney walking out of the lake naked with the water glistening on her breasts, the way she would touch him and the explosion of feeling, her look of triumph when Misty was walking out of his life for good, so many memories of both of them.

Somehow finding the courage, maybe from the memories or maybe just from time, he heads on to his house. Parking alongside Whitney's car, he wonders what the next few minutes of his life are going to be like. Life with Whitney during the past few years has failed to endear either one of them to each other. Constant fighting and bickering make the boys upset and Cole, the oldest, is beginning to have trouble in school. No matter what the teachers say, Nick knows why Cole is acting out. It is time for the two of them to come to some kind of truce or take a break from each other. Nick believes deep down a break is in their future. He knows he needs to pay attention and keep his boys safe and happy throughout the next few weeks.

Whitney hears Nick's car pull in and she can feel her heart beating in her ears. She knows it will be important in the next few minutes for her to stand her ground. She knows Nick's smooth-talking attitude is going to infuriate her and she needs to remain calm. His actions over the past few weeks had confirmed what she already knew, and it was time he realized it as well. Misty Jenkins had risen again somehow and this time, Whitney was not going to be the only villain. Suddenly remembering the day when Misty walked out of both of their lives, she feels ill and ashamed. Shaking off her thoughts, she sits down at their kitchen table and waits for Nick.

The Bank (Present)

For several minutes Tom Fraser's office is as quiet as a tomb, Jonathan and Misty sit in chairs facing Tom. It is making her very uncomfortable Tom seems to be unable to stop staring at her. Jonathan puts his hand on Misty's leg and squeezes it. Taking this as a sign he wants her to initiate the conversation, she smiles at Tom and says, "Tom, I'm sure this is quite a shock for you. My appearance has to have put a wrench in your plan, but I'm here to assure you Jonathan and I are more than willing to work with the bank." Coming out of his stupor, Tom looks at Misty and chuckles. "You have no idea, Misty. I and most of Millersville thought you were never coming back. The bank even spent some time looking for you before we approached Jonathan about the property. I must say you did a very good job of being invisible because there was no sign of Misty Jenkins in any of our searches." Misty responds with a shy grin, "A girl can't tell all her secrets, can she? I didn't want to be found and when it is that important to you, you make it happen." Tom looks at her and smiles, but she recognizes he is angry. Wanting to see this through for Jonathan, she tempers her response. "Jonathan and I are united now. Our family farm means everything to us, and we have decided if it's possible, Jonathan just wants to farm small. With that being said, we would like to, with the help of our bank, come up with the best solution for the town and for us."

Hearing her, Tom feels a spark of enthusiasm. Maybe Misty's appearance is going to be a good thing. Sitting back in his chair, he smiles and remarks, "Now the landscape has changed and we can reevaluate the whole project. "What would you like to discuss?" Looking over at Jonathan, she realizes they might be successful in selling the property for the best possible price for all parties involved. "I understand the farm is being touted because of the land attached to it and they need to capitalize on the value of the land and the land's proximity to the highway. No one knows the land like Jonathan and me. Some of the area has beautiful vistas which would be enticing to anyone who wants to build there. I want the bank to work with us to subdivide the property into two acre lots and position the price to be attractive." Fraser's attitude has now done a 180 and her bullshit antennas are up and firing. She knows Jonathan wants to sell so badly and since her arrival is still fresh, she is afraid he will accept the first good offer Fraser submits. She pauses and sits forward in her chair

Focusing on Fraser, she ventures in, "Tell us Tom, the previous offers, were they attractive for the bank and for Jonathan?" Hesitating for a moment, Tom realizes he needs to be careful with his response. "Well, there were a few lucrative offers." He hesitates again, carefully weighing his response. "They weren't pursued because of what appeared to be a lack of cooperation from Jonathan at the time. Do you agree with that perception Jonathan?" To avoid giving Jonathan time to answer, she smiles uneasily, and quickly responds, "Well we know why that was happening don't we. So, can we put all this rhetoric aside and focus on getting this done? I'm here now and not going anywhere until this deal is successful."

Jonathan can't believe what he is hearing, but it is definitely putting a smile on his face. Tom Fraser finds himself re-evaluating his plan and Jonathan knows Misty will give him all the time he needs to get it right.

Realizing his whole plan is now in the trash, Tom changes his attitude and with a genuine smile looks across his desk at the two of them. "As a representative of the bank, Misty, I would like to welcome you home to Millersville and I will do my best to put together an offer which will be beneficial to both of us. We will put all the past issues aside and move forward. Give us a day or so. The bank and I will work toward getting new offers on the table." Feeling the energy coming from Jonathan takes all of Misty's control not to look at him. This is what he wanted to happen. "*It is going to be a trying time but, in the end, it will be the best thing for our family*, she thinks to herself. *It is now in the hands of the bank and all we can do now is wait.*" Relieved it has gone well, Misty stands and shakes Tom's hand. Jonathan follows and together they leave the bank.

Tom is glad the meeting it is over and it appears to have gone well. But believing the situation is still fragile he picks up the phone to begin the details of re-negotiation without delay.

Walking out to the street together, Misty and Jonathan stop, and Jonathan looks over at Misty. "We need to go somewhere so you can open that envelope, Misty. Maybe there is something in there which will give us information Dad wanted us to have. From what you have told me, it seems it was important to him you find it if anything happened to him." Looking up at my brother I realize how much he has changed since I left. The evidence of losing our Father before he could make amends is conspicuous. The gravity of his loss is apparent in his face and his appearance. Those imperceptible by one's eyes, is carried in silence by his spirit. The envelope I realize may contain the information which would absolve him from the guilt of his failure to pay more attention to my dad's work to prove the danger of the electric company's attempt to cover up the harmful impact of magnetic energy escaping from its electric lines. "Ok let's go to the park and get to an area where we can sit quietly and go over all of this together," I answer.

Driving out to the park, we watch the cars and trucks pass us, and the familiar yellow school bus stopping to pick up children, Jonathan grabs my arm and speaks softly, "Misty, do you really understand how much this town missed you? There were a few people who were negative and vocal when you first left. As time went on, they quieted down. For the people who knew, the ones who knew how Nick hurt you, it was a long time before they finally accepted you were gone and may not ever come back. Now you are back Misty, and you are so different, but some of those people who were verbal with their opinions when you left are still here and I don't want you to be hurt by the talk which might start." Smiling up at him, I laugh, "Jonathan, don't worry about me. I have changed a lot since that teenage girl whose heart was devastated. I'm a lot tougher and there isn't anything which will keep me from staying here. Being back here is something I wasn't sure I could do, but now I find I love it again and I am not leaving. Let's walk over to this picnic table and sit and find out what our Father has left for us to delve into." Sitting down Misty took the envelope and opened it. Pulling out note paper showing their Dad's handwriting she felt some trepidation. Was this going to change everything for them? Jonathan was tapping his fingers on the table incessantly. "Stop with the finger tapping you are driving me crazy. Let me concentrate on this and then I will read out loud to you." "Ok Misty, just read it so we can figure out what we need to do if anything? Quietly reading the paper, I take a couple of minutes to absorb what he wrote. Raising my eyes to his, I smile and say, "You know Jonathan, our Dad was something else. He had enough sense to write this to us so we would have a chance. He knew it would only work if I came back and we were a unified front."

Jonathan couldn't speak for a moment then, "So what does that say about me?" "Jonathan, it says nothing other than he was protecting us even after death. We need to find that box. It has everything we need to bring down the towers and hurt the Electric Company. But more than that prove Dad was murdered."

Whitney & Nick (Present)

Wondering what the outcome will be is unnerving Nick. It is time now to be the man Misty had always thought he was. Knowing Whitney is sitting at their kitchen table waiting for him, gives him a kind of weird comfort because of its sameness. This part of their life probably isn't going to have a fairytale ending. He knows it is time for this travesty of a marriage to change. The guilt and remorse during their years together had cultivated, for each of them, a burden which fostered feelings of resentment and regret between them. Now overwhelming for both of them, those feelings have to be resolved, their relationship mended and restored if their marriage was to survive.

Pushing the kitchen door open, he sees Whitney sitting there with her head in her hands. Feeling a moment of concern, he touches her shoulder and asks, "Whitney, are you ok?" Feeling Nick's hand on her shoulder makes her shudder and want to shrug her shoulders to remove his hand. An intense feeling of sadness comes over her and with those feelings reflecting in her eyes she looks up at Nick. "Hey." Nick stepped away from her. He wanted to be able to sit down and look at her face to face. "Whitney, we need to talk," he said quietly. "I know, Nick, it's been a long time coming and it's time we tell each other the truth." "Ok, and no matter what we decide we are going to make sure our boys are not on the injury report of our team, right?" requests Nick. "I want to tell you how I've been feeling over the last few weeks, Nick. It might not make a lot of sense to you but its how it is for me," Whitney said. "There is no way to describe the past few years of our life and how your obsessive commitment to your football program, work, your bank duties, the volunteer work you do, and all of your friendships you have cultivated without the inclusion of me, since high school have been for me. While you were doing all those things, I was trying very hard to be a good wife and Mother. But you know what, Nick, I failed terribly. I have felt like a bystander in your life, relegated to the sidelines as an observer instead of a participant. I have carried with me these years the guilt of the deceit I perpetrated to have you be with me," Whitney sobs.

Looking away, Nick tries to maintain his composure. He knew Whitney and he did not want things to escalate and the mudslinging to begin. "Nick, do you know for the last twenty years I have done a phenomenal job forgetting Misty and the day we drove her out of our lives? Recently though, there have been these nagging thoughts of her, wondering how she is, where she is, how what we did affected her life and happiness. All I could think about then was being with you no matter what the cost. The price of our action was my best friend. On purpose, I sacrificed her so I could be with you. It is a devastating truth that has stalked me through all these years of our marriage. You betrayed her too, Nick!" By this time Whitney is screaming and crying.

She jumps up knocking the chair over and moves toward Nick. "What were we thinking?" she shouts. "How could we have both been so wrong to her?" Now quietly sobbing, "Nick, she was our best friend, not just your girlfriend but your friend. She wasn't just my best friend, she was like my sister and what did I do? I destroyed her. We destroyed her Nick," she continues to rage, her eyes filling with disgust for both of them.

For a moment Nick is not sure what Whitney is going to do next. She stands there staring at him for a moment. Then she picks up the chair which had fallen on the floor and sits down across from him. Looking at Whitney with apprehension, he wonders how to tell her he thinks Misty is back in Millersville. Instead, he responds, "Whitney, I know, it's been something we have both been living with for a long time. I think we have never shared it with each other because we have been too ashamed, and fearful the disclosure of it would finally ruin our marriage. So much of the guilt and anger has done nothing but silently deplete us both. We need to admit to each other we both knew what we were doing twenty years ago at the lake. You had an agenda, and you were determined for it to come to fruition. I was selfish and gullible, Whitney. You were attractive, seductive, and desirable and at that moment I lusted you, but Misty was my heart. I loved her. You know, Whitney, if you hadn't walked out of the lake that day, we wouldn't be sitting here today. I would be married to Misty now and life as we know it would be entirely different."

Trying to quell her anger and keep her patience knowing Nick was being sincere, she paused for a moment before she spoke. "Yes, you are right, Nick. Those images haunt me now when I sit here alone. However, Nick, I remember the day Misty walked down the road away from us. It was her decision. She didn't have to leave, she could have faced us and maybe things would have been different," Whitney rationalized. "Is this what you really think, Whitney?" exclaims Nick. "Your memory deceives you because what we did to her is something back then would have been hard to face and forgive no matter how tough she was. We flaunted our relationship in front of her. Don't you remember what you said that day, the smirk on your face as you gloated, and me, just standing there, letting her go, with no attempt from me to keep her from leaving?"

"Over the years we have changed the story. We have changed the truth of it, so we weren't completely at fault. Except guess what, Whitney, we were and after all this time, it has caught up to us." Whitney lowered her head to the table and several minutes passed. Slowly looking up at Nick, she bowed her head in acknowledgment. Muttering under her breath, she said, "What the hell do you think has been wrong with me over the past few years, the drinking, the mood swings, the lack of affection and more than anything my suspicions of you? Do you think those things just happened to me or were you so caught up in your own life and so-called success it did not matter? I think the latter is the case."

"Also, Nick, there is something going on in this town and it has to do with this woman, Morgan. Ever since she arrived here things have been different." Trying to navigate the path Whitney's dialogue is taking, Nick decides to tell her what he has been thinking about the woman, Morgan. Cautiously Nick begins, "Whitney, I want you to realize what I am about to tell you may seem somewhat bizarre, but I assure you I've done a lot of thinking about it." The tone of Nick's voice made Whitney pay attention. Something was on his mind, and just the fact he wanted to share it with her was monumental. His inner most thoughts weren't something she had privy to over the last few years or ever, now that she thought about it. Sitting back in her chair and adopting a serene expression she looks at her husband of twenty years and tries to smile. "Whatever you need to say, Nick, it will be ok, she assures him. Just say what is on your mind. Nothing will shock me. Our past has taken care of that for both of us."

Brett, Seth and Olivia (Present)

Smiling at Brett, Olivia says, "Your Mother must have taken a liking to Morgan. I've never heard her described as animated and if this is truly the case, then she felt some kind of kinship with Morgan." Brett realizes his next few words are going to impact both Olivia and Seth. Forming his words carefully, he speaks softly to Olivia with Seth listening in. "It was almost eerie how Mother was talking to Morgan. No one could have interrupted their conversation and I was just a spectator during an event. Believe it or not my Mother was the main attraction. Morgan's attention to Mother's story was intense and now looking back on the day, that was weird in itself. We all know Mother's personality is not one which attracts too many people, only the ones who love her." Morgan's reaction was so surprising it took me several minutes to figure out the landscape I was navigating."

Turning to look at his best friend, Seth begins, "Many years ago, the farm Jack was visiting all the time was a very prosperous one. Jenkins was by far one of the best farmers in the county. Olivia, you remember, all the times we went out there to help Jonathan and Misty with the farm work. His Dad was always whitewashing the buildings, scraping the ground, and constantly working to make his farm the best. How many times were we recruited to help get the hay in and run wagons when they were chopping up the corn?" Olivia laughs, "Those are some of the best memories I have of the summers around here. Nothing was better than getting all hot and sweaty, right Seth?" she chuckled. Brett, trying not to sound impatient asks, "Who is Misty?" "Misty was there working right with us up until her senior summer." Olivia speaks so quietly, Brett has to lean down close to her so he can hear what she is saying. "Misty is Jonathan's younger sister." "Why have I not ever met her?" Brett asks Olivia. "She suddenly left Millersville right after graduation and we have not seen her or heard from her since." Seth continued, "Her father was devastated. We never found out where she went but we have a pretty good idea why she left. We've never talked about it to Jonathan, and as you know, he really hasn't been around until lately."

Now Brett's curiosity was getting the best of him. "Ok you two, why do you think she left or is this some kind of town secret?" Seth looks so serious, Brett wonders if he is exactly right, it is a secret. "No, it isn't a secret, but it is something that is not talked about. Sometimes I wonder if anyone even thinks about her anymore. Jonathan gave up the hope long ago she would come back some day." "I don't know why I never heard Jack say anything about her," Brett remarks. "Not that I listened much to Jack during those years, but still Mother would have said something. On second thought, no I don't think she would have cared what was going on with Jack then. Those years were very difficult at home because of his obsession with the Jenkins." Anyway Seth, tell me, "Why did she leave?"

Olivia was getting visibly upset, "Seth please stop. This doesn't do anything but flash back to dreadful memories." Getting up and putting his arm around his wife, he continued with the story. "Brett, you know Nick Darlington, right?" Olivia noticed the lines in Brett's forehead get more pronounced proving he was getting a little irritated. "Yeah, I know him, can't say I like him much. He comes in here quite a bit. He seems full of himself if you ask me." "Somehow it doesn't surprise me," laughs Seth. Brett continues, "A few of the patrons who seem to migrate here are not what I envision for this establishment. I am grateful though to have as many engaging and enjoyable patrons of the Tavern as I do."

Completely changing the subject, Olivia chimes in, "You need and want to settle down, so why not just take the plunge and tell Morgan exactly how you feel." "If you two are finished being philosophical I would like to continue with my conversation," quips Seth. "Ok, we will let you have the floor, please do continue, my dear," laughs Olivia. Seth grins and bows. "Thank you, Olivia, he quips in return and forges on. "Nick and Misty were high school sweethearts and were inseparable. Everyone expected them to marry someday. But as their senior year began, Nick was beginning to get scholarship offers from a lot of colleges. He was touted as being one of the best high school quarterbacks in the region. However, most of the college programs were small and the school he really wanted to come knocking was the University of Michigan. The stress of worrying about whether or not Michigan was going to offer anything to him and Misty dealing with her family drama began to wear heavily on both of them." Seth looks at Olivia and asks, "Liv, do you want to pick up here and tell the rest of it." Olivia's eyes tear up for a moment, then pulling herself together wishing she did not have to retell this part of the story, she begins talking softly. Brett finds himself leaning closer to Olivia because he can barely hear her voice.

"Misty's family reputation was under fire because of her dad's preoccupation with the electromagnetic fields and the stray current emanating from the electrical towers. He was so involved in his theory that the public's health was in danger, he began to neglect his farm and his family." Olivia paused, "A lot of people were questioning her dad's stability because they didn't understand what he was doing. We didn't know this until much later, but even Nick's high school football coach was indirectly putting pressure on Nick to rethink his relationship with Misty," Olivia crosses her arms as if to ward off the sad memories. Scanning the bar making sure everything was running smoothly, Brett turns back to Olivia and Seth. "Did you guys know then this was going on with the two of them?' Seth shook his head. "We were young and enjoying our lives in college. No one could have ever predicted what happened next." Standing up as if she couldn't sit any longer, Olivia continues. "Whitney was Misty's best friend.

They had been friends since childhood. As long as we can remember they were linked together like sisters. Wherever Misty was, Whitney was never far behind."

Coughing from stifling a swallow of his drink, Brett managed to say, "Whitney, Nick's wife? What the hell?" Seth and Olivia look at each other knowing the catastrophe bestowed it's humiliation on Misty and the Jenkins family. Touching Brett's arm to calm him, Olivia replied in detail, "We had no idea what was actually happening. Misty and Whitney were just like any other girls getting ready for the senior prom. They were all worrying about dates, of course not Misty, but Whitney was almost obsessed with wanting someone to ask her. She was trying to make it Misty's job to find her a date. Every day at lunch, conversations were all about the prom and who Misty or Nick was going to get to ask Whitney."

"The prom was just a few days away and they were all getting excited about the night and the after-prom weekend, most of us always felt were the best part of the whole event. This was the one weekend in a teenager's life parents were more lenient and also the weekend many virginities were lost. Just before the big event, Whitney suddenly became extremely confident about having a date, but she was keeping who it was under wraps. No one could have predicted what was going to unfold later."

The noise level in the tavern was getting higher and Brett needed to go help one of his bartenders with a difficult customer. "I'll be right back, please don't leave." Seth laughs, "Don't worry we'll be right here. We aren't going anywhere."

Nick and Whitney (Present)

Nick is failing trying to read Whitney's expression. She looks so calm sitting there he wonders whether he should tell her his suspicion. He decides it is only fair to confess to her what he suspects, since most of her life, his life and theirs have been linked to Misty. Hesitation stalking him, his determination finally triumphs. "Whitney, you know we never heard from Misty again after that summer. I tried to go and see her after that day when we destroyed her life, but Jonathan wouldn't let me anywhere near her. Even after we were first married, I tried to talk to him about Misty. I never told you, but after her dad's funeral I sat in my car and waited to see if I could see her. There was not even a glimpse of her and now remembering that day, I don't know how I could have missed her, unless she was there but looked different." Finding herself becoming alarmed, Whitney strikes back, "Why this is crazy Nick! She could have been there, but if she didn't want to see you, I am sure she just made herself scarce." Realizing this conversation was starting to upset Whitney, he decides he shouldn't drag it out. He should just tell her his suspicion. "Whitney, you know the woman Morgan you spoke about who just recently moved into town. She is renting a house next to Seth and Olivia's." "What does she have to do with any of the conversations we are having about Misty?" complained Whitney. Nick lowered his head and quietly said, "Whitney, I believe Morgan is Misty?" Standing up with an abruptness knocking her chair over again, she stared at Nick in disbelief. "Have you lost your mind? Why in the world would you think Morgan is Misty? Nick knew this was going to seem like some kind of pathetic attempt to assuage his guilt about everything that had happened so many years ago, but he was almost sure there was something about Morgan which made him think he was looking at Misty. "Tell me Nick you really don't think she is Misty. What has she done or said which gives you even the slightest inkling they are one in the same? Because if you can't tell me something, concrete, I'm going to wonder what in the hell is going on inside that head of yours."

Trying to convince Whitney is going to be more difficult than he thought, because he can't put his finger on exactly what it is makes him so sure Morgan and Misty are one in the same. "*I need proof, solid proof,*" he thinks to himself. "*I am going to find a way to show her Morgan is Misty, and then come back to Whitney with evidence.*" "Whitney, I know this is more than you want to deal with right now, but I'm not going crazy. Let's just forget I even brought it up. Let's figure out what the next chapter in our lives is going to be. I don't want you worrying about something which might not even be true."

Calmly, Whitney looked at her husband and with as little emotion as possible, she said, "After a lot of soul searching during the past several days Nick, I think we need to take a break. We have been drifting apart for years now. I think this will be the best for all of us. The boys don't need to see their parents this way. We will be better parents separate than we are now together. Too much hurt for both of us has accumulated over the years. It has never been addressed by either of us, much less together as husband and wife. We mourned separately in silence the death of our first child, and we still manage her loss alone. Since then, it feels like we have partitioned most of our life together. She was why we got married to begin with and I have struggled with the thought lately if I had never gotten pregnant, you would be with Misty today." Moving toward Whitney, Nick reaches for her and for one-minute Whitney let's go and wraps her arms around the love of her life. Finally, she has admitted to herself, what she has always known but never acknowledged she has never been the love of "his" life.

Nick and Whitney sat quietly reflecting on the past few hours and trying to grasp the implications which lingered in the air. Whitney tried to gather her thoughts before she speaks again to Nick. Knowing her husband like she does, she knows it is going to be hard for him to let go of his perceived vision of his life. Things need to change no matter what this will be a good thing for the two of them. It was time now for the guilt of the last twenty years to be lifted and their lives free of old regrets, and Nick had to release Misty and leave her in the past. She leans across to him, takes his hand and says softly, "Nick if you want to leave, don't feel obligated to stay here with me. Truly, I am fine. It's time for you to find the truth about what has been eating at you for the last few months. Go and see whether your suspicions are right and if they are be sure to come back and share them with me because we both need to be able to reconcile Misty." Nick rose from his seat and coming over to Whitney, he bends down and kisses the top of her head. "Thank you, Whitney," he whispers. Her composure is on verge of cracking, but she looks up at Nick and smiles. As soon as she hears the car start, she lays her head down on her arms and weeps. She cries for her boys, for herself, and she cries for Misty and the time they have lost together in their life.

After what seems like hours, she leans back exhausted and drained. Deep down she knows this is going to be the best for her and the boys. Nick had always been a great father, and nothing will keep him from continuing to be the best Dad he can be to the two of them. As for the rest of it, he was so sure of his suspicions that she knew he would pursue them until he found Misty. She truly believed his desire and need to find Misty was as much for himself as it was for her.

Brett, Seth and Olivia (Present)

Meanwhile at the bar, Brett ends up throwing out the disorderly patron and generously gives everyone in the bar a drink on the house. Finally working his way back to Seth and Olivia, he stops just long enough to quickly recognize some of his regulars. He can't stop wondering what the ending is going to be to the story Seth and Olivia are telling him. He has a funny feeling in his gut he hasn't felt since he was a kid. In those days, every time Jack would have too many cocktails at night, he always worried about his Mother. Jack was not a very nice person to begin with, but after his vodka every day, he became contemptible.

Finally getting back to his friends, Brett sits down and looks over at Seth and says, "Continue please." Seth begins to proceed with the rest of the story, when Brett delays him by asking, "What dilemma was Misty facing with college? Olivia smiles and Seth continues the story. "She really wanted to go to Michigan with Nick, and probably could have had an academic scholarship. But the amount of the scholarship was not enough to completely cover the expenses. She decided to go to the University of Arizona who offered her a full scholarship, however, she hadn't told Nick yet. Unfortunately, Whitney decided it was her time to be in the spotlight." Feeling uneasy about what Seth was going to say next, Brett shook his head and spoke. "Whitney is still vying for the spotlight, except now the light doesn't shine so favorably on her.

"Olivia quietly said, "Oh Brett, you have no idea! Whitney ended up going to the Prom with Nick." Brett looks dumbfounded, "What! Why would Whitney be Nick's date when Misty was his girlfriend." "Well regrettably that is the end of the story. We are not exactly sure what happened but there was some kind of confrontation between Nick, Misty and Whitney right before the Prom," exclaims Olivia.

Brett looks at them like they had both lost their minds. "This couple had been sweethearts all through high school and when it came to the biggest event in high school, they decided not to go to the Prom together. It must have been one hell of a confrontation! Do you really think they had any kind of chance to stay together after that event?" insists Brett. Hearing the indignation in Brett's voice had Seth and Olivia remembering the surprise and sadness they felt during a time which should have been nostalgic but exciting.

"Wow, that's quite a story," Brett exclaims. "I would love to hear more, but I really need to pay attention to the patrons now." Hugging Olivia and shaking Seth's hand, he begins to work his way around his bar, all the while contemplating the story Seth and Olivia had told him.

Finally getting to his office, he shuts the door, sinks into the chair at his desk to relax and closes his eyes. The story of Misty, Seth and Olivia recounted begins to intrigue him. He is curious as well about the demeanor of Morgan when his mother portrayed Jack's involvement with Jenkins and his farm.

Walking back out to the bar, he finds his head bartender. "Hey, can you close up for me tonight I'm going to get out of here?" "Sure, Brett, I've got it. Go ahead and take the rest of the night off. I'll cash everything out and put it all in the safe for you to go over tomorrow morning." Brett puts his arm around her shoulders and with meaningful thanks takes his leave of the bar.

Brett decides to take a drive around Millersville to ponder the story Olivia and Seth told him about Jack, a farmer, Carl Jenkins, Nick, Whitney and a girl named Misty. Immersed in his thoughts, he drives to a small park just blocks from the Tavern, he decides to pull in and park to have less distraction from his consideration of the story. "Twenty years ago, are they kidding me? What in the world could have happened to make this woman leave home and not come back?"

Thinking about his own family, stopped him for a minute. Jack was nothing like a father, but he knew it was as much his fault as Jack's. In his own way, he tried. He had to admit to himself many times he just didn't respond to Jack's efforts. When his mother had married Jack Callahan, Brett was 13 years old and believed he could take care of his Mother. There was no need for another man to come into their life. Jack meant well but Brett could never fully accept him. He always made Jack feel as if he was intruding and now looking back, Brett realizes he had been unfair to Jack. Shaking off the memories, he decides he needs to find out more about the story and this girl Misty Jenkins and what happened between Jack and her family.

Morgan (Present)

The rest of the day was pretty uneventful, and Morgan needed to regroup. It seemed like ever since Jonathan had become part of her life again, it was like riding a rollercoaster of emotional ups and downs. Reading the letter Dad left for her she believes now her gut feeling is right.

"I am sure he didn't die from natural causes. Something or someone was responsible," she demanded aloud. Hopefully Jonathan will realize now Dad really was onto something. The electric company would have never been so interested in Dad's comings and goings if he wasn't close to exposing the release of stray current permeating the County. She can't stop repeating his last words, *"Misty, if you are reading this you have to know something bad has happened to me."*

The information in the letter confirms what she has believed all along Jack Callahan and his army buddy, Charlie Kemp were not salesmen, or friends of the farming community, but actually were representatives of the electric company. They showed up every other day asking questions, telling Carl Jenkins they needed to take samples of the corn and the milk, which gave them way too much access to the farm. Just the fact he wrote down his worry told so much. He was afraid something was going to happen. She could feel his panic through his words describing the stalking, the sabotage of the milk tank, and the rumors running throughout

Millersville. She could see now how it made Jonathan very uneasy. She wanted to scream at him, "Where were you when all of this was going on?" She understands too it is the past, and she has to forgive him and herself as well. Most of all, she can't stop thinking about Brett and Elizabeth. Doubtful of her intentions, Morgan wanted to spend more time with Elizabeth to figure out what her relationship really was with Jack. When talking about those times when Jack was involved with her dad at the farm, Elizabeth almost became wistful and that didn't correlate with the memories she had of Jack.

Tomorrow is a new day, and I am going to be sure to catch up with Brett early before he gets busy with the bar, she decides. Maybe I will be able to convince him to visit his Mother again before she leaves on Holiday. I know deep down there is more to Elizabeth Callahan than meets the eye.

Thinking about the visit with Elizabeth agitates her. Her coined responses and her perfect demeanor are a contradiction of everything she had gleaned from Brett about his Mother. Shaking off her agitation, she wanders outside onto the porch. It is such a nice day and the symphony of birds singing for their enjoyment and hers was very calming. Sitting down relishing the moment in her rocker, she suddenly hears Seth yell, "Olivia, can you get out here and help me, I am up here trying to hold this birdfeeder. Where do you want me to hang it?" Leaning over the porch railing, Morgan yells over "For Pete's sake, Seth what are you doing?" Seth's head spun around toward Morgan. Looking at Morgan, his memory jerked backed in time. He almost fell off the ladder. Misty's Mother said that all the time. Whenever one of them was getting into trouble, she would say "For Pete's sake, you kids, what are you doing?" Seth regaining his composure yells back, "Hey you, it looks like I'm hanging out here on my ladder, waiting for MY WIFE, to get out here and tell me where she wants this hummingbird feeder." Laughing, Morgan moves off the porch and walks over to Seth. "Well, it looks to me where you want to hang it would be the perfect place. I'm sure wherever you hang it, Olivia will like it too."

Suddenly the sliding glass door opens, and Olivia spirals out the door never noticing Morgan, "Honest to John, Seth what is all the yelling about?" Before she realizes her mistake, Morgan blurts out, "Hey Olivia, this is crazy, my Mother said that all the time." Really, that's amazing because I thought it was just something said around here." Trying to move away from the train of conversation, Morgan informs Olivia, what all the consternation was with Seth. "Olivia, Seth just can't hang this hummingbird feeder without your opinion. I told him it was fine where he was going to put it, but he's been up there yelling for you to come out." Olivia laughs and looks up at where Seth is trying to hang the birdfeeder. "Seth, honey, can you move it over to the other branch which has the pretty leaves on it. I think it will look better on that branch." Smothering a laugh, Morgan looks up at Seth and winks. "I see what you mean, Seth. Maybe I should take my leave and let you two decide." Looking down at her and smiling, Seth replies, "You are smart, Morgan, you best get moving while it's safe to leave. You stay much longer, and you will be commanded to get up on the ladder with me and help."

Waving to Olivia, she decides to go into town and walk around. "It's such a nice day, she says to herself and I am feeling better about the farm, Jonathan and even Brett. I have a good feeling now about what is going on in my life."

Nick (Present)

Driving down his street, Nick felt sad for every year he and Whitney spent deceiving each other, occupying the space in their home as two people who were married and parents but in the end nothing but familiar strangers. The requirements of their lives seem to envelope every waking moment. Somehow Whitney seems to have pulled herself from the precipice of bitterness and hopefully would now be moving toward less guilt of what happened with Misty, he hoped.

Moving slowly, because of construction, he had the chance to look around at the town which had given him so much happiness and brought him pain as well. There is such a nostalgic atmosphere within the streets of Millersville he thought. So many people who went to school here came back after college to settle here. The town is filled with the same faces as twenty years ago but just older and wiser, *or at least that's what we want to think*, he remarked to himself. Hearing a horn beep, he focuses on the traffic in front of him. He realizes he needs to stop at the bank before he pursues any notion of finding the proof, he promised Whitney. He pulls over. Getting out of the car he decides to walk a bit before he goes to the bank to see Tom Fraser. He dreads what Tom is going to tell him about the Jenkins project. Walking down Main Street he sees group of people studying the layout of the town. Millersville has several gift shops and a book shop,

Barneys, which was offering entertainment to the weekend visitor. The locals were moving through the construction impatiently, but vehicles were moving at a snail's pace.

Deciding he has a few minutes, Nick sits down on one of the many benches along Main Street. Watching the people and cars, Nick finds himself getting sleepy. Laying his head back for a few minutes, he thinks about the last week of his life and how much life changes when you least expect it. Whitney will be fine, he reassures himself. He feels pretty confident she is going to feel a lot better about today when she sleeps on it. Before he knows it almost a half an hour has passed. Now close to being late to his meeting at the bank, he hurries along Main Street. As he approaches the bank, he looks across the street and sees Morgan walking toward the intersection. Knowing his next move may change everything for him and a lot of other people, he yells, Misty! Nothing in his wildest imagination, prepared him for what happened next. All the times he dreamed of seeing her again never did he think it would be like this. Morgan stops and quickly turns around, looks and locks eyes with him. For what seemed like minutes, the noise surrounding them went quiet. Then it started again, and Morgan turned and hurried across the intersection. Nick starts to follow her and then realizes he is supposed to be in the bank seeing Tom Fraser. With just minutes to spare he walks into the lobby, his head spinning and his heart beating so loudly he is sure the bank employees can hear it.

Quickly he moves down the hallway toward Tom's office. Knocking on his office door a little too hard, causes Tom to yank the door open, "What the devil is going on? Jeez Nick, are you trying to break my door down?" Looking hard at Nick, he lowers his voice, and says "Damn, Nick, you look like you saw a ghost." Laughing shakily, Nick says quietly, "I think I just did!" You will never believe this when I tell you this. I just saw Misty Jenkins outside." Trying to keep his face as neutral as possible, Tom replies, "Who did you just see, Misty? You are working too much, Nick or not getting enough sleep because you can't possibly be talking about Misty Jenkins."

The confidence Misty and Jonathan had bestowed on him that he would keep her return as quiet as he could, required him to act as skeptical as possible. He needed to move Nick along with this because it wasn't going to help the bank, himself or the Jenkins' if Nick Darlington started trying to interject his opinion into the negotiations. Nick looks out the window as if trying to have her materialize again. Struggling with his thoughts, he turns and says, "Tom, I have been a lot of things in my life, but crazy I'm not. There is a woman who moved into town a few weeks ago. Her motions and her mannerisms, even her voice is are so much like Misty's. It has become even more apparent in the last few days. She has been overly interested in Seth and Olivia's granddaughter's health and asked a lot of questions. I understand she has been hanging around Brett Compton and even went out to see his Mother, Elizabeth Callahan. We both know the implications which could be there with her visiting Elizabeth. It's been haunting my every waking moment and today I saw her across the street and took a chance." Tom, wanting Nick to continue, said, "Good Lord, man what did you do?" Smiling with the attitude Nick always seems to have, he laughs and says, "I yelled her name and you'll never believe it, she turned around and just stood there. It was like time stood still, I couldn't do anything but stare at her."

Tom found himself feeling very uneasy. How was he going to respond to this without betraying Misty's confidence in him? Taking a deep breath, he expressed his concern. "Nick is you sure this woman was turning around to look at you. Couldn't she have been just looking out of curiosity when she heard someone yell?" Annoyed, Nick answers vehemently. "It wasn't like that, she reacted automatically because she heard her name. Tom, I'm telling you, Misty Jenkins is back in town, I'm sure of it." Watching Nick carefully, Tom motions for him to come with him back to the vault. "Nick, I really want you to think about the implications of what you are saying. We are on the verge of settling a proposal we have presented to Jonathan and if there is anything which could jeopardize the deal, it would be a huge loss to the bank. I need you to drop your suspicions now about whether or not Misty Jenkins is in town. This whole project has been subject to so many delays and problems, the fact it could be signed, sealed and delivered this week is just short of a miracle. There is no way I or anyone else on the Board is going to accept your small shred of evidence Misty is back, so I suggest again, that you drop it."

Feeling claustrophobic in the vault, Nick moves just outside of the door but keeps secluded from the rest of the bank customers and personnel. "Tom, I have no intention of jeopardizing the Jenkins deal, on the contrary, if Misty is in town there is a reason why and I am determined to find out what it is. Tom knew better than to argue with Nick at this point, because his personality would prove true to what most people thought about him, which was he would be irritatingly persistent. Deciding it is time to move the meeting along, Tom puts his hand on Nick's shoulder and assures him there will have to be more proof Misty is back in Millersville before the bank would make any assumptions. Nick recognizes staying at the bank talking to Tom is a waste of his time and he decides to leave the bank and try to find more evidence that Misty is back.

Morgan and Nick (Present)

Hurrying along Main Street, Morgan is trying her best to keep herself together. What in the world had possessed Nick to yell out her real name, a name she had not used in more than twenty years, yet she just used it once again? She realizes Jonathan's mood has done a 180 since they reunited which has given him so much enthusiasm and ambition. She is in a quandary about what she should do. *I cannot believe I let my guard down and turned around when Nick yelled. What in the world was I thinking? She asks herself. What's done is done Morgan, just leave it alone. No matter what is going to happen now, it is time to find out what Elizabeth Callahan knows.* I decide though that first I need to get home, drive out to the farm, and warn Jonathan. Knowing Nick, he is not going to let this go and the first person he will want to question will be Jonathan.

She arrives home somewhat out of breath. Grabbing her car keys, she hurries out to her car. Just as she backs out of the garage, someone bangs on her window, jerking to a stop, she looks up and Nick is staring at her. Trying to stay in character, she rolls down her window and with a nervous laugh she asks, "Good grief, Nick, what in the world is matter with you, banging on my window? If you are looking for Seth and Olivia, I don't know where they went and I am late getting somewhere so if you would move, I will be on my way. Putting her car back in gear, she starts to back up. Suddenly Nick's arm reaches in past her and shifts her car back into Park. Pulling open the driver's side door, he extends his hand and pronounces, "I think it's time you and I have a talk, Misty or do you want me to call you Morgan? Which is it, the name you've been running around town calling yourself or your real name which is Misty- Misty Jenkins of Millersville, girlfriend of Nick Darlington, sister to Jonathan Jenkins, any of this ringing a bell with you or are you going to deny that is who you are?" Watching Nick carefully while he is stating his suspicions, I realize my heart is beating fast and I feel a stinging in my eyes. Instead of what I thought I would feel, which was anger, I feel sadness. Tears begin to blur my eyes. I duck my head quickly hoping Nick won't notice.

Getting out of the car, steeling myself from anymore displays of emotion, I observe a couple of the neighbors across the street are looking over at us. I take Nick's arms and say, "Why don't you come up and sit on my porch. I'll go in and get some iced tea and we can talk. Nick cannot believe his ears. He follows her up on her porch determined he is going to get her to admit this ridiculous facade.

Watching her go into the house he begins to doubt himself. She seemed calm and matter of fact with his diatribe which now thinking back made him seem desperate. Feeling uneasy, he recognizes he needs to get out of there before she comes back out.

Quickly moving toward the steps, he starts to hurry down them, and then he hears a voice he thought he would never hear again. Misty had dropped her adopted accent and softly says, "Nick, please come back up here, it's time we talk." Feeling like he is in a kind of time warp, he walks back up and sits down.

For several minutes they just sit there quietly lost in thought, silence cloaking both of them with memories. Brimming with emotion Nick does not know whether to be happy she is here or furious she had never come back. All the feelings of hurt, guilt, regret, and loss they felt and still harbored were struggling to be released. Taking a deep breath Morgan spoke. "Nick, I'm sure you have a lot of questions. You are right, I am Misty Jenkins and I have come back to Millersville to mend the past." Hearing her say what he had been thinking was almost more than he could bear.

Sitting there now knowing the truth, he couldn't think of anything to say. Looking over at her, he tries to see the girl he had spent most of his high school years with and the only one he had wanted to be with for the rest of his life. Seeing Nick staring at her was becoming uncomfortable. She knew the longer he said nothing, the more questions he was going to have. Her emotions were seesawing all over the place, yet she was successful in appearing very calm.

Figuring she had the most to explain, Morgan sits back in her chair and begins. "Nick, it was time for me to come back home.

There are things I need to clear up. I just wanted to come, do what was needed and leave. Instead, I have found many feelings of my life here rekindled in me. Anger, anxiety, loss, and fear play hopscotch with my memories of laughter, family, love, and friendships from my past. Inevitably the pain and rejection I felt that summer started to bubble back up to the surface. Over the past twenty years I have attempted to forget what happened that summer, and as we both know, most of those feelings have to do with you and Whitney." But Nick, the longer I am here the more I realize this is my home and I want to stay.

Hearing Misty speak rescued Nick from his journey in memories. "Why has it taken you so long to come home? And why did you feel you had to change the way you looked? Don't you know how much you have been missed here? There are so many things I want to say to you Misty, except I don't know where to begin." Wishing she didn't need to pursue it, but knowing she has to, she assembles strength and calm and commences. "Why don't you begin with why you and Whitney decided to ruin my senior year or has that day faded from your memory. Because if it has faded, I can refresh it for you," she said, anger surfacing born again from pain. Hearing the distress in Misty's voice, he knows he has to tell her what the last twenty years have been without her. "Misty, please believe me when I tell you my life and my marriage have been less than blissful, but I couldn't just leave her when she said she was pregnant with our baby."

I feel like I have been punched in the stomach. Breathing is becoming difficult. My heart is beating in my ears like a drum and I realize my eyes are leaking tears. I feel as though I am going to faint. Nick moves to help me and somehow, I am able to discourage him. I manage to stand up and move to the railing of the porch. Leaning against the railing, feeling as those it is swaying, I want to scream. I manage to look at Nick. "Do you have any idea Nick, what that day and the days following were like for me? All our dreams were being trampled and you were tiptoeing through a landmine of lies and deceit all the while knowing Whitney was doing all she could to capture you. I should have recognized something was going on. She was my best friend Nick, and you were the love of my life. The two of you betrayed me, sleeping together, and then parading your conquest in front of me, and now you tell me Whitney got pregnant that night? Going to the Prom it seems was the least of the issues I actually faced then. That didn't matter to the two of you did it? Whitney practically was strutting down your street and you just stood there and let her continue knowing what it was doing to me." I am sobbing now.

"It happened so fast," Nick declares. You and I were struggling with our college and the issues with your Dad. Michigan was looming in my future. It had become more than I could manage. It was all I could think about. I am ashamed Misty." I sit trying to keep myself still, wondering how I am going to respond to his excuses. My anger and pain at the memory merged, exploding like volcanic lava paralyzing my judgment. All the work I had put in to come to grips with what happened, and the changes I had made in the past suddenly became engulfed, and then submerged in a sea of unbridled emotion. Nick and Whitney and the impact of their actions changed my life. I wasn't going to let Nick off the hook. His life had been unchanged, and he is sitting here trying to tell me how devastated he was. I was there, I saw his reaction to Whitney's declaration and the look in his eyes hurt me more than Whitney bragging about her sexual conquest. "Nick, stop! Your life looks good from where I am, father to two boys on the same track as their father, athletes, Board member at the bank, football coach, and a hero to the town. I don't think your life is so bad."

Suddenly Nick's attitude changed. "What do you know about how my life has been or is now? Were you here?" Giving a look of exasperation, he said, "No I don't think so. You ran off instead of facing what had happened." Rising from my chair, I begin to pace back and forth on the porch. Turning suddenly, I shouted, "Is that what you think, I ran away? Do you have any idea what was going on at home during that time, or were you too caught up in your Michigan scholarship chances to notice? My Dad was going off the rails; he wanted to help all those people who were having health issues because of the electromagnetic fields. Did you know every Saturday night, they went out with their friends to a dance hall? Did you know suddenly their friends no longer asked my parents to go with them? Did you know their accounts were put on hold at the feed store, because the owner wondered if Dad was losing it? No, of course you didn't because I didn't tell you." Standing then to face her, Nick shouts back, "Why Misty, why didn't you tell me what was going on? Maybe things would have been different; I could have helped you deal with it." Laughing almost hysterically, "Really Nick, You, what were you going to do? You just said you couldn't manage what you had on your plate at the time. We were in high school, we were 17 years old, what were you going to do to help me deal with the humiliation my family was experiencing? Do you even care now to know how many people he helped?"

Sitting down I lie my head back, and quietly say, "Nick it doesn't matter whether you knew or not. What happened with Whitney would have happened eventually. I know that now. You can stand there and say things would have been different, and maybe they would have been for a while. But eventually it would have been someone else, it's just who you were then." Knowing deep down inside Misty was right, it took him a minute to speak. Tears slid down his face. "I am sorry, Misty. I hope I am a different man today."

I know my feelings are still wounded, and now they are thrashing about once again. I thought somehow, they could no longer surface. I was mad about how it happened and why I left, but in this moment, I feel sadness. Night is cloaking us now, but the sky is filled with stars. My eyes change with the scenery and looking up, I see a shooting star. Is it possible it could mean something, a star falling from the sky?

Nick suddenly stands up and tells me he needs to go talk to Whitney. Nodding, I walk him from the porch to his car. Right before he opens his door, I say to him. "Nick, remember we are all guilty, be easy with Whitney. None of this was fair to any of us and I need, for my own good, to finally let it go, and so do you. We need to remember that, OK?" Part of me could barely fathom the words I heard myself say "we are all guilty" and I recognize it has taken me an arduous journey on a long road to wind up here.

I realize the past had defined me and I still have to reconcile my feelings for Nick. The anger and hurt I felt has haunted me for the last twenty years. It is time to address those who were the participants, Whitney, Nick and even me. We were all guilty for the actions which defined us. We need to figure out a way to resolve our issues with each other no matter what the outcome may be.

Morgan (Present)

Now that Nick is gone, I realize how drained I feel. Sitting back down on the porch furniture, I lay my head back and close my eyes. For a moment, I let myself go back to the day when Nick and Whitney confessed their secret. Waiting for the anger to bubble up, I am surprised to feel only sadness and regret. So many people's lives changed that day and for so many years I thought Whitney and Nick were happily living their lives. I was wrong. A year ago, I would have been ecstatic. Now I feel sadness for the two of them and for their boys.

Hearing a door slam, I come out of my distressing thoughts and see Seth and Olivia have come home. I start down the steps, Olivia with Seth closely behind her coming down the sidewalk. "Hey, you guys, how are you? I am sorry I have not been available today. It was crazy downtown, and I had a lot of errands to run." Olivia speaks first, "It's been the same for us, except we ended our crazy day at the Tavern. We thought we would have seen you there." "It was a busy day and time got away from me. I've got some wine in the refrigerator, would you two like a glass?" Looking back at Seth, Olivia raises her eyebrows and Seth nods. "Sure Morgan, red or white?" "Actually, Olivia, I've got a bottle of both. I spent some time riding around taking pictures and I came across a winery not far out of town. So, I stopped, had a tasting and decided it was pretty good. So, what will it be red or white?" "Look at you, stopping at wineries, remarks Olivia laughing out loud. I'll take a glass of white and Seth will have a glass of red." Walking into the house, I look back over my shoulder and say, "Riding throughout the area really makes me feel at home" "Well aren't you just the wine connoisseur touting the best wine in the county," laughs Olivia as she hears the screen door open and Morgan emerges. "Yes, and now wine seems perfect to celebrate time with my two best friends. Oh, I saw your friend Nick by the bank today. He stopped and talked to me." "He did? That is unusual for him. He usually likes to be the one recognized and acknowledged. "Yes, I'm not sure why he stopped me. I was walking to the Deli to get the local paper and he suddenly appeared in front of me. We talked for a few minutes and then he said he had to leave for a meeting at the bank." Seth rolled his eyes and said, "You know Morgan, I have known Nick for a long time and there is never a time he does anything by accident. He has an agenda when he walks out the door so seeing you was not pure happenstance. It was in his mind so if he would see you, he was prepared."

Taking a deep breath, and moving closer to them, I ask them if they will come up and sit down on the porch. I just sat there less than two hours ago telling Nick who I was, and it has left me a little disconcerted for the moment. It seems however like this is going to be it. It seems to me, now is the time to explain to Seth and Olivia who I really am and the reasons I have stayed away so long. Seth looks at Olivia and then at me, puts his hand first on Olivia's arm, then on mine and says to me, "Morgan, Olivia and I are positive we can help you through whatever is going on right now."

I wonder how I am going to explain all of this to them. I take a sip of my wine pause a moment trying to find the words to confess to them I am Jonathan's long-lost sister? In a voice earnest with friendship I begin. "I want to tell you both you have been great friends to me since I've come to Millersville, and I really appreciate your openness and friendship. The time we've spent at the Tavern talking has been just what I needed when coming back here. When I told you both about the day, I spent riding around the area and went by the Jenkins Farm, I wasn't being completely honest with you. I actually went there to see my family's farm. The walks downtown and the rides with Brett are all on roads I know like the back of my hand. My teenage years were spent riding around on these roads. I am Misty. The words come easier than I expected. Understanding what made me leave and why I have come back may be hard for you to accept, but I am here now and don't have any plans on leaving." Seth and Olivia look at each other and then look at me. Managing to keep their emotions under control but failing, Seth and Olivia get up and grab me out of my chair, "Misty, is it really you?" Seth reaches for me and gently sits me down.

Sitting there trying to get myself together, images of home and family pour through my mind. "More than anything I have wanted to be able to tell you, who had been friends and supporters of my family for years, I had finally come home. Looking at them know I can see the young version of them standing in our driveway with Jonathan. Yesterday and today had joined hands and brought me home.

Seth and Olivia were brimming over with questions and after the initial shock for all of them, it became easier for Morgan to talk to them about how she felt back then with all of the rumors floating around about her family and the relationship between Nick, Whitney and herself. Thankfully, they were a great audience and more than anything they didn't judge. Seth though was feeling anger toward Nick which was distracting him from the conversation which was now taking place between Olivia and Misty or Morgan, whoever. Breaking into their conversation, Seth tempers down his anger. He understands Misty was the victim in this trilogy, but he can't stop himself from asking. "Misty, I know both of them betrayed you. Nick was weak and wrong to succumb to Whitney's seduction and Whitney disregarded your feelings and your friendship to have what she wanted knowing the pain you would feel. Why though did you give up so easily, Morgan? Why didn't you stay and fight for Nick?" I delay my answer for a moment to assemble the words to the conclusion

I had reached myself years after. Then, looking at both of them I explain, "Seth, then it was devastating to me. My family was trying to recover from the shock of my Mother's death. Nick was leaving for Michigan and I was unable to attend Michigan with him. I was leaving to attend college at the University of Arizona. After my Mom died, my Dad became more obsessed with trying to determine exactly how the electromagnetic fields were causing sickness to people. He directly blamed it for Mom's disease. It was such a sad and difficult time for me. I had to go. Two people I loved and trusted had shattered me."

"Staying here facing the remnants of it was too much for me with everything else which was going on in my life." I begin to cry again, softly at first, and then tears began to slide like raindrops. Olivia gathered me in her arms. "Oh Misty, we wish we could have been there for you. Whenever we asked Jonathan about you and what you were up to, he would get so irritated we finally stopped asking him. You understand don't you, he was our best friend, and you were his little sister." Smiling gently at Olivia, "Please I know it's Ok. I left that summer for school and never came home. Dad had become wrapped up in studying stray currents from the towers, helping those who were sick and challenging the electric company. Jonathan and Dad were struggling with their relationship because of the farm. I didn't feel welcome at home anymore."

"Eventually I graduated from college and moved again. When Jonathan called me to tell me Dad had died my world once again felt like it was crashing down around me. Part of me wasn't surprised when I got the call. Jonathan could barely talk but he really didn't have to, I knew Dad had died. He found him out in the field lying between the tractor and the corn wagon. Nothing can prepare you for the shock of hearing such news and I was no different. I asked if he knew how he died." "I'm not exactly sure yet, but it appears he had a heart attack," he told me. "A heart attack? Olivia, he was as strong as an Ox. It had something to do with those damn stray currents, I know it. I felt as if it was my fault then, Olivia. I had left home, left them alone for so long. I wasn't even there to assist him with the funeral arrangements. I told him I was sorry I wasn't there to help him. I knew his wife Sarah would take care of arrangements with him, but I should have been there." Olivia looked at me with such sadness in her eyes. "Misty, you can't carry the blame of this on your shoulders. Sara is so quiet and doesn't always appear to be a strong partner to Jonathan, but we know differently. She is one of the main reasons he has been working with the bank. Their livelihood is at risk and she is the motivation behind wanting the sale of the land to go through. Seth and I believe without Sara, Jonathan may have not survived the demise of the farm."

"It took me several days to gather the courage to decide to come back for his funeral. When I finally arranged to go my flight was delayed by weather. I missed the funeral and was pulling up just as the last person left the cemetery. I felt somehow, I had been spared seeing everyone and saved from enduring a goodbye to my father in front of everyone. I know it sounds terrible, but you have no idea what we had gone through as a family. The chance Nick was close by prevented me from staying long, but I am home now."

When I said that, I realized I really was home now. By the time Morgan finished the sentence, Olivia was crying. Staring at me through eyes rimmed with tears. "I am so sorry, Misty. Your pain must have been enormous. Please forgive us for not paying attention back then." "Oh Olivia, we were all so young then, too caught up in ourselves and too naïve to realize what the future would bring. In the years between then and now, I have gathered much to me. I am more observant now, more determined in paying attention to the present, and learning from the past without allowing it to discourage me from believing in myself and others."

"I understand now why you were so concerned at Cissy's," Olivia said. "I thought several times since then about the look you had on your face and wondered what made you so concerned. What did you feel when you were there, Morgan?" Continuing the subject, but changing the direction, Morgan answered, "Those towers are old and have to be dropping stray current, Olivia. Abigail is sick with a blood disease and the percentage of people who are sick with some kind of blood disease or terminal cancer is high when they live near power lines. I have been living with that knowledge for years. I have kept it quiet because my family's reputation is so tainted; I have not yet been able to think of a possible way for me to come forward with what I know. Plus, I need proof and I believe it's here somewhere in this town."

"I just found out Jack Callahan was Brett's stepfather. Please tell me how I'm going to figure this out when Brett's stepfather is the man who worked for the electric company and caused so much trouble for my dad, and he is the man who is trying to capture my heart?"

Seth knew his next few sentences were going to be very instrumental on how Misty, "*Wow, I am calling her Misty, and miracles do happen.*" was going to proceed. "Misty, Brett's relationship with his stepfather wasn't good and I think you have seen enough of his relationship with his Mother to know it also has its issues. Olivia and I have always been very respectful to Elizabeth and at the same time, we have listened to Brett. Over the past several years, we have become very close to him. He has always been somewhat of a loner, but he has a kind of magnetism which draws others close. His personality is what keeps his bar busy. He is friendly to everyone. Misty, when he took over the Tavern, he was determined and committed to change the stigma of racism which hovered in the background of the bar."

"At the time he encountered a good amount of resistance from some of the patrons." I smile, "Oh yes, I remember, grimacing at the memory. The African Americans, or colored as they were called then, always came in the door that entered the Tavern from Bailey Street and they always sat in a separate section of the bar." Nodding Seth says, "You are exactly right, but he closed up the door and expanded his table area. Everyone now comes in the front door and sits together at the bar. When that happened, Olivia and I decided he was someone we wanted to call our friend."

"Our friendship with Brett helped fill the void we felt when Jonathan became withdrawn and detached. Misty, he was our best friend. There wasn't anything we thought could separate us, but when your Mom and then your Dad died, he changed. No matter what we did, we couldn't reach him. He just shut down and with it came the neglect and eventually the demise of a working farm."

Trying to hold back tears, I motion to the two of them to look up. "See the sky above us. Up there I see an expansive universe with bright and guiding stars. I can see my future there. My life began in this town under this very sky. I feel it is sending me an invitation to come home. I have ignored it for far too long. My brother needs me, and I know the two of you are going to help me sort this entire out. I need to know what happened to my

Dad. How did he die? Jonathan never said, just that he found him lying dead in the field." Seth looks at Olivia and with that look the two of them move me, pulling me out of the chair to my feet. We wrap our arms around each other. With a determination which contradicts our state of emotion, we grab one another's hands and look up. Seth speaks first, "We are going to work together and the power of three is greater than one." Olivia struggling with her words squeezes both of their hands, "We love you Misty, and together we will find out what happened to your Dad and restore the legacy he left for the two of you." Looking at the two of them, I realize what family and friendship is truly about. It doesn't matter if there is a common thread of blood; it too is an unmistakable bond of hearts, an invisible connection, and an immeasurable gift for keeps. Hugging one another we stood there for an indeterminate amount of time. For the first time in a long time, I didn't feel alone.

It is late but Seth, Olivia and I agree we are hungry, so we decide to go out to the Tavern. I am a little worried because Brett will be there and there is no guarantee Seth and Olivia will be able to keep from mentioning our conversation. I don't want Brett to find out unexpectedly. I need to tell him myself. Pulling in we notice the bar is really busy, and I breathe a sigh of relief. Brett will be occupied with all of the operations of the Tavern and won't have as much time to stand and talk with us.

Walking in the first person I see is Whitney. She is sitting by herself at the end of the bar and I can tell by her body language she is unhappy. We move to the other side of the bar where there are some seats available. They are right where I met Seth and Olivia as Morgan just a few weeks ago. It is ironic now they know the truth and we sit where I portrayed myself as someone new to the area. "Hey, are you somewhere else?" asks Olivia. Smiling and squeezing her arm, I say "Yes I was. I was just remembering the first day when I arrived here. It was just a day after I came back when I knew this would be the place where I would find information about the fabric of Millersville after being gone for so long. Little did I know you and Seth were sitting right here. Do you know the shock I had that day?" Laughing Olivia taps Seth on the arm, "Hey are you paying attention? Do you hear this woman? She thought we would have the inside scoop of Millersville." Seth looks over at Misty, "You had us pegged from the start. Olivia and I have always been very active in Millersville. When the farm started to deteriorate, we reached out to Jonathan to help but he shut us out. After that we focused our time volunteering for the local sport teams and that's how we became so close to Nick. I knew something had happened back then, but we were older than the two of you and we had just gotten married. It doesn't seem right now looking back, but I hope you understand it just wasn't important to us at the time. We were young and just starting out."

Scanning the bar, I see a lot of familiar faces and suddenly realize they don't know who I really am. Funny it is what I wanted when I came back here, but now incredibly it has changed for me. It is still a problem that my family's reputation has not been exonerated. Jonathan and I will have to journey back in time together to put the pieces together which will mend the fabric of our family name and make us whole again.

Entranced in her thoughts of the overwhelming events of the last few days, Whitney was oblivious to the music and the conversations around her. Her mind was in another place. A slight smile crossed her face. In a voice barely audible, Whitney said to herself, "finally things are going to change." Her thoughts continued, Nick's everyday presence will be gone and now I can for once focus on myself. The boys will need me, but then I have always been the one there for them. She admitted to herself though Nick had done his share and she knew nothing would keep him from continuing in his support of them.

A familiar voice interrupts her distraction. Looking up she sees Seth and Olivia sitting on the other side the bar. Suddenly her breath catches, sitting next to them is Morgan. Realizing she is holding her breath, she inhales a deep intake of air. Trying not to think about Nick, the closeness the three are exhibiting finds her plunged into memory of friendship.

Unexpectedly she finds herself tearing up. Blinking rapidly, she begins looking around to make sure no one is watching. The last thing I need is someone to start asking questions she thinks. Deciding it is time to go home, she gets up to leave.

Nick and Whitney (Present)

Nick finds himself driving all around the county trying to come to grips with the last two hours. Misty is back. His mind is traveling a mile a minute and he can't focus on anything. Pulling over, he lays his head on the steering wheel and tries to calm down. The love of his life is back, and he can't figure out why he feels the way he does. Looking at her was surreal. Knowing she is Misty but seeing someone who looks completely different overwhelms him. Hearing her voice and looking at her face complicates his thoughts. The pain in her voice and its change into anger brought back all the memories of that summer. Whitney naked walking out of the lake, Misty striding away from the house while Whitney and Nick stood there watching. Whitney losing the baby, the guilt which consumed her then her new lease on life, the birth of the boys all brought the past flooding his mind, and his heart. He knew he needed desperately to bring himself back to the present.

Today's events were going to have so many ramifications extending way past those of us who were there that day. Now the bank, the investors and the community of Millersville were involved. Not only in a personal collision but also an economic impact because the bank was going to be interested in Misty's reappearance. Torn between going to Whitney and the bank, Nick decided it was important to go back home and talk with Whitney.

Whitney pulled into her driveway and sees Nick's car is there. Sitting there she wonders what would happen and what they would do if Misty really ever came back. Finally getting out of the car she braces herself for Nick's new plan on finding out if Morgan is Misty Jenkins. Walking in their front door, she hears Nick upstairs rummaging around. Yelling up the stairs, "Nick what are you doing up there?" "Trying to find a carton I brought from my house when we moved here. It has old pictures from high school in it of Misty and me," muttered Nick. Struggling to hear what Nick said Whitney went upstairs to see what he was doing. Walking into their bedroom she sees Nick standing on a small ladder they kept upstairs for changing light bulbs. "Nick why are you so intent on finding this carton. I'm pretty sure it's not in there because I just cleaned out the closet a couple of weeks ago," Nick pulled his head out of the closet and stood up, annoyed he said, "What did you do with the carton then, because it isn't in here anymore and it was here not too long ago. So, again where is it, Whitney?" Realizing Nick was starting to get angry she left the room and went down to the garage. Rummaging through an old chest they kept in the garage she found it. Hearing Nick come through the door, she turns around with the carton in her hand and asks him, "What is so important in this carton? I've never seen you so intense on finding something before. There wasn't anything in there but some old pictures from High School. I kept your football photos and some of them were of the two of us but the rest of them weren't important." Nick looked like he was going to explode. "Whitney in there was pictures of Misty and me from high school. I wanted to keep those pictures so where are they now?" "What difference does it make those pictures are gone? Those times weren't something we needed to remember so do you want to tell me why you want them now after all these years?" demanded Whitney. Nick found himself struggling to speak, he looked at the woman he had been married to for almost twenty years, the Mother of his boys and wondered how he was going to tell her the girl who had been her best friend all through high school has come home.

Finding his voice, Nick quietly asks for Whitney to sit down. "Whitney, I have something to tell you. I realize this probably won't change anything for us, but it still will have an effect on our future whatever that may be." "The Morgan woman again," she muttered to herself. She had already heard too much from him about her, but she pulled out a chair and sat down. Nick began, "Whitney, you know my suspicions of the woman who calls herself Morgan. It seems as though I might have been right about her," he said softly, hoping not to aggravate her more. Straining to maintain some form of dignity, Whitney looked at her husband of twenty years. "Nick, what in the world are you talking about saying you were right. She is some kind of photographer who is taking pictures of our area for a magazine article about small towns in America," Whitney stated emphatically. "Nick, she continued, your need to free yourself of the guilt about Misty is making you crazy. I told you this before, stop it, and let it go. We've never had to think about what happened then, until now. Why now, Nick? This obsession you have developed about this woman is unhealthy. You are plagued by her. Why Nick?" She repeated in frustration and fear. Yes fear, was the part she tried hard to dismiss each time he spoke of her. Please help me to understand."

He knew his next words were going to make Whitney think he had really gone crazy, but he needed to tell her he knew for sure now Misty was home. "Whitney, I did something that even when I did it, I thought to myself, *"What in the world are you doing Nick? This isn't going to turn out how you think it will or want it to be."* "The woman, Morgan, has constantly been on my mind and I couldn't figure out why. So, I started to watch her closely whenever I was around her."

Staring at Nick, all she can do is nod for him to go on. Continuing, "Seth and Olivia have befriended her since she arrived, and they always invite her out with them. Since they are also my friends, I have been around her frequently. It was during those times when I felt like there was something familiar about her. I couldn't shake the feeling. The tilt of her head, the movement of her hands and the way she walks were so unnerving. My eyes were telling me she was just some woman who had decided to stop in Millersville on her way to wherever, but my gut kept telling me something completely different." Whitney questioned sarcastically, "What was your heart telling you?" Knowing Whitney, Nick knew she was trying her hardest not to stand up and walk out, but he needed her to stay and listen. "Please, Whitney, I know you have doubted my love and commitment to you a long time now, but I am doing this to help us. You need to hear this so please let me finish."

She wanted to tell Nick she could care less about his suspicions surrounding this woman Morgan, but something was telling her to stay and listen. Almost in a whisper, "Go ahead, Nick, she said." Nick felt his stomach churning with worry knowing both of their lives had now changed and he wanted Whitney to be able to absorb what had happened. Taking a deep breath, he began, "I had to go to the bank to see Tom Fraser. It was a short meeting so I thought I would take a walk down to the paper store and pick up a lottery ticket. As I was waiting to cross the street, I saw Morgan. She was walking toward the Hotel and I hurried across the street so I could walk behind her." Whitney couldn't help herself, "Why would you do that, are you stalking her?" "No, Whitney, but I had a hunch and I wanted to play it out. So, when I got closer to her, I called out her name."

Rolling her eyes at Nick, Whitney quipped, "Well I guess she turned around if you called out to her, so where is this going, Nick." Nick moved from his chair, knelt down in front of Whitney and grabbed her hands. "Whitney, she did turn around, but I didn't call out Morgan, I called out Misty."

Getting a sick feeling in her stomach, alarm now resounding in her voice, "What do you mean you called out, Misty?" Whitney couldn't believe what she was about to say, "She turned around?" Nick squeezing her hands, "Yes, Whitney she did and for just a moment she looked at me and I knew it was her." "Nick, why would she come back to Millersville now? This woman doesn't look anything like Misty," Whitney emphatically responded. "Besides, Nick, why would Misty come back here now? You are grasping at this, Nick, because of the past and your guilt. Nothing is going to change for us, if that's what you are thinking,"

Struggling with his emotions, Nick knew Whitney was going to react this way, but he had to prove to her Misty was back. "Whitney, listen, I doubted myself some too, but I knew she was renting the house next to Seth and Olivia, so I went there and confronted her. She tried to deny it at first, but then it was like some kind of epiphany happened to her because suddenly she looked at me and told me to come up and sit with her on the porch."

Whitney couldn't believe what she was hearing. She knew now with certainty her suspicions all these years that Nick had never gotten over Misty were correct. Apprehension and fear began to replace frustration and started to well up inside her. Trying to contain it, she replied, "Nick, why? Why would she come back now and disguise herself so no one would know her? What's the point? The point is she didn't want any of us to know." Standing up and moving to look out the window, he ran his fingers through his hair and said, "Whitney, all those same thoughts went through my head when I sat there looking at her. I really don't know. I do know she is going to be helping Jonathan and beyond that I'm really not sure."

"Well, Nick if what you say is true and she is really Misty, then there is more to this situation than you think. She is up to something," Whitney declared. "Whitney, we need to go to her as a couple and talk with her," Nick quickly responded. "What for, Nick?" Whitney demanded. "It isn't over is it? It's never been over for most of our marriage has it? Admit it, you have never gotten over her and all the times you told me how much you loved me when you were making love to me, you were talking to Misty. I never could understand why you would sometimes not look at me when we were making love. Your eyes were would be diverted or closed and now I understand. You could see Misty then instead of me." Her voice quivered unexpectedly. She gathered herself then, pushed back the chair, walked over and stood in front of him. "No, my darling husband, she said unequivocally, I don't want to go see her with you, but you can be damned sure I will see her." Nick knew not to push Whitney anymore, he told her he would pick up the boys from school and get them ready for practice.

Brett, Morgan and Elizabeth (Present)

Grappling with his thoughts about Morgan, Brett moves around the Tavern to make sure all his customers are happy. Morgan's eyes follow him. She is uneasy and still coming to terms with her visit with Nick. Her thoughts are weighing on her mind so much that at first, she doesn't hear Olivia say Whitney has left suddenly, until she repeats it again. Morgan shook off her thoughts and said, "Really I didn't even see her here." Olivia laughs, "Yeah, she was sitting across from us, but she seemed unlike herself. Normally she gets sloshed and then gets loud, but today she looked like she wanted to sink inside herself so nobody would notice her. It was very obvious she didn't want anyone to talk to her. When I looked over there again, she was gone." Wondering what is going on with Whitney, Morgan couldn't help but think Nick had shared our conversation.

Brett is now working his way over to her and by the time he reaches her side, all she can do is lean against him. A total weariness washes over her and it is all she can do to pay attention to Olivia's banter with Brett. Looking up at Brett, she whispers, "Can we get out of here? I am tired all of sudden and would like to go home." Smiling, Brett quietly says, "Just wait here for a few minutes so I can talk to my staff and remind them of a few things, then I will take you home." With that, he walks back over to the other side of the bar and through the swinging door. Seth tries not to upset Morgan, but says, "Hey are you going to tell him? It would not be fair for him to find out from someone else. We aren't going to, but you don't know what frame of mind Nick is in and if he were to get to Brett before you could tell him it would be really bad." Knowing Seth was right, Morgan quietly says, "I know Seth, it will have to be the right time for me to tell Brett, but you can rest assured Nick won't say anything. He is going to be handling Whitney plus he has a role in the bank project relating to the farm." Seeing Brett walking toward her, she hugs Seth and Olivia whispering, "I don't want the two of you to worry about me. I'm home now and I won't be leaving. I am going to help Jonathan regain some respect for himself and our family no matter what the outcome of the farm sale might be. My family needs healing and it has a chance to begin with my coming home and will finish when the mystery of my Dad's death is resolved."

Turning away, she walks up to Brett takes his hand in hers, "Let's go, we need some quiet time together." she says softly. Moving toward the tavern door, she stops and looks back at her friends, smiles, and wave. It is her way of telling them she will see them again, assuring them this time she won't leave! Walking out together, I wrap my arms around him and pull him close. "We should take a ride and enjoy the beautiful afternoon. There is somewhere I think we ought to go." Smiling and hugging her closer, Brett laughs and says, "Where might that be?" Getting to his car, I open the door and say, "We should go and visit your

Mother. Didn't she say she was leaving soon? I think you should see her before you go, and it would be a reason for me to get to know her better." Frowning slightly, Brett muttered, "Mother doesn't like impromptu visits, but I guess it would be alright. You should know Elizabeth doesn't like to be surprised. Everything she does is planned and then controlled to her liking." Suddenly laughing, he said, "so let's take a ride over there, however, remember we will go there at our own risk." Smiling at Brett but thinking, *"That is just what, I want for her to be surprised."*

Riding along with Brett, the atmosphere is uneasy, and I don't want to upset him before we arrive at his Mother's house. This visit may not be pleasant for Elizabeth, but nothing is going to stop me now. I am definitely not going to pressure her too far, but it is time to find out what happened during that time between Jack and my Dad. Somehow, I know it will make her uncomfortable and I need to venture into a conversation with Brett. Keep it light, I instruct myself. Confident I will be careful, and I am ready, I reach for his hand and begin, "I know, Brett, you told me your Mother doesn't like surprises, but do you think if we tell her how happy we are to see her and how we want to wish her a safe trip she won't give you such a hard time?"

Staring out of the windshield, Brett takes a deep breath, "You know, Morgan, I really don't know. My life with her has been very fragmented, when I was very young, she was so happy, but then when she met Jack she changed. Suddenly material things became more important. It was all about who she and Jack were entertaining. It seemed to me I became a responsibility more than a son to her. Much of the time I felt diminished."

"During those years the lawyers and the court appearances were constant. The persistent phone calls coming from the lawyer asking questions about my visits with my real father annoyed Jack and caused my mother a great deal of anguish. The banishment I felt then has, in some ways stayed with me. I have never been able to completely erase the feelings of that time in my life." He quickly proceeded with, "Nothing though would have stopped her when it came to my success as an adult and I owe her because without her, Morgan, I wouldn't be the person I am today."

Listening to Brett, I find myself admiring his honesty and loving him for it. I realize how little I know about him. I have been so concentrated on my family, my mission to discover what really happened to my father, the state and situation of the farm, and Nick and Whitney which I have almost completely ignored really getting to know him. 'Self-absorbed' in other words, I say chastising myself.

Pulling up to his Mother's house, I am interrupted in my silent dialogue with myself but promise I will continue the conversation later. I look over at him and take his hand, "Brett, I know it must have been difficult remembering those changes in your mother and their effect on her relationship with you when sharing them with me. Please know I want to understand and be a part of your journey to come to terms with and resolve the consequences which continue to travel with you. Now, though let's go inside and visit her before she goes on holiday." Brett leaned over and hugged me, "Morgan, I'm so glad you suggested we stop over here today. I just hope our unexpected visit is received graciously."

Arriving at Elizabeth's house suddenly makes my heart stop for a second. Here is my chance to find out something, anything that will help Jonathan and I understand the importance of Jack's interest in my father. Brett grabs my hand and smiles, "Well we have arrived, Morgan, are you ready. "You know, Brett, I am ready. Trying to relieve his apprehension, I took his hand again and I looked at him. "I believe your Mother will be happy to see you. Those days which caused the changes in her and your relationship with her are over. Jack is gone. You and your mother have a new chance at life if you want to get to really know each other again. So, what are we waiting for, let's go," I laugh?

Walking up to the front door I know this is going to be a monumental day for me, but I have Brett to think about and I don't want to damage the relationship we have. I see his hand slightly tremble when opening the door. Touching his arm softly, I smile, "You've got this, she doesn't bite, you know." Brett laughs, you would be surprised, I will have to show you my bite marks later," with that he rings the bell, and we wait. We can hear Elizabeth footsteps nearing the door. The curtains on the side windows of the door move and I see Elizabeth looking to see who is at the door. For a split second I see the look on her face, which is not one of pleasure at seeing who is ringing the bell, but the mask came down and with much aplomb she opens the door and steps out to welcome us. "Brett, what a surprise, you didn't let me know you were coming over, let alone bringing a guest. I haven't even had my afternoon tea yet," she pronounces. I can feel Brett tense up, so I quickly move and hug Elizabeth saying, "Well you look stunning, why don't we go inside so we can have tea." Elizabeth smiles, leans in and gives Brett a hug. "Let's go inside and make ourselves comfortable. Morgan I just love the jacket you have on, so bohemian looking." "Elizabeth, thank you, it is just something I picked up on my way across country at this little shop in a small town outside of Austin, TX."

Leading us into her formal sitting room, she turns to Brett motioning for him to take her arm, leaving me to follow behind them. As we walk into the sitting room, Brett looks at me and says, "Mother likes to sit on the loveseat so she can put her feet up, so just grab one of the other seats." Finding myself tensing up, I suddenly realize he is doing what is rote because his whole life he has catered to his Mother. If there is any chance of him having a healthy relationship with another woman, he is going to have to release himself from the hold she has over him. Her dominance over him is an indication to me of the power she has had over the men in her life.

It is becoming more apparent than ever I need to get her to set aside her control so I can discover her real personality. At this point, I am suspicious Elizabeth knows more than is evident about Jack and his involvement with my dad and the farm, and I am determined to find out what happened and the truth of it all. There is more at stake than just my family's reputation. I have my own family, I remind myself and it is more important now than ever to clear our family's name. Following Brett's request for me to take another seat, I begin with unshakable resolve, to commence my deciphering of Elizabeth.

We settle in and Brett and Elizabeth catch up on the news of Millersville. They talk about Elizabeth's garden and the flowers which are becoming popular for English gardens. Watching them I realize how attuned Brett is to his Mother which makes me realize to have any kind of relationship with Brett in the future I need to tread lightly. Interjecting into their conversation, I say, "Elizabeth, I would love to come over some day and work with you in your garden. My gardening skills are limited, and Brett has told me about all your flowers. If you would share some of your knowledge with me, I would be the best student." I lean forward, "Please don't feel any pressure, I actually have a slightly green thumb, so I won't fumble too much over your expertise."

Elizabeth had no other choice than to respond to me, "Morgan, nothing would please me more, come over anytime, but remember I will be leaving soon." I lean back and think nothing will suit me more than to spend some time with Elizabeth by myself. I am sure she knows more about what transpired between Jack and my Dad. Brett looks at me and I realize his expression is one of amazement. I know he is astonished by what just happened between his Mother and me. I am amazed myself that she accepted my request and is willing to share her garden with me.

Smiling slightly, Elizabeth gets up and moves to look out the window. For a few minutes there is an uncomfortable silence, and then she turns. Her face had been in shadow and I realize it was done on purpose. She didn't want me to see her expression. Her countenance then had reflected her displeasure at having to extend the invitation to me for the sake of her son. Brett stands, reaches out and hugs his Mother. Her composure softens and Elizabeth smiles and motions for me to stand with them while looking out at her garden. Moving to stand with Brett and his Mother, I find myself feeling sad.

Deep down, I feel Elizabeth knows more about my dad and Jack's visits than she lets on. Brett, knowing his mother had never liked unexpected company, even his, thought it was time to leave while things were going well. I promise her I will call when I can come over to garden with her. Brett hugs and kisses his Mother on the cheek, and I turn back and wave again before pulling out of the driveway.

Once Brett and Morgan had gone, Elizabeth turned and began to walk through entire the house, something she had not done in a long time. So many memories swarmed around her, as she walked from room to room. Jack, sitting in his chair reading with the sunlight fading dispelling its last rays of light through the glass. She thought about all the times she spent alone waiting for Jack to come back and tell her something new about his activities in Millersville.

Time and time again she had waited for some kind of revelation, but the only thing demonstrated to her was his frustration. He had become obsessed in his attempt to find the out the agenda of Carl Jenkins. Every day there was something else changing the landscape and the emotional ups and downs had become detrimental to their relationship.

Elizabeth wandered throughout her house replaying old memories. Finding herself navigating the memories of her past was all because Brett had developed a relationship with this girl, Morgan Kiernan. Her persistent curiosity of Jack and his work made Elizabeth uncomfortable. The questions she asked, and her familiarity with the events made it seem as though she had been a part of that life. It had been years since Elizabeth had thought about any of the particulars leading up to that fateful day. She had safely sealed and locked them away long ago. They were protected from remembering, but the girl had made her remember. On top of that, Brett seemed infatuated with her which made it worse.

Whitney and Morgan (Present)

"So, what do you have on your agenda for the rest of the day, Morgan?" asks Brett. Knowing the underlying meaning to his question, I struggle with my feelings. I really want to spend the afternoon with him, but I have this feeling my life is going to be unraveling shortly and I need to get ahead of it. Smiling at Brett, I put my hand in his, "Actually, I need to go home, I had planned to do some crafting with Olivia and I've already can-celled once. You know Olivia, she will never let me live it down if I cancel again." Trying to hide his disappointment, he leans over and kisses her, "Morgan, it's fine, you won't be crafting all day, so I'll call you later after I check on the Tavern. Maybe we can get together then." As we pull up to my house, I smile, "Brett, this sounds like a plan. Olivia and I should be finished before cocktail hour. You know Seth doesn't let anyone interfere with his Scotch." Leaning over to kiss him, I put my hand on his cheek and say, "Thank you for today." Opening the door, I step out and head up to my house.

As Brett is pulling away, I see a car moving down the road very slowly. Wondering who it is, I hesitate on my front step. The car pulls over in front of the house and Whitney emerges from the car. She walks around the car to the sidewalk and just stands there staring. Rationally I know I should feel relieved she showed up, but my heart is beating fast and I feel weak. Motioning her to come up to the porch, I walk ahead of her and sit down. Whitney gradually moves toward the porch hesitating on the steps. Wanting desperately to keep my composure, I wave my hand motioning her to sit down. I am sitting opposite her and wondering how I am going to handle the next few minutes.

Looking over at her, I smile and say, "Whitney, I'm assuming you are here because Nick told you about our visit. I thought maybe you might come. I guess you have a lot of questions." Whitney found herself staring at Morgan, trying to see her best friend Misty. Finally finding her voice, she says, "This is more than crazy, you know. How is it possible that you are Misty? If you are, why are you here? You left over 20 years ago. You have been gone for so long, why now? And somehow, I really don't think you are who you say you are. Why would you tell my husband you were his long-lost girlfriend?" Feeling herself becoming outraged, Whitney says, "Who cares if you are Misty Jenkins? If so, you left Millersville in disgrace, your family's reputation has been destroyed and your brother is a loser. I realize my anger of long ago, safely kept at bay these many years, has now returned. Today has given it the chance to show itself again and I realize I have not ever completely let it go. Now I can tell her now for the first time how wrong she was and release the hurt that left its signs littered on the paths I've walked since then. Except now is not the time, I tell myself.

Restoring my family's reputation and finding out why my Dad died is what is important now. Hearing Whitney's diatribe just tells me she hasn't let it go. I lean toward her, "Whitney, there is no other way to say this but just to dive right in. Nick is right. I came back and I don't look anything like I did when I left. There is much I need to tell you and I have struggled for years trying to decide what would be the best way. There are so many things you don't know. The relationship that you, I and Nick had is all part of that time. Those things you said about my brother are uncalled for. Nothing Jonathan did have an impact on you or Nick, your guilt just worked on your conscious and I am not going to sit here and listen to you berate my family or me. You did this, Whitney, you wanted to have Nick by sleeping with him. Don't think I don't know what your intention was then. Sleeping with him was your way to have him for yourself and eventually your ticket out of Millersville, but that didn't happen did it? You got pregnant. His football career ended. Yes, I know about that too! Do you know what it did to me? Nick and I had plans and all of that was destroyed the day when you decided to tell me about your relationship with Nick. Except, Whitney, it wasn't a relationship was it? It was a one-night stand except you got what you wanted. You got rid of me. All the days and nights crying, sick, missing my family, and worst of all not sure how I was going to go on. There were things going on between Nick and me you weren't privy to, but we were working them out."

"Somehow, though you managed to get to him, and with all of the other problems I was facing, it was a devastating time for me. I was alone after I left, my Dad died, which you knew, and I could barely bring myself to come back here to say goodbye to him. Changing my appearance allowed me to come home without having any interaction with any of you as Misty. I didn't want to deal with the two of you Whitney, but now I am. Now, what do you think will come from all of this? What purpose does it really serve?"

Nearing tears, Whitney put her head down and whispered, "Misty, I'm sorry, so very sorry! I have carried so much guilt. I've tried to drink my guilt away and I kidded myself that it did. Except now I have a problem so drinking is the last thing I should be doing. Somehow, all of this has helped me see what is wrong in my life and right now it is Nick. I realize now, and I think I have always known he has never stopped loving you. I have realized more than ever in the last few hours. Misty, no matter what you do to change yourself when you have someone your heart loves, that love is for always. "Whitney, it may be true, but love scorned and lost is an expedition by the heart and mind through time. The roads traveled cannot be anticipated and the pilgrimage is long. But it can be a serious motivator and that is what helped me to come back here and now to face both of you. My journey to this place has not been an easy one. My energy now is directed at supporting Jonathan, finding out what happened to my Dad and becoming a family again."

"Nick was my first love and the memory, though dimmed in intensity will remain a part of me I know I won't forget. He is a memory now Whitney I am no threat to you." Whitney leaned over and touched my hand, "Misty, Nick's love hasn't dimmed, and it has always been right under the surface." With that Whitney stood up to leave, "No matter what you think of me Misty, I hope you stay in Millersville. The town has never been the same at least not for me."

Now that Whitney has left, I feel emotionally drained. I lay my head back to rest for a little while. There is time before I need to meet Brett later. Just as I doze off, I think how good it feels to have finally talked to both Nick and Whitney. I have come through it feeling strong.

The Bank (Present)

While Whitney's visit to Misty was going on, Jonathan was waiting in the lobby of the bank for Tom Fraser. Someone is calling his name. Jonathan looks up to see Nick walking toward him with an intense look on his face which causes Jonathan to feel slight irritation. "Nick, what can I do for you? I only have a few minutes before my meeting so make it quick." Diving right in, Nick says, "Jonathan, I know Misty is back. Don't bother to deny it because I have already talked to her." Jonathan tries to look as nonchalant as possible and says, "Yes it was quite a surprise for me, and I guess it must have been the same for you, but then you are one of the main reasons she left." Shaking his head, Nick says, "I'm just glad she's back." At that moment, Tom Fraser's assistant walks up to tell Jonathan Tom is ready for his meeting with him. "Stay away from her, Nick. She doesn't need you now or want you either." Walking away from Nick, he smiles. It is good to know Misty had been able to handle seeing Nick.

Extending his hand to Tom Fraser, he says, "So Tom I hope you have good news for me from the investors." The smile on Tom's face, gave Jonathan hope, the last few times in this office, the atmosphere was not as positive. Tom motions for Jonathan to sit down with him in his conference area. "Jonathan, I have good news! The investors have met and worked out a deal I feel will be attractive to you. Our economy is struggling right now and small businesses have always been the backbone of our economy. The bank understands and we as a group have decided keeping a business like yours in our town is in our best interest as well as yours."

Stunned Jonathan was finding it hard to find his voice, "Tom, did I hear you correctly. What are you saying?" Tom laughs, "Jonathan, I have to apologize for the laughter but the incredulous look on your face is so touching. Yes, we are going to make it possible for you to get your farm back up and running." Trying to maintain some kind of composure, Jonathan can do nothing but nod. "Jonathan, there are a lot of conditions to this Agreement, but those are something we can go over at a later date. All you need to know right now is we are going to help you get back to farming," replies Tom. Finally, Jonathan lifts his head, looks at Tom and says, "If there was ever a time in my life, I could be so thankful, now would be the time. I think I owe you an apology because I really believed you were against me right from the beginning." Honestly, Jonathan, we didn't think you had it in you to farm again, but when Misty showed up that day, even though she didn't say much, her demeanor spoke many silent words. It was like nothing was going to stop her and, in this day, and age, we don't see that resilience much anymore. Her commitment to family and the desire to make something great was very evident. Then Nick Darlington came back with a glowing review of the capabilities of the farm."

Tom stands up and moves to his desk shuffling some papers and produces some paperwork for Jonathan to review and sign. "Jonathan, these are preliminary documents for you to review. Once you and Misty have reviewed them please give me a call with any questions and we can set an appointment for you to come in and sign them. There will be a local farm equipment company calling you to help with the buying of any new equipment. Rest assured we are confident this company will be helpful, because the owner farms a lot of the ground in this county. He has been a friend to farmers since he established his main business here."

Thanking Tom, Jonathan takes his leave from the bank and hurries to his car. I need to see Misty to tell her what just transpired, and the impact Nick had on the deal. She is not going to be happy about it but hopefully the fact we will be able to save the farm will be enough to calm her down, he says to himself.

After leaving the bank Jonathan rode around reliving the words of Tom Fraser. He drove back to the farm and parked in one of the fields. Looking around, he understands the impact of his neglect. He realizes he has always loved his sister. He also recognizes now he loves her even more for her courage and strength. Together we will work to regain our family's legacy and continue to farm, he thought to himself. Instinctively he closed his eyes to picture it and could see his Dad smiling when they shipped their first load of milk again. He needed to see Misty. Smiling he backs out of the field and heads over to Misty's house.

Meanwhile, as soon as Jonathan left the bank, Tom picked up the phone and placed a call to the bank's Chief Financial Officer to let him know he has met with Jonathan Jenkins. He informs him he has given Jonathan the paperwork with the terms and conditions he believes will satisfy Jonathan's expectations and will in short order make a windfall profit for the bank.

Olivia and Jonathan (Present)

Something was disturbing my dream, I could hear a kind of ringing. It kept touching the outside of my dream like someone was ringing a bell. Suddenly, I wake up and realize it's my doorbell ringing. Struggling awake, I get up and move to my front door. Peering in the door is Olivia. Opening it, I hear Olivia say, "Oh my, did I wake you?" Trying to stifle a yawn, I manage a sleepy smile. "I knew we were going to the Tavern tonight, so I called Brett and said I wanted to stop by and see you before heading over there. He asked if I could bring you." Frowning suddenly, "You didn't say you were coming over to talk to Misty, did you? "Of course not, silly. Seth and I are here to support you and that means waiting for you to talk to Brett. We are so happy you came back. We will do whatever it takes to make sure you stay here and are happy." Smiling, "I know Olivia, I just have to take a quick shower and then I will be ready to go. Just make yourself at home." "Misty, while you get ready, I am going to run home. I will get ready myself and be back in about an hour. Will that work?" This was just what I needed to hear. My mind needed some time to reboot before seeing Brett and Seth too for that matter. "Sure, just come in the back door when you get back, there is some wine in the refrigerator so help yourself, ok?" With that Olivia left and I went back to start my shower.

Standing in the shower under the hot water I think about the last few days. So many things have happened, and the effects are spinning around in my mind, Nick following me and Whitney showing up to confront me, Seth and Olivia being so supportive and then Brett feeling like there is something going on he doesn't quite understand. The impact on all of us has been difficult.

I turn the shower water temperature cooler to wake me up from the lingering drowsy feeling from my nap, wrap myself in a soft bath towel and stand in front of my closet to find something to wear to the Tavern. I realize looking at the sparse choice of evening wear it might be time to do some shopping. The selection of clothing in front of me is a testament of how little I cared about dressing nicely for anyone before now. Just as I pick out a blouse and a pair of jeans, I hear my doorbell. Yelling out, "Olivia, I told you to come on in when you got back."

Dressing quickly, running a brush through my hair and throwing some lip gloss on, I head out of the bedroom down to my kitchen. Sitting comfortably at my counter, is my brother Jonathan with a big grin on his face. "Well don't you look like the cat who ate the canary. What's with the big smile?" I asked. Hardly able to contain himself, Jonathan gets up and gives me a big hug. Putting his arms gently on my shoulders he pushes me back so he can look at me and he says something which is music to my ears. "Misty, the bank is going to help us get back to farming. Can you believe it? The farm will be able to have cows again, new tractors, cornfields growing, and it is all because of you." Smiling just as broadly I say, "Me, what do I have to do with it?" "You have everything to do with this Misty. Coming back here, supporting me and just being you. It has been what the bank wanted all along, a unified front and that's what we gave them. We stood together!" exclaims Jonathan. Hugging him, I prepare to speak. Then my throat begins to tighten allowing me to speak in barely a whisper, "Dad and Mom would be so proud of you, Jonathan. I am so proud of you."

There is something I want to make sure you are clear on though. I will support you in all of this, but I did not come back here to become a farmer again. My throat loosens and I continue. I will be in the background cheering you on and supporting you. "This is what you always loved, Jonathan. I think you became distraught and distracted after Dad died. You looked at the farm as Dad's life and lost sight of the fact it was your life as well. I know you will make it into a successful farm once again. You know Misty, I don't think I ever let myself believe what you are saying, but I know it is the truth. I always felt it was Dad's farm and life. In reality though, it was mine too. Thank you, Misty, he said with tears in his eyes. I will have my life again now, and I will build it into an even greater farm for both of us to have.

Now though I need to tell you the rest of my conversation with Tom Fraser. "Misty, Nick had some input into the bank's decision. Apparently, he told Tom good things about us. I am surprised at Nick's input but then again, nothing should surprise me about Nick Darlington," says Jonathan quietly.

The door slams and in comes Olivia. "Hey Jonathan, fancy seeing you here today hanging out with my dear friend, Morgan." Laughing out loud, Jonathan looks over at Misty and then back at Olivia and says, "Olivia, I'm sure you must be mistaken. This is my sister, Misty." Practically leaping into Jonathan's arms, Olivia screams, "Isn't it wonderful, she came home, Jonathan! She came back to Millersville and we, all of us, are not going to let her ever leave again." Putting Olivia down, and pulling his sister close, he says, "Olivia, in all of the time I have known you, and that is since you were born, he laughs, that was probably the most prophetic thing you have ever said, and I love you for it." "Well Jonathan you need to come with us and celebrate. Misty are you ready to go because by now everybody is there and you know how Seth is about having to wait for me."

Heading back to my bedroom to touch up my makeup and get my pocketbook, I yell out, "I'll be ready in a couple of minutes. Jonathan, why don't you head over to the Tavern and I'll catch a ride with Olivia because I'm not quite ready yet." Rolling his eyes at Olivia, he says, "Some things never change. Ok Misty, I'll see you there." As Jonathan walks out the door, Olivia comes over and hugs me. "Misty, nothing has pleased me more than to see the two of you in the same room conversing like family. Seth and I have struggled with Jonathan's withdrawal over the last few years and now everything feels so normal.

Smiling at Olivia, I declare, "Well then let's go and have some fun tonight. We deserve it. Just remember I have to figure out when to tell Brett. I realize I need to do it sooner than later. I am going to visit his Mother tomorrow by myself..." Stopping me right in the middle of my sentence, Olivia looks anxiously at me. "Whatever for? Why would you subject yourself to this kind of torment? She is not a nice woman. It has always made Seth and I wonder how Brett turned out to be such a nice person." "Oh, come on, Olivia, she doesn't bite! I admired her gardens, and she extended an invitation to me to do some gardening with her. It might have all been done for Brett's sake. I don't care what her reasons are Olivia, I want to go, if only for Brett. A slight look of annoyance shows on Olivia's face, but then disappears. Olivia waves her hand in the air, "Let's go before Jonathan thinks we're not coming and leaves." "Olivia, wait! I need to check and make sure I turned off my curling iron, I say as I turn and head for my bedroom. I see my curling light on in my bathroom as I go through the bedroom door and I hear my cell phone ringing which is lying on the table by the front door. "Hey Olivia, can you get that for me. Just take a message and tell them I'll call them back whoever it is." I yell. I shake my head, well at least it wasn't the iron, and I laugh to myself shutting it off. "Ok I've got it," Olivia yells. "Hello, you have reached Morgan Kiernan's phone, Olivia speaking." There is dead silence on the other end, Olivia says again, "Hello, may I help you? "Yes, is my Mom around?" Olivia freezes in place. "I'm sorry. I think you might have the wrong number." Hearing a sigh on the other end, "No, I don't think so. This is Morgan Kiernan's phone, right?"

By the time I reach the kitchen and see the look on Olivia's face, I know who is calling Olivia sees me, hands me the phone and heads out the door. Putting the phone up to my ear, "I hear, "Mom, what is going on there. You said you were going to keep in touch with me and I haven't heard from you. Did you find what you were looking for?" "Heidi, I'm so sorry, I know it's been weeks since I talked to you. I was so close, I decided to stop in Millersville. First though how are you Heidi?" "I am fine, Mom. I want to know how you are and why you haven't called. "Oh Heidi, I have taken lots of pictures and seen so many people I haven't seen in such a long time." I'm about to run out and they are waiting for me, but I promise you I will call you tomorrow and tell you all about it." With a tremulous voice, Heidi says, "Ok Mom, please call me tomorrow. I want to talk to you. I need to know when you are coming home."

Walking into the Tavern seeing my brother laughing with his friends and conversing with the bartender, allows me to hesitate a minute so I can pull myself together. I feel the tears begin to well up in my eyes at the sight of it. Olivia walking ahead of me is talking with everyone along the bar, so I move past her and get to Seth and Jonathan without delay. "Hey, you two, what does a girl have to do to get a drink around here?" "Hold your horses' girl, always so damn impatient," laughs Jonathan. Seth smacks his arm, watch how loud you say that. Remember she is Morgan Kiernan, not your sister for all of those who are in here watching and listening."

Putting my hand on Jonathan's shoulder, I lean in and whisper, "There are a few more things I need to take care of before I can openly say I'm Misty Jenkins, so please be patient and understanding. He wanted to grab her in a hug but couldn't, so instead he reaches over and grabbed Seth's arm. "You know how lucky we are, Seth? Life has a way of healing old wounds and friendships blossom again. You and Olivia have been my dear friends for so long and I've neglected both of you. I am going to change that here and now. Your kindness and friendship for my sister has even outdone our friendship, and for that I will always be grateful." Olivia walks up just as Jonathan finishes, and knowing the implication of the comment, she walks over and hugs Morgan. Morgan whispers, "Olivia, I will explain Heidi, I promise, just later when we are alone." Olivia hugs her again and sits down next to Seth.

The rest of the night was pretty uneventful. Brett was there but was really busy and didn't get much time to spend with any of us. We made eye contact several times and I am assured he is still feeling good about the two of us.

It was getting late and time to get home. Jonathan appearing to have had a little too much to drink walks over to me to let me know he is leaving, Seth is going to drive him home and Olivia and I are going to pick up Seth from there. I pull him aside for a moment and in a lowered voice, "Jonathan there is evidence in this town there was more to the interaction between Jack, Charlie and the electric company and I am going to find it. Dad wasn't crazy and you need to remember that in the next few months. Things are going to get uneasy but making the farm a working farm and successful is what you need to concentrate on now. I will take care of the rest." Looking at his little sister, Jonathan was once again amazed at her strength and he has finally forgiven her for leaving. The revelation which came over him made him feel the best he had in years.

We are getting ready to leave, and I see Brett walking over to us. Hey, Olivia can we wait a few minutes before we leave, I want to talk to Brett?" "Of course, I wasn't really ready to leave yet anyway and since Jonathan is being driven home, we can stay for a while." Brett appears at my elbow, "Are you guys leaving?" I finally have a free minute to come over here and see you." Smiling at him, I grab his hand and squeeze it, "I am so glad you are able to get over here before we leave.

Seth and Olivia's friend Jonathan has the need to get home assisted. He apparently had a lot to celebrate today." "Really, that's good. I'm glad Seth and Olivia brought him into celebrate. I don't really know him very well. He lives out on a farm on the outskirts of town, but he's never come in here very much," replies Brett.

Deciding it is time to remind Brett of my visit, I wait for him to finish talking with Olivia. "Hey, do you remember tomorrow is my visit with your Mother? I plan on going over there after lunch because she wanted to wait until it was a little warmer for us to work outside." Brett's whole demeanor changed which took me back. I know he is uneasy about the visit, but his reaction startled me. "Hey, what's with the frown, everything is going to be fine. Remember she invited me, so she is definitely ready for me to come over. I'm not going to be there very long. I'm not going until after lunch." Knowing who he was talking to, Brett cautions his words. "Morgan, I know, except I also know my Mother and nothing she does is without a plan. Her plan with you is unknown to me which is what concerns me. I care about both of you and don't want to deal with a situation which might make me take sides." Hearing Brett say those words makes me realize whatever the outcome of this journey is going to be, it will impact all of the people I care about, past and present.

I get up early. It's a beautiful day. The sun is shining, and clouds are scarce in a blue bird color sky. Feeling emotionally charged, I decide after getting something to eat I will take a walk before I head downtown. I sit down by the window in the comfortable rocker graced with needle work cushions of irises and snap dragons and sip my morning coffee. I see Seth outside on his patio drinking his coffee. Waving to him through the window, he motions for me to come over and sit with him. Walking over, I laugh out loud as Seth says, "Well Morgan, you have a little hop in your step. What is on your calendar for the day?" Sitting down on a patio chair cushioned with fabric scattered with butterflies I reply "Funny you should ask me that today, Seth. I have a garden date with Brett's Mother, Elizabeth."

Trying to hide his surprise, Seth says, "Really, and what precipitated this visit. Elizabeth is not known for being very hospitable and least of all to someone who has captured her son's attention." I smile at Seth while thinking, *He has her pegged that's for sure.* "You know Seth, Elizabeth's husband Jack knew my parents, especially my father. Jack worked for the Electric Company and spent a lot of time at my parents' farm on its behalf. Maybe Jack shared information on circumstances which occurred after I left with Elizabeth and she can shed some light on the events that happened during that time. Also, she is Brett's mother and since Brett and I are dating I would like to get to know her a little better."

Not wanting to upset Misty, Seth decides to minimize his knowledge of what was going on then. He felt like it was a betrayal of his friendship with Brett and it was all in the past now anyway. "I didn't really know Brett's stepdad very well. It seemed like he wasn't home much when I was there and if he was, he always stayed up in his study. Plus remember I didn't get to know Brett until we were out of high school. He went to a private school. You did know that didn't you, Misty?" Putting her angst aside, she smiles at Seth, "Yes I do remember Brett saying something about it. Well, I better get back I have to do a few things downtown before I head over to Elizabeth's. Figuring it wouldn't do any good to tell her it was a bad idea to go over there, Seth just smiles and says, "Ok, stop over when you get back and we will have cocktails." "That sounds great," I say as I walk across their yard to mine stopping to sniff the Gardenias along the way.

Finishing my makeup and drying my hair, I decide to return Heidi's call. Grabbing my cell phone, I call and wait for her to pick up. Hearing her voice sends a wave of warmth and love through me. "Hello, my girl, how are you doing? We didn't get enough time to talk last night. I'm sorry I had to rush out so quickly." "Hey Mom, I'm doing alright but I want you to come home soon, or I'm going to fly there. I know you needed to take this trip to figure out things, but I miss you." I miss you too, Heidi." Hearing her sigh, I say, "Please is patient Heidi. I have decided I would love for you to let me fly you here. You could use a little time off. It would be great if you could get here by your birthday. It would be terrific for us to celebrate your 21st birthday together. I have rented the cutest house and we can stay here and vacation together for a week." "Ok that sounds great, Mom. I will put in for those days off and get my airline ticket bought. What airport do I fly into and how far away is it from Millersville? Heidi asks. "Not far at all, just about a 30-minute ride, you can call me when you land and by the time you get your luggage, I will be out front. With a wide grin, bordering on laughter of joy, I say, I can't wait to see you!" "Me too, and I can take some extra time if I need it," Heidi replied. Smiling at my daughter's planning, I say, "Ok, I'll make sure to call you tomorrow and find out what dates you are coming and what your flight times are so I can have everything arranged for you."

"Today, I am riding out farther in the County and taking some pictures of a property of a person I met who has a beautiful garden. She has a magnificently designed English garden. It will make for some really great pictures, so I've got to run for now. Please stay safe and I love you." "Ok, Mom. See you soon." "I can hardly wait. Bye. Sitting down on my couch, I lay my head back and think of everything which has happened. It seems life is beginning to turn around and the events of the years during my absence seem closer to resolution. Jonathan will now be able to farm again. Hopefully soon, I will be able to get some answers and learn what happened to dad the day they found him lying lifeless in the field. Getting up, I grab my keys and head downtown. Eventually, I am going to have to figure out Brett and what impact all of this is going to have on him and our relationship. Now, though, I need to get downtown, finish some errands and then head over to Elizabeth's.

Nick and Morgan (Present)

Millersville is a beautiful town and today and I see it in a whole new light. Suddenly it feels like home again and nothing except my daughter makes me happier than the feeling of being home. My visit to Elizabeth's isn't for a few hours yet and sitting with Seth this morning delayed my breakfast, so I head to the Diner. Hopefully, Susie is working because I would love to talk with her again.

Walking in, my old habits come forward. I scan the diner to see who is there. Feeling safe, I find a booth to sit down and relax. Susie sees me and waves. I wave back and let her know I need a menu. Sitting back and closing my eyes for a few moments, I listen to all the sounds and conversations going on around me. This is what small towns around here are all about. Dairy farmers talking about milk prices, vegetable farmers who just got back from the market complaining about asparagus prices, Moms getting together for their book club and the few strangers who have stopped in for a bite to eat discussing the results of yesterday's sporting events. They are the sounds of home I hear, and I realize why I love Millersville. Snapping me out of my reverie is no other than Nick. "Hey Misty, I mean Morgan, may I sit down with you and talk?"

Looking up at him standing next to the booth, I can't help but smile. His demeanor is almost tentative and somehow it amuses me. "Sure Nick, sit down. Have you had breakfast? I haven't ordered yet." Sliding into the booth, Nick runs his hand through his hair and averts his eyes from mine. I reach over, put his hand in mine and hold it for a minute. "Nick, we have years of history and so many memories between us. We have known each other since we were kids. It doesn't matter now what happened. I've already tossed away too many years of my life because of you, Whitney and Millersville." Lifting his eyes to look into mine, Nick smiles and takes my other hand in his. "Misty, I couldn't stop thinking about everything last night. I hardly slept. It's so surreal. You look so different but yet you seem so much the same. All the times we spent together played like a movie in my mind, except it never had an ending and now we have another chance." I move my hand from his, lay my fingers on his lips and whisper. "Nick, please don't. Today can't find its way back to twenty years ago.

We aren't the same people now. They say time heals everything, but time has only given me the energy to understand and resolve the happenings back then. One thing I know for certain is you will always have a place in the memories of my heart. The last twenty years I have tried not to spend time there." I realize now those years are captured, placed and set. They are in a space of time which will always be a part of me. I move my hand away from his lips and smile at him, startled at the feeling of my words.

There are more people coming into the diner and some of the patrons are looking our way. Nick is well known in Millersville and it seems as though we are drawing some attention. It doesn't seem to be bothering Nick. He looks at me and I can tell he is struggling with his words. "Misty, I have never stopped loving you and I have known that all these years. Nick lays his head into his hands and runs his fingers through his hair again.

When he raises his head from his hands, I see one lone tear has found its way to the edge of his eye. "I realize I have a family I have to take care of Misty, and Whitney will I think, need me now more than ever," he whispers as the tear finds its way down his cheek. I hear my lips release the words, "Nick, I've got to go. I recognize in this unexpected moment that I am not able to address my own emotions. "I've got to go." I hear me say again. I stand up to leave, hesitate and stop beside him. Placing my hand on his shoulder I say, "I can't Nick, not right now," I can't.

Driving home, I struggle to hold back the tears. Seeing his turmoil took me back to our time together and looking at him I could see the Nick of twenty years ago. All the signs of passing years and stress lines were gone and his love for me then had traveled through twenty years of time. Feelings of then, now, those years in between are cresting and waning all over me again. Anguish, loss, strength and resolve all travel together. Then, unexpected, love interrupts again. Finally reaching my porch, I sit down and rest my head against the railing. I look at my watch. It is almost time for me to leave for Elizabeth's. Pulling myself together I head inside to get ready to leave.

Elizabeth and Morgan (Present)

I find myself actually looking forward to visiting her gardens, having loved flowers and their beauty. The fascination I've had with the gardens which provide a home for them to bloom and grow. While driving, my eyes are drawn to landscapes adorning homes along the way. It is a wonder to me why my attention has not been attracted to them before. I reach Elizabeth's and pulling in the driveway I see a beautiful backyard with magnificent hollyhocks, hydrangeas and foxglove. I know there is more than I can see from where I am. I leave my car and instinctively head back toward her gardens. As I turn into the back yard there is a patio table set with two lovely place settings, a container of iced tea, and Elizabeth waving to me from the window. "Make yourself at home. I will be out in a minute." Turning to her, I wave, walk to the patio and sit down. Smiling Elizabeth walks onto the patio. "Morgan, I'm so glad you have such an appreciation for flowers and the beauty they bring when they live among us. "Let's walk, shall we?" Elizabeth offers her arm, and we walk arm in arm through her garden. As we walk, she explains to me each flower and plant. We walk while she teaches me about the elements of her garden and how each came to be. I realize then much of her life has been planted in this garden. I notice there is a pattern to each section. Meandering along the side of the back yard I catch the Honeysuckle scent of Bougainvillea.

As we walk, she tells stories of Jack and Brett but mostly Brett. Her demeanor changes whenever she talks about Jack. My former husband, Jack, never understood the enchantment of flowers for me. He thought it was a waste of time, but the creation and enjoyment it brings has always been a gift to me." She asks if I would like to go inside and have some tea. Walking beside her, I realize the similarity between Brett and Elizabeth. Their walk is the same, the way they hold their head when looking at you and most of all, the inflection they have in their voice which always makes you think they are asking a question. We walk inside.

Immediately Elizabeth guides me into a very formal living room which I had not seen when I visited her with Brett. It is what you would expect in a home where there would often be formal entertainment. There is a grand piano with pictures of distinguished looking family members, a large formal sofa, and love seat surrounded by several precisely placed fabric covered chairs. Smiling, I slide my fingers gently across the keys of the piano. "My Mother was a very accomplished pianist and she wanted me to follow in her footsteps. I tried, but found it wasn't the "cool" thing to do when I was in High School, so I stopped. I regret it terribly now that I am an adult." Laughing quietly, Elizabeth says, "Most things we are asked to do when we are young, we dismiss, but we all change our tune when we become older." Her eyes seem reflecting. "There are so many things I would change now if

I had the chance, but unfortunately that is life. We live with our choices as bad as some may have been. We have to rise up and continue knowing something was important enough at the time to drive us to do whatever we did."

Heading toward the solarium where we are going to spend the rest of our afternoon, I look at all the artwork. The sculptures and artwork are evidence of wealth. Taking all of this in, I realize why Brett is the man he has become. I think he wanted to prove to himself and his Mother he didn't need the wealth he grew up in, he could make a living doing hard work and being a solid businessman.

Reaching the solarium, we comfortably sit on the settee and for a moment we just looked at each other. Elizabeth breaks the silence first, "Morgan, I understand from Brett you are quite the photographer. Maybe you could take some pictures of the gardens, I'm sure there are some very photogenic opportunities out there. He also said you weren't from around here. Have you relocated here permanently?" Finding myself at a loss for words, I stand up to look out the window at the gardens. "I would love to take pictures of your gardens, Elizabeth, flowers make great subjects. Maybe you could be in some of the pictures. I understand there is a section in next month's Home & Garden in the paper which is going to be dedicated to local gardens. Yours would be a great addition to the section and I would be happy to take the photos. It is getting late and I know Brett is probably chomping at the bit for me to get to the Tavern.

Elizabeth has been the ultimate hostess and recognizing our visit is concluding, rises from her seat. Standing, I mention how much I have enjoyed my visit "Elizabeth, I have had such a nice time visiting you today and your gardens are just beautiful." "You know, Morgan, I had some doubts about you when I first met you but after today, I realize it is true first impressions aren't always right. I am happy you enjoyed your visit. "Would it be ok for me to use your bathroom? All the tea we had is making it imperative I use it soon," I say laughingly. "Follow me, I'll show you where to go."

As we move through the solarium I look back and smile. We are walking down a long hall and Elizabeth says, "I'm taking you to the guest bathroom please enjoy the lotions and soaps I have on display. No one ever visits anymore so they haven't been used and I would love if you could experience the scents I have placed there." Opening the door, I see a bathroom posing as an oasis of serenity. *A bathroom Oasis! Incredible!* Moving into the room, I see a grand Jacuzzi tub. I take a moment to picture it lined with candles, filled with bubble bath, and a bottle of wine next to a crystal glass resting on the windowsill adorned with plants. Her choice of color for the walls, the tile on the floor and all the accruements blend perfectly with one another. Elizabeth Callahan is all about appearance and it is evident throughout her home.

Remembering Jack Callahan, the image of the two of them together doesn't seem to work for me. He was too smooth, always knew something about everything and when no one was paying attention, was very watchful. I wash my hands and looking in the mirror I realize my hair is disheveled from the breeze in the garden. Glancing around the bathroom I try to think where Elizabeth would keep a hairbrush. I see a small vanity with a mirror sitting in the corner. I pull the middle drawer open and find Bobbie pins and other hair fasteners. There are a couple of drawers on the side, so I open the top drawer and there are hairbrushes, combs and other items. Finishing, I look around for hairspray. The little cupboard door in the front of the vanity looks like a perfect spot to keep hairspray so I quickly open it. Inside, instead of hairspray, I see newspapers, and other papers bound with a rubber band. I move the papers aside, hoping there is hairspray behind them. Suddenly I am startled. I find my eyes looking at a canister. I recognize the canister. It looks just like my dad's! His was designed by my grandfather and there is not another like it in existence. It is my dad's. I am sure of it. I open the lid and there etched in the underside of the lid are my grandfather's initials. I cannot believe my eyes. Why would Elizabeth have it? Quickly, I close the vanity and exit the bathroom. Morgan, are you alright?" asks

Elizabeth. Taking a deep breath, I say "Oh my, Elizabeth, it is so beautiful! I never expected to see a bathroom so lovely. Walking down the hallway through the drawing room, Elizabeth moves to touch my arm. "Morgan, I'm so glad you enjoyed your time here. Thank you, Elizabeth for such a nice visit. As we reach the front door, Elizabeth turns to me "I'm so glad you came today, Morgan. It was very enjoyable to me to have you walk through the gardens. Hopefully, I will see you again."

Moving down the steps to the sidewalk, I feel my heart beating so fast I almost can't speak. Waving my hand, I manage to say, "I had a great time and I hope to see you again soon." Gratefully I get in my car and pull away. Driving the short distance home, there are so many thoughts racing through my mind. How did dad's container get there? What does this mean? Whose help can I depend on to find out? Where do I begin? Is it related to Jack, Elizabeth? Is it related to my dad's death?

Though the distance to my house is not far, it seems like a long time before I pull into the driveway. Just as I turn off the car, I hear my phone ringing. Answering it, I hear Heidi say, "Hi Mom. "I called earlier. Did you get a chance to listen to my message?" "Oh Heidi, I am so glad you called. I did get your message. I'll call you back in a little while, I just pulled in the driveway." "Sure Mom, no rush." I hang up the phone, still shaken.

Suddenly, there is a knock on the car window. Startled, I look up and there is Brett. "I am sorry to alarm you Morgan, but we have to go. Go, where? His voice trembling, he says, Abigail has died.

TO BE CONTINUED....

CPSIA information can be obtained
at www.ICGtesting.com
Printed in the USA
LVHW081807071022
730138LV00014B/466